Death
of a
Fox

Death
of a
Fox

A Cabin by the Lake Mystery

Linda Norlander

LEVEL
BEST BOOKS

Author Photo Credit: Jerry Mathiason

First edition

ISBN: 978-1-68512-370-3

Cover art by Level Best Designs

This book was professionally typeset on Reedsy.
Find out more at reedsy.com

For Grace Stone who inspired this story

Contents

Praise for A Cabin by the Lake Mysteries

Praise for Death of a Fox

"The Minnesota landscape, as well as the characters who inhabit this world, are rendered with compelling precision, and the descriptions are vivid and sympathetic. Highly recommended."—Lori Robbins, award winning author of the On Pointe Mystery Series

"A haunted former sanitorium, a missing boy, mysterious family secrets, a greedy ex-husband—this complex mystery set in northern Minnesota has more than enough intrigue to make the book a page-turner."—Charlotte Stuart, award-winning author of the Discount Detective Series

"*Death of a Fox* is a haunting tale of deeply buried ancient family secrets mingled with a few mysteries of a more modern vintage. Linda Norlander has created a smart heroine, a lush setting, and an abundance of strange goings-on to make this a page-turner I couldn't put down. I absolutely loved it!"—Annette Dashofy, *USA Today* bestselling author of the Zoe Chambers Mystery Series

Praise for Death of a Snow Ghost

"*Death of a Snow Ghost,* the third in the 'Cabin by the Lake' series by Linda Norlander, is a nicely layered blend of small-town mystery and big-time corruption. Author Linda Norlander weaves an intriguing tale of murder, cross-border trafficking of newborns, indifferent cops, and occasionally problematic long-distance romance, all within the confines of a small town locked in the grip of a cold and snowy northern Minnesota winter. It was a fun read!"—Gregory Stout, author of *Lost Little Girl* and *The Gone Man*.

Chapter One: Apple Pie

I sat on my rock by the lake, admiring the lime green of the newly budded aspen and birch across the water on Bear Island. The snow and cold of the winter had finally given way to spring on Lake Larissa. I thought about spring in New York, with the trees waking from their winter slumber and the greening of the parks. It should have been a time of renewal, except I remembered how the thaw and the warmth always brought out the smell of a winter's worth of garbage and trash in the streets.

Spring on Lake Larissa smelled of rebirth, like nowhere I'd ever been. With that in mind, I finished my coffee and walked into the cabin to read the latest edition of *The Killdeer Times,* our local paper.

I was following the story of a missing seventeen-year-old who disappeared from the Camp Six program for troubled teenagers located in the western part of the county. A week into the search, all they'd found was an overturned canoe on Waagosh Lake and a backpack with some clothing in it. The story was the big news in Jackpine County. His parents were offering a large reward for finding him.

Jilly, my friend from the *Times,* had told me the program had been a source of local gossip ever since it took over an abandoned logging camp two years ago.

"They say it's run like a military boot camp, and it's supposed to straighten out wayward youth. I hear it's more like a prisoner-of-war camp run by a bunch of thugs in camo."

What we didn't need here in the quiet Northwoods was an army of amateurs possibly carrying guns. I set the article down, patted Bronte, my dog, on the head, and told her, "Not my problem. I hope they find the kid—alive."

Bronte, as usual, had no opinion.

After brewing another pot of coffee, I opened the latest manuscript I'd contracted to edit. The author sent a little note:

> Dear Jamie,
>
> You come highly recommended. I have worked on this story for several years and feel it is ready for final edits. I hope you enjoy "Apple Pie a'la Murder." As you'll see, it's a cozy murder mystery with a few recipes added for tasty reading.
>
> Sincerely,
> Opal Harris

Bronte wagged her tail as only a chocolate lab mix can while I read the note. "Well, girl, I think I'm in for another editing ride. Recipes are not my area of expertise. I hope my old Betty Crocker cookbook will help me out."

My editing business had been steady throughout the winter despite a few detours involving a Minnesota version of human trafficking. With a combination of editing, selling an article to a major magazine, and a small compensation from the City of New York, I'd weathered my first Minnesota deep freeze. I looked forward to a calm spring.

The calm of my spring ended abruptly before I could finish page one of *Apple Pie* where Opal reveals that the narrator is a pot-bellied pig named Apple Pie. As I expressed my dismay in the form of a swear word, the phone rang.

Clarence, my octogenarian lawyer friend, and sometime employer, greeted me. "So, how is my New York mobster tree hugger?" With my New York accent, some people around here still thought I belonged to the *Sopranos* family.

"I'm about to embark on research about pigs. And how are you?"

"What is the word they use for us old guys? Spry?"

"Sounds like you are in good form." I set down the first page of the manuscript with a quiet sigh. Clarence never called simply to chat. "What can I do for you?"

"I have a client who could use your help."

I felt a headache coming on. "Oh? Please tell me it doesn't involve any kind of intrigue." Clarence and I had had several adventures together since I moved to Northern Minnesota a year ago.

Clarence laughed. "Hope not. She's old and wants to tell her story but needs some help sorting it out."

"If she's looking for a ghostwriter, I'm not what she wants." One of my New York friends once contracted to ghostwrite a memoir by a not-so-well-known off-Broadway theater director. It turned out he wanted it done like a Shakespearean play. She backed out after two days.

"No. I believe it's written but needs some editing."

"Hmmm." Did I want to take this on? "I'm not sure I'd be the best person for her. I'm a decent editor, and I used to write a lot of poetry, but personal memoir?" I shook my head.

"Well, then. Let's sweeten the pot a little. She lives in the western part of the county on a property that used to be a TB sanatorium called 'Gooseberry Acres.' They say it's haunted."

The haunted part intrigued me. "You mean like ghosts of old patients?"

"I'm not clear on the details, but you might find an interesting history. Plus, it's right across Waagosh Lake from where that young man disappeared. Could be interesting."

"Clarence, you know I'm done snooping into places where I don't belong. I don't think I should go anywhere near that part of the county. I have a nasty habit of getting sucked into things..." I let the end of the sentence hang.

Clarence tsked. "I don't think you have anything to worry about. Nella is just an old woman who wants to write something for posterity. No intrigue—really."

Famous last words. "Promise me she hasn't written it in Shakespearean English, and I might consider it."

Clarence laughed. "I seriously doubt it. The lady is an expert on the history of sanatoriums since she grew up there."

I felt an obligation to Clarence. He'd gotten me out of a jam or two in my short year in my cabin by the lake. "Okay, I'll at least talk to her."

"I'm exhausted by your enthusiasm."

I imagined the sparkle in his eyes when he spoke. We arranged to meet this mystery person tomorrow.

Turning back to *Apple Pie,* I found the body of the murder victim on page three. "Opal isn't wasting any time, I guess." Fortunately for the deceased, Apple Pie the pig was more interested in solving the murders than eating the remains.

Chapter Two: Miss Nella

The next morning, Clarence gave me a history lesson as we drove west of town into state forest land.

"Nella Fox's father was an ex-military physician who owned and ran Gooseberry Acres as a private sanatorium. It catered to a relatively exclusive clientele. She grew up on the property. Left home to attend college and then came back. Her father wanted her to be a doctor, but it was hard for women to be admitted to medical school in those days. I think her degree was in history. She never married, but there was a rumor about a romance that left her heartbroken. I would let her take the lead on that part of her history."

"Intriguing. It's a sensitive subject?"

Clarence adjusted his bow tie. "It's said she was young when she fell in love. Might have been one of the patients, which would have sent Dr. Fox into a storm. He did not like her mingling with the residents of his hospital."

"Ah, a mystery. Fortunately, not one for me to solve."

Clarence laughed. "I think you've solved your share for this year."

A young deer stood at the side of the road. I slowed down, remembering the stories my state trooper friends told me about deer damage to cars and lives. It watched me with its ears pricked before bounding off into the woods, its white tail held high.

Clarence didn't appear to notice the deer. "I recall listening at the parlor door as a young lad while my parents talked about Dr. Fox. They said something was 'off' about the sanatorium. Unfortunately, they caught me spying, cuffed my ears, and I never heard what 'off' might have meant."

"What happened to Gooseberry Acres? I didn't even know a sanatorium had existed in Jackpine County."

"It closed in the late fifties. By then, they had better treatment for TB, and Dr. Fox was getting on in years. I suspect he suffered from dementia. The buildings fell into disrepair, and several of them burned. About twenty years ago, a group of developers from the Twin Cities came up with a plan to build a resort, but it never went anywhere. Nella refused to sell."

"Do you know why?"

Clarence shrugged. "It was her home. She'd never gone far from it other than college."

We drove by stands of pine and aspen. The beginnings of new growth greened the forest floor. Trillium poked through with their white blossoms. It was a glorious spring day. A time for rebirth.

I kept that sense of optimism until I spotted several crows picking at a lump in the road. I slowed to let them fly away. They were working on the carcass of a skunk, and the smell permeated the air.

Clarence noted it. "Poor driver who hit that creature. His car will stink for weeks."

So much for paradise, I thought.

Pointing ahead, Clarence commented, "Up there, about five miles is the camp where they lost the young lad. They say the compound is fenced in with barbed wire. Not that I've seen it, of course."

"Sounds like something out of a horror movie." The less I heard about this Camp Six, the better.

A mile beyond the dead skunk, Clarence directed me onto a gravel lane. The remains of a long-neglected stone gateway with a "No Trespassing" sign were the only indication the sanatorium existed. The driveway was in worse shape than mine—hardly more than two ruts with grass growing in between. "Doesn't look like she has much traffic or has done much maintenance." I didn't want to think about what the road was like in the dead of winter.

"Nella is pretty much a recluse. She has been ever since her father died. There's a sad story in it somewhere. Maybe it will be in her memoirs."

After bumping down the tree-lined lane for a half mile, we came to a weedy clearing filled with tall brown grass and tangles of bushes just starting to green up. A large, three-story building stood at the end. Paint peeled from the weather-beaten siding, and most of the third-floor dormers were boarded up. The roof over the front portico sagged, and the wooden shingles were slick with moss. An older pickup truck was parked near the front door.

To the left, as we faced the building, was a covered walkway. Parts of the roof had caved in, and most of the screens on the walkway were either riddled with holes or missing. The walkway ended with a weedy foundation and a crumbling brick chimney.

"This doesn't look very welcoming."

"Vandals, fires, and neglect have taken most of the buildings over the years."

To the right of the old hospital stood a gray stucco house with an open porch. The house was in better shape than the main building. The roof looked new, although the white trim around the windows and porch was peeling like the main building.

Clarence pointed at it. "That's where Miss Nella lives. It had always been the doctor's residence."

I pulled up close to the walk to the house and turned off the car. I needed a few moments to take this place in. In contrast to the weedy neglected grounds and the dilapidated look of the house, rows of red and yellow tulips lined the sidewalk to the porch. On either side of the house, lilacs were ready to bloom. A budding oak tree stood in the front yard, surrounded by a mowed lawn.

"Looks like she keeps the yard up."

Clarence didn't reply as he fumbled with his seat belt. I walked to the passenger side to help him out. He'd taken a fall in late winter and was still a little unsteady on his feet.

"Let me escort you." I held out my arm.

"Getting old is not for the weak-willed," he grunted as he stood up.

On either side of the front door were large picture windows looking out over the porch. Both were covered in dark drapes. I pointed them out. "Not very inviting."

"As I said, Miss Nella has become quite a recluse."

I wondered if something was motivating her to write her memoirs now.

When I rang the doorbell, I heard a soft chiming inside. Clarence waited beside me, leaning on his cane.

Footsteps approached, and the door was opened by a plain-looking woman in her early fifties. She wore a faded pair of jeans and a flowered smock top. Her dark hair was streaked with gray and pulled into a ponytail. A shiny, intricate barrette held her bangs back. The piece of jewelry didn't fit with her drab appearance. She peered at us through the screen door. "Yes?"

Clarence took a step forward. "Hello. I'm Clarence Engstrom, Miss Nella's lawyer. She asked me to come with my assistant." He pointed at me.

The woman scowled. "She didn't let me know you were coming." Abruptly she turned and walked deeper into the house.

"Weren't we expected?" The scene at the door puzzled me.

Clarence cleared his throat. "Ah, that's a fair question."

"What? Is this a surprise visit?"

Clarence touched my arm as if to calm me. "I'll explain later. Meanwhile, let's see where we get with Nurse Ratched."

"Ratched?" It took me a moment to put the name together with *One Flew Over the Cuckoo's Nest.* I glowered at Clarence. "What have you gotten me into?"

Clarence chuckled but didn't reply.

I was about to say something more when the woman who opened the door strode back. "Humph...she says you can come in."

She opened the door with an expression like she was letting rats into her house. Clarence and I slipped past her into the dimly lit hallway. The house was a four-square style of the 1920s, with rooms on either side of the hallway and a staircase leading up to the second floor.

Immediately I noted how warm the house was—overheated for the time of the year.

Clarence was the first to speak. "I'm sorry, I didn't get your name?"

The woman pressed her lips together like she was gritting her teeth. "Barrett Fox."

I held out my hand. "Nice to meet you. I'm Jamie Forest." Barrett ignored my outstretched hand and led us into a darkened parlor.

The room was lit with a floor lamp next to an elderly woman with her white hair pulled back into a neat bun. She wore thick glasses that magnified her eyes. The lamp emitted a soft yellow glow that couldn't permeate the dark corners of the room. The woman sat in an easy chair, her legs resting on a hassock. She was wrapped in a colorful afghan. Behind her, the walls were lined with bookshelves crammed with books that hadn't been touched for decades.

Barrett stood at the door like a sentry as we entered. Without greeting us, the woman said, "Barrett, you may go now, and close the door behind you."

Barrett opened her mouth, and for a moment, I thought she'd refuse. The woman repeated in a louder voice, "You may go now. Come back in fifteen minutes with coffee."

When the door finally closed, Clarence walked over to the easy chair and took her outstretched hand. "Nella, I see you are as bossy as ever."

She replied with a titter. "You always were a charmer, you old fart."

This was not the conversation I had expected. The Miss Nella I'd conjured up from what little Clarence had told me was a severe old maid with no sense of humor. I'd assumed that Barrett was simply a younger version of her.

"And you are the poet?" Miss Nella beckoned to me.

I bent down and took her hand. "I'm Jamie Forest. I'm afraid I'm a lapsed poet. Too busy with other people's work."

Clarence and I sat down on the couch. I noted how he winced when he sat. His hip was bothering him. I'd tried to get him to see the doctor after his fall, and he'd said, "When it's broken, I'll see the doctor. Until then, nature will take its course."

Miss Nella surprised me again when she whispered, "We need to talk very quietly. Sometimes they listen."

Perhaps Miss Nella was a little demented.

Clarence whispered back, "We'll be quick then."

The darkness of this room, the heat, and the whispering sent a shiver down my back. At least I didn't have the tingling in the nape of my neck that signaled danger. I couldn't wait to get Clarence back in the car to hear the whole story.

"You know those military people have come by a couple of times. They said they're looking for a boy." Miss Nella shook her head. "Now, why would they want to bother me?"

Clarence leaned close to her. "It seems the lad disappeared from their camp across the lake. Maybe they thought he came here."

"Nonsense. Ed would have let me know if that child had come here."

I refrained from asking who Ed was. Clarence could explain later.

"Well, my friend," Clarence smiled at Miss Nella. "Let's get down to business before your cousin comes back."

Miss Nella motioned me away. "Young woman, could you step outside for a moment while Clarence and I talk? I'll call you back in when I'm ready."

Dismissed already. I walked out into the gloomy hallway and studied the faded wallpaper. It was a grayish flower pattern that had darkened over the years. I guessed that at one time, it had been a very expensive item. From somewhere in the rear, I heard voices—a male and a female. It sounded like they were arguing.

"I don't understand. We just bought milk, and we're out." Barrett's voice was higher and strained.

"Relax, Barry. You probably just lost track."

I followed the hallway back to the kitchen where Barrett was pouring water into a Mr. Coffee.

"Hello," I greeted them. Barrett stared at me as if she'd seen a ghost. The man turned, and the first thing I noticed about him was the thick head of dark hair. He had a tanned, lined face and a square jaw. His face and the way he carried himself reminded me of an actor in action films. Ruggedly handsome. Next to him, Barrett appeared even more plain and dowdy even though I saw the resemblance in the shape of her face and the hazel color of her eyes.

For a moment, the man appeared startled. Suddenly he broke out into a dazzling smile indicative of a very good cosmetic dentist. "Oh, you must be the visitor."

I found myself a little speechless in the glow of his presence. I shook it off very quickly when I realized he reminded me of an older version of my ex-husband, Andrew, the actor.

He held his hand out to me. "I'm Tucker, Barrett's brother. We're helping our cousin Nella...." He let his voice drop in a dramatic way. "She's not well, you know."

Before I could ask him what he meant, Clarence called. "Jamie, we're ready for you."

When I walked into the parlor, Clarence was putting some folded papers into the inside pocket of his suit coat. Miss Nella's hands rested on her lap, and her eyes were closed.

I cleared my throat. "What can I do for you?"

She opened her eyes with a benevolent smile. "Clarence tells me you are quite talented."

If keeping my wits about me when an author wanted her main character to be a pot-bellied pig, I guess I had some talent. I merely nodded. "I have some loyal customers."

Clarence interrupted. "Miss Nella would like you to edit her memoirs. She's willing to pay your standard fee, of course."

I squatted down next to her chair. "Are you finished writing them?" I was afraid she wanted me to ghostwrite them.

She took my hand. "Oh, my dear, I've been writing them most of my life. I need someone to organize them."

I pictured cartons of notebooks dating back to God knows when. She must have read the expression on my face. "I have pared them down. It's been a project of mine for many years, but now my eyesight is failing, and it's time for someone to have a fresh look at them."

I'd edited memoirs in the past. Often, I found the writers to be sincere and boring. I always asked before I took the project on, "Who is your audience?" If the hope was to be on the best-seller list, I usually turned them down.

"Miss Nella, who do you see reading this when it's done?" I expected her to talk about historical societies or university archives. She replied in a tight voice, "The families of the people who lived and died here and the seekers of truth. That's all."

Seekers of truth? I was taken aback. What were the secrets of this crumbling old place?

Chapter Three: The Memoir

We were interrupted when Barrett walked in carrying a tray with the Mr. Coffee carafe and three mismatched mugs. She set it down on the coffee table in front of the sofa hard enough that the mugs clanked together. "Hope you don't take cream. I wasn't prepared for guests, and we're out of milk."

I felt more unwelcome by the moment as she glared at Miss Nella. Miss Nella ignored her. "Black is fine, Barrett. Can you pour me half a cup?"

To her credit, Barrett made a good cup of coffee. I complimented her. "Not everyone knows how to make coffee around here."

For a moment, it looked like she was going to smile before she formed her lips into a thin line and walked out.

I watched the expression on Clarence's face darken. He opened his mouth as if to say something, then changed his mind. I jumped in instead. "Barrett is...ah...rather stern." I really meant to say "rude and disrespectful."

Miss Nella lifted the coffee to her lips and set it back down without taking any. "I'm fortunate to have her. Most people don't want to live out here in the midst of this." She pointed to the window. "Some of the locals still believe the place is contaminated and they could catch a disease. Others think it's haunted." She paused with a faraway expression. "And maybe it is."

I had questions about Barrett and Tucker but decided I'd wait and ask Clarence. We fell into silence as we drank the coffee.

Miss Nella finally spoke up. "I think it's time for my nap. Jamie, would you be a dear and get Tucker to carry this out to your car?" She pointed to a cardboard box filled to the top with notebooks and papers.

I stepped out into the hallway and nearly tripped over Tucker. Had he been listening at the door? "Miss Nella would like you to carry a box to my car."

"Right-oh." He straightened up with a mock salute. Again, he reminded me of my ex, and I did an involuntary shudder.

After he'd hefted the box and walked out of the parlor, Miss Nella beckoned me. "I know the papers are a mess, but maybe you could sort through them and come back next week so we can talk."

"Should we set up a time?"

"Oh no, dear. Surprise is the best, but don't come in the afternoon because I like to nap." She looked beyond me with a wistful expression. "Sometimes I dream about the way things should have been."

Clarence stood with a little groan. "I believe it's time to go. And if you'll excuse me, I'll use the facilities before we get back on the road."

Tucker waited for me by my red Ford Escape. I opened the back hatch. "Slide them in here."

"It's quite a collection," he grunted, pushing the box in. "Wonder what it contains."

I sensed this wasn't an idle comment. Tucker wanted to know what was in the box.

"I guess I'll find out."

"I hope you can share." His dazzling smile nearly blinded me.

We were interrupted by the approach of a Black SUV. Tucker and I watched as it pulled up next to my car. A Camp Six logo in white was painted on the door. The two men inside wore military-style camo.

Tucker groaned. "Man, these guys are persistent. I told the last ones we haven't seen their lost camper."

The driver rolled down the window. "Any chance you've spotted this kid? He goes by the name Tally—short for Talbert." He held out a flier with a photo of the missing boy. The boy had a rounded face and long blond hair swept to the side.

The driver continued. "His hair is shorter now in keeping with the camp rules."

14

I shook my head. "Sorry. This is my first time here, and I guarantee I haven't seen anyone under the age of forty."

The driver did not smile as he waved the photo toward Tucker. I noticed a subtle change in Tucker's expression, and it brought back memories of Andrew, my ex, when he was working his way into a role.

He took the photo scratching his head. "When did you say you lost him?"

The driver flinched with the word "lost." "He went AWOL a week ago."

"Hmmm." Tucker pressed his lips together. "I seem to recall I was coming back from town—maybe it was that day—and I saw a truck pull over and pick up a hitchhiker. Could it have been him?"

The driver glanced over at his partner, who nodded. "Could be. What direction was he going?"

Tucker peered up at the sky. "Well, since I was coming back here and he was on the other side of the road, I'd say he was headed for town." He paused. "Yes, and I think it was a kid. But I could be wrong. Is that helpful?"

"Yessir. That's a great help." He rolled up the window and backed around.

Tucker waved as the vehicle bumped down the driveway.

I stared at him. "Are you telling the truth?"

Tucker smiled and said nothing.

The Camp Six car was gone by the time Clarence stepped outside. When he reached us, I was sure I could see the pain etched on his face. Before opening the car door, he turned to Tucker. "Take good care of Nella." I thought I heard a hint of threat in his voice.

Tucker saluted with his false British voice. "Right-oh."

Once we were buckled in, I spoke to Clarence. "Before you came out, a couple of men from Camp Six showed up."

Clarence nodded. "I saw them. What did Tucker say?"

"He told them he might have seen the kid hitchhiking."

"Good. Might keep them away from here. They upset Nella."

Chapter Four: That Couple

I stopped the car in front of the crumbling hospital. "Clarence, I know you enough to sense you are worried. What's going on? It's more than all the stuff about a missing kid on the other side of the lake."

He took a deep breath and let it out with a whistle. "Nella contacted me about a month ago. She wanted to make sure her will and estate were in order. When I talked with her on the phone, she was whispering. 'I don't want them to hear.' At first, I thought maybe she was getting a little senile, but when I asked her who *they* were, she said, 'That couple.'"

"You mean Barrett and Tucker?"

"That's what I assume."

Before we could continue, an old man, wearing a blue work shirt and dirty jeans, approached the driver's side of the car. He carried a rifle.

"Who is that?"

Clarence smiled. "Ah, it's Ed. I think he wants to talk."

"Who?"

"He's the old caretaker. Been part of Gooseberry Acres since he was a child."

Clarence rolled down his window. "Fine day, Ed."

He stared at Clarence for a moment with a pinched expression. It seemed to me, watching from the driver's side, that he was trying to figure out who Clarence was.

Clarence stuck out his hand. "Clarence Engstrom. I'm Nella's lawyer. We met a couple of years ago. Remember?"

Ed continued to stare for a moment before he growled. "You got business with her?"

Was he being curious or protective?

"Oh, you know me, always up to trouble."

Apparently, Ed didn't have a sense of humor. "I don't want no trouble. Those soldier guys have been sniffing around. They say they're looking for a lost kid. No kids here."

Clarence chuckled. "Nella is lucky to have you looking after the place."

Ed paused, "Well, don't steal stuff, okay? I got a rifle."

"I'll keep that in mind. But for now, my assistant and I need to get going." He rolled up his window and nodded to me. I put the Escape in drive and started down the road. Through the rear view mirror, I saw Ed standing in front of the abandoned hospital. For a second, I was sure that I saw something like a ghostly face staring out one of the dirty windows on the second floor. I blinked, and it was gone.

"Ghost?" I whispered.

"Excuse me?" Clarence turned to me.

I shook my head. "Nothing. Thought I saw something in the window of the hospital."

He nodded. "Oh yes. That building is haunted—no doubt about it."

Clarence's words didn't surprise me as much as his tone. He sounded completely serious. I felt something like a spider kiss on the back of my neck.

When we reached the main road, I stopped and took a deep breath. "Honestly, Clarence, if I didn't know better, I'd say we were stuck in the middle of a horror movie script complete with a militia and a psycho-caretaker."

I expected Clarence to laugh. He rubbed his chin with a tight set to his lips. "Not good. Not good at all."

Rays from the sun dappled the road as we drove back to Killdeer. Clarence filled me in a little more on the history of Gooseberry Acres. "After it shut down, some of the locals dubbed it Ghostberry Acres. People in the area claimed they heard strange howling at night."

"Ghosts of the dead patients?"

"More likely timber wolves. It's wild country around the estate."

The highway was empty except for a couple of cars heading west. As we passed a clearing, I saw an eagle soar and land in the one tall pine still standing. Clarence spotted it, too.

"Bad wildfire here a couple of years ago, but look how the earth is renewing itself." He pointed to the seedlings shooting up among the dry grasses.

I waited for him to tell me more about Gooseberry Acres and the Fox family, but he lapsed into silence.

After a few miles, I reached over and patted his leg. "Come on, Clarence. Tell me more about what you know. You're worried about Miss Nella, but what do you suspect?"

"She wants the land to go for a state park. Told me when I did her will ten years ago that she had no heirs, and other than leaving some money for Ed, the rest would be donated."

"Barrett and Tucker called her a cousin. Does that mean she has relatives?"

"They showed up out of the blue about three months ago. Said their father told them about Gooseberry Acres and the Fox family on his deathbed. He asked them to promise that they would check it out."

I thought through what Clarence had told me about the Fox family. "Barrett and Tucker are shirttail relatives?"

Clarence gripped the cane with both hands. "It turns out Dr. Fox had a brother. They claim to be his children. And that's part of why I'm worried. When Nella told me they were relatives, I looked her straight in the eyes and said, 'I thought you said you had no family.' She became so quiet I wondered if she'd fallen asleep. When she did speak, she said, 'Oh, they're Judd's children—or so they say.'"

"Judd?"

"Dr. Fox's younger brother. Nella said he was a bit of a scoundrel, and her father had lost contact with him long ago."

Something struck me as being clearly off with both Barrett and Tucker. Perhaps they were scam artists who stumbled across an article about Gooseberry Acres.

"Gooseberry Acres could bring a tidy sum if a developer wanted the land.

It's surrounded by wilderness and borders Waagosh Lake. The lake is deep and clear and undeveloped except for that youth camp place." Clarence's voice dropped off. "A person can't be too careful."

"I'll see if I can find anything about them on social media. If they are scammers, though, I'd think they would be careful about what they posted."

"In my experience as a lawyer, I've found that criminals can be amazingly stupid."

We arrived in town before Clarence could tell me more about the value of the land and Nella's plan for it. I dropped him off at his house. Lorraine, his neighbor, and housekeeper, had already planted the hanging baskets for the porch. The contrast between this house and Nella's was notable. Clarence's had a lively, well cared for look, and Nella's, even with the tulips in the front, looked like it died years ago.

I walked him up the sidewalk. "Clarence, you really should get that hip looked at."

"I'd say you were conspiring with Lorraine."

"We're all worried about you."

"Poppycock! I'll know when I need to see a doctor."

"Boy, have you got your old crank suit on today." I opened the front door for him. "None of us want to pick you up off the floor."

He turned to me. "Let's get Nella straightened out, and then I promise I'll see whatever doctor you can come up with."

"Deal."

As I drove out of town to my cabin by the lake, I had a growing sense of urgency. I wasn't sure if it was about Clarence and his hip or Miss Nella and the weird people surrounding her. Tomorrow I would start reading through the box of memoirs.

Chapter Five: Jim in Washington

Once home, I lugged the box into the cabin. Bronte nearly tripped me in her enthusiasm to greet me. Much as I loved her, she could be a pain, especially when she needed attention.

"Let me get this heavy thing in," I grunted. "Then you can have a pat on the head."

I dropped the box with a thud on the kitchen table. "Next time, I'll have you bring it in."

Bronte woofed as if she agreed. I squatted down and gave her the requisite hugs and pats before adding a scoop of dog chow to her dish. It was time to have some tea and sit on my rock by the lake. The rock was my thinking place, and as I stared at the box, I decided I really needed to think.

The sun had warmed the rock, and the lake washed gently onto the shoreline. The water was crystal clear with an odor of freshness enhanced by the deep springs feeding it. "If I could capture that scent, I could be rich."

Bronte wagged her tail, hoping I meant to throw her a stick. Instead, I scratched behind her ears. "Sorry, girl. I'm not in the mood to throw sticks right now." As if she'd understood my words, she loped up the hill, dug under a pile of wet leaves, and retrieved a rawhide chew that she'd left in the yard over the winter.

My head was filled with a mixture of anxiety. First was the weirdness of Gooseberry Acres, complicated by the presence of the pseudo-commandos from Camp Six. Second was the ongoing saga of my love life. Jim Monroe, the State trooper who shared my bed when he was around, was currently in Washington DC at a six-week training session on internet forensics. When he finished the training, a job in the Twin Cities awaited him. I was torn between hoping he'd fail the training and come back to Jackpine County and feeling guilt over wanting him to flunk the class. Our relationship, never totally affirmed, was currently on shaky ground. On top of that, his bright-eyed little son was still undergoing treatment for leukemia in the Twin Cities.

I took a deep breath of the fresh air, noticing the faint fragrance of blossoming wildflowers mingled with the scent of pines. If he asked, would I move to the cities to be with him? Would I be a stepmother to Jake?

"I don't know."

Bronte bounded over at the sound of my voice and settled at my feet.

When I'd finished the tea, I walked back up the slope to the cabin and let myself in. Bronte stayed behind, preoccupied with her rawhide. My phone, sitting next to the box, pinged with a text, hopefully from Jim.

To my disappointment, it was from a number I did not recognize. **Hey, J Long time. Let's talk.**

I stared at the message. The only person who ever called me J was Andrew, my ex-husband. We'd had no communication since the divorce was finalized in New York, and he'd moved in with his Venezuelan makeup artist/model. Andrew had taken up with her after he won the role of Mr. Right Digestion for a probiotics company. After nearly two years of being Andrew-free, I had no desire to chat with him.

Bronte barked at the door to be let in as I paced with the phone in my hand. How had he gotten my number?

The phone pinged again. **Owe you a big apology for bad behavior.**

This had to be a joke. One thing I'd learned through my less-than-perfect marriage was that Andrew never apologized. If anything went wrong for him, somehow it was my fault or his agent's fault or his mother's fault.

I let Bronte in. She followed me as I moved from the living area to the kitchen and back. Maybe someone had hacked his phone. I texted back one word. **Andrew?**

Within moments of sending the text, my phone rang. It was the same number as the text. My reluctance was overruled by curiosity. I answered the call. "Andrew?"

"Jamie? Wow, so glad you answered." His voice reeked of boyishness, the same boyishness that had attracted me ten years ago.

"Andrew," I repeated.

"Uh, it's been a while. I thought I'd check in."

A "check-in" for Andrew usually meant he wanted something. "Andrew, is everything all right?"

The line was quiet for a moment. I sat on the couch while Bronte stared at me with a worried expression.

"Well, sure." The boyishness had dropped from his voice.

"What's wrong?"

"I…uh…well, I'm in Minnesota and thought it would be nice to see you."

In Minnesota? What the hell was a New York City boy doing here? I held back the urge to say, *I don't want to see you again—ever.* Instead, I kept my voice noncommittal. "Oh?"

"I'm in Minneapolis checking out the Guthrie Theater. Auditions, you know."

I wondered if the venerable Guthrie Theater would want someone whose main claim to fame was wearing green tights while playing Mr. Right Digestion. "Yes?"

"Well, I thought I could drive up and see you."

The excuses scrolled through my brain—too busy, lots of deadlines, the dog doesn't like strangers, I'm about to hop a plane for Iceland—but I couldn't lie even to Andrew. "I guess we could meet for coffee. When were you thinking?"

His tone brightened. "How about tomorrow?"

"Andrew, it's a five-hour drive in good weather. You sure you want to come that far for coffee?"

He laughed, and an old feeling tickled at my chest. I used to love his laughter—deep and hearty. "I can handle it. If I get tired, don't you have a Motel Six or something between here and there?"

Andrew was not a Motel Six kind of a guy. Even when we were scraping pennies and he had an out-of-town audition, he always stayed at top hotels.

I worked two and sometimes three jobs to help pay for them.

I should have asked him more questions, been more sociable on the phone, but more than ever, I wanted the call to end. "Listen, Andrew, I need to go. If you can get to Killdeer in the early afternoon, let's meet at the Loonfeather on the main street. Text me when you're close, and I'll drive in."

"Uh, okay."

Was he taken aback by my abruptness? If so, good.

"See you tomorrow." I ended the call. My shoulders were so tensed I had to concentrate on relaxing them. It was amazing to me how his voice caused such a visceral reaction in my body. Maybe it had to do with that final I-want-a-divorce conversation, where he actually said, "Jamie, it's not me, it's you...."

I set the phone down and closed my eyes. Why did Andrew want to see me? At least I could tell him I didn't have any money. He's the one who should be rolling in it. As far as I knew, Mr. Right Digestion paid him well. Oh, and would he be bringing his Venezuelan model Destiny? Yes, she called herself Destiny even though I knew her real name was Consuela.

I smiled, thinking about how she would turn heads in town.

Ten minutes later, the phone rang again. This time it was Jim calling from Washington.

"Hi, Jamie, what's new?"

I opened my mouth to tell him about the surprise call from Andrew and found I couldn't tell him. After a pause, I filled him in on the trip to Gooseberry Acres, Miss Nella, and the cousins. Then I added, "Besides all of this, there's a kid who went missing near Gooseberry."

"Aha, another thing for you to get involved in."

I shuddered, picturing the blond kid with the round face. "Not on your life. And as for Miss Nella and Company, I'm not sure I want to take this on. I'll tell you more, once I've gone through the papers she sent home with me. It might be a much bigger project than I can handle. Besides, I already have a pig to deal with."

"What?"

I laughed and told him about *Apple Pie* and the murder mystery. He told me Jake was doing well, being cared for by his maternal grandmother. Jake's mom, Maria, was still in rehab and wouldn't be released until June. "He says he misses you and wants to come back to the cabin and sleep on the couch with Bronte."

Smiling, I pictured Bronte mothering him on his few visits last winter. Jake, at five, thought it was a real treat to sleep on the lumpy sofa with Bronte snoring at his feet.

As the conversation wound down, guilt gripped my body. I should tell him about Andrew, but for reasons I didn't fully understand, I couldn't. Maybe Andrew was a chapter in my old life and Jim in my new, and I didn't want them to blend. Maybe something else...

"Uh, you still there?"

"Oh, sorry. Distracted, I guess."

"Well, stay out of trouble. I've still got a couple more weeks before I get back."

I'd learned in my thirty-some years that a lot could happen in a couple weeks.

After I ended the call, I retreated once again to my rock by the lake. This time with a beer. As the sun set behind Bear Island, yellowish rays spiking through the tall pines, I wondered what I would say to Andrew. How's life with Destiny? What are you doing straying from New York City? Why the hell are you here?

Bronte trotted out of the woods with a stick. I picked it up and hurled it up the slope noting the happy wag of her tail. Oh, to have a simple life of sticks and rawhide chews.

I concentrated on erasing thoughts of both Andrew and Jim and instead admired the serenity of Lake Larissa. It had been almost exactly a year since I'd arrived at the old family cabin to begin my new life. I remembered my dismay at the state of the building. The last time I'd seen it was when Dad and I had come to scatter Mother's ashes. At sixteen, all I'd wanted was to do the job and get back to the big city.

In the sixteen years since then, Dad had rented the cabin to summer people but put very little into maintenance. With almost all the money left from his estate, I'd upgraded the plumbing, electricity, septic system, and kitchen. Now, a year later, I barely eked out a living with my freelance editing, but I loved living here.

Bronte settled at my feet with the stick and chewed it apart. My friend Rob had dropped her off last summer as a rescue dog. I'd told him emphatically, "I don't want a dog. I had a pet—my ex-husband—and it hadn't worked out so well. I don't want another." He'd ignored my remark and replied, "You need her."

Sometimes people can be so right.

A little breeze rustled the leftover leaves from last fall. As they swirled down the hill, thoughts of Andrew came back to me. He'd hate this place. I pointed to the lake. "Too quiet. Not enough drama. Too few people around to adore him." Bronte ignored me and continued to tear at the bark of the stick. "And too much work for him." Jim, on the other hand, loved the woods and the lake, and the wilderness surrounding the cabin.

Would I show Andrew this place? A piece of me wanted to be able to say to him, "Look, I made it without you."

I finished my beer without answering the question.

Chapter Six: The Fox Family

After sitting on my rock and thinking about Andrew, I walked up to the cabin in a foul mood. The earth must have sensed it because a bank of clouds rolled in, obscuring the golden sunset and turning the skies an iron gray. A chill wind scraped through the pines as the sky darkened.

In all my years in New York City, I'd hardly noticed the weather. When I stepped outside, it was sunny, raining, or snowing. Simple. Here my body recognized the subtle changes in the air pressure. An almost imperceptible ache grew in my jaw as the low front moved in. I smelled the rain before it began to pelt tiny ice balls from overhead. Standing in the doorway, I watched the sleet and hoped the temperature wouldn't drop enough to cause a late-spring frost. Behind the cabin where I'd tilled a small garden, fragile little seedlings were just poking through.

I ate a supper of homemade chicken soup to the sound of rain on the roof. I barely had room for the soup bowl on the table because of the box from Miss Nella and the *Apple Pie* manuscript spread over much of the surface. The soup was watery and tasted like I'd added too much sage and thyme and not enough salt. I grabbed the pot, slipped on my shoes, and ran with it through the rain to the compost box, dumping it into the pile of leaves and debris.

It wasn't until I was back in the cabin, drying my face with a towel, that I realized the reaction to the soup and weather was really about Andrew. How dare he show up in my life again!

With a huge sigh, I surveyed the table. What to tackle first? Murder or memoir? Remembering the hint of intrigue about Tucker and Barrett, I laughed. Maybe there was a murder in the memoir. Thinking about the ruin of the hospital and the neglected grounds, I shuddered and opted for a pot-bellied pig over Miss Nella's memoir.

Grunting, I hefted the box of journals off the table and shoved it in the corner. Tonight, I needed to concentrate on fiction, even if the narrator was a pig. Before going too far into *Apple Pie a'la Murder,* I looked up pot-bellied pigs to find out what kind of pets they were.

Bronte curled up on her rug in the living room while I scanned the internet. "Did you know pot-bellied pigs can be sociable like dogs, except they are intelligent?"

Bronte didn't stir. I figured the only time she'd be interested in pot-bellied pigs was if I brought one home as a pet. As I read about them, I decided they might have the capability of solving a murder, especially if you promised to feed them. They were friendly but could get aggressive, especially around food. They were also easily bored and required a lot of attention. Sounded a lot like Andrew to me.

I read the first chapter of *Apple Pie* and noted the author seemed more interested in writing about food (from the pig's standpoint) than solving the murder. Apple Pie narrated, "The body of Chef Mac's sous chef lay between me and the refrigerator. I knew she'd put the leftover coq au vin on the top shelf, and I was determined to get at it. She'd used a dryer, zestier red wine, and I wanted to know how it paired with the chicken."

Already I was growing to like Apple Pie. He had an honesty about him that often escaped humans.

That night I lay awake in bed listening to the rhythm of falling rain. When I closed my eyes, I saw an image of my wedding photo with Andrew now packed away in a box in the loft. Instead of doing the traditional walk down the aisle church ceremony, we chose a small park in Queens, and a friend with a mail-order ordination performed the ceremony. I wore a pink mini-dress and a flowered headband. Andrew wore jeans and a Hawaiian shirt. We thought we were very cool. The wedding high lasted three months until Andrew was turned down for an acting role he thought was his. The tantrum he threw destroyed two plates and several of our wedding present wine glasses.

I sighed and rolled onto my side to see Bronte's hairy back as she curled up next to me. Bronte didn't throw tantrums, sneak money out of my billfold, and, above all, didn't carry around a wounded ego every time someone said, "No." In retrospect, I'd spent most of my marriage enabling Andrew's bad behavior. I wondered if Destiny was doing the same.

After tossing and turning and disturbing my dog's sleep, I got up and took an ibuprofen. I was tempted to grab the phone and text Andrew to tell him not to come. Still, I was curious. I thought about the first chapter of *Apple Pie* when he said, "It was either curiosity or bad mushrooms that killed Mac's sous chef, and I was determined to find out who did it."

If a pot-bellied pig could solve a murder mystery, I could spend an hour with Andrew.

When I finally fell asleep, I entered into the recurring dream that I was in a holding cell in Queens and couldn't move because my feet were glued to the dank cement floor. Beyond the haze that was the cell, someone waited.

I woke with a start to see soft light from the dawn filtering through the window. Bronte lifted her head and gave my shoulder a quick lick. I threw the covers off, still feeling heavy and groggy from the dream.

When I let Bronte out, I was met with the cool fresh damp of the newly washed forest around my house. Waves from Lake Larissa gently licked the shoreline.

Bronte trotted outside to attend to her morning business and chase a squirrel. I wished I felt as refreshed as the air around me. But I knew I had to deal with Andrew.

To keep my mind off him, I lugged the box of Miss Nella's diaries back onto the table. When I slipped the cover off, I was immediately aware of the dusty smell of old paper. The box had probably been stored in the attic. Peering in, I saw a pile of diaries and a couple of scrapbooks. The top diary appeared to be the most recent and was dated ten years ago.

It opened to January 1st and a list of Miss Nella's resolutions. Some of them were mundane—*this year I will balance the books faithfully every month.*

Others were cryptic—*will plant a tea rose at his site and won't let it die this time.*

Miss Nella wrote in a large, looping style with run-on sentences and little punctuation. It appeared to be a stream of consciousness with little focus. How could this be converted into a memoir? Especially when much of it was a record of the everyday commonplace. *Chickadees in front yard pecking away. Heard a dog barking last night. Furnace fan squeaks. Need to have Ed check it out.*

"Hmmm." I rummaged through the box and found one dated seventy-five years ago. Miss Nella must have been about fifteen.

The writing was smaller, more careful, and done in complete sentences. On January first, when she was a teenager, she listed one resolution: *I will be perfect for Papa and will stop complaining about Punky.*

I stared at the faded ink. "Who is Punky? Someone who worked on the estate or maybe a patient?"

The next five entries were more typical of a fifteen-year-old. She wrote about school and how one of the boys was sweet on her. *He's a honey but not nearly as handsome as the new patient. The nurses call him Dash even though his name is Joshua. No one could be better looking!*

Her words had such a tone of youth and innocence. Did she have a crush on one of the patients?

Scanning the next couple of pages, I found a note in February referring to her father. *Papa lost another patient last night. He gets so sad when it happens even though he knows he can't save them all. They say my mother knew how to calm Papa. I can't do it even though I try.*

The next entry, three weeks later, made no mention of her family. She wrote a long paragraph about school and hoping someone would ask her to the spring dance. *If only Dash wasn't sick. Everyone would be so surprised if he took me to the dance. Someday when he's better, I'm going to be brave and talk to him.*

Bronte whined at the door. I put the diary back in the box and decided to sift through it later. When I set it into the box, a small black-and-white photo slipped out. I caught it and held it to the light. It was taken in front of the house. Four people stood squinting at the camera. The oldest was a tall man wearing wire-rimmed glasses. Next to him, a shorter, younger man, and in front of the two of them, a young girl in a frilly dress and a toddler in a sailor suit.

Was this the Fox family? Dr. Fox, Nella, an unnamed child, and someone else. I brought the photo closer to the light and was startled at the resemblance between the shorter man and Tucker Fox. Both had the same square jaw and the wide smile. I guessed this was Judd, the uncle who became known as a scoundrel. And the little boy, was he Punky? I'd have to ask Miss Nella the next time I saw her.

I checked the clock. It was time to think about what I would wear to have coffee with Andrew. If he was after money, I didn't want to look like I had any.

Chapter Seven: The Lawsuit

The text came in just after noon. **Should arrive in an hour.**

I texted a thumbs-up emoji even though I didn't feel like this was a thumbs-up situation. Since I was showered and ready to go, I decided to leave early and make a quick stop to talk with Clarence about the Miss Nella project. As I brushed my teeth, I noted how much my dark brown hair had grown out since I'd last seen Andrew. It fell to my shoulders and, with all the fresh air and exercise, had a healthy sheen to it. Back in those final days of marriage, when I was so stressed, my hair had become brittle and thin.

I pulled on a plain black long-sleeved T-shirt and a pair of clean jeans. After brushing my teeth, I brushed my hair and warned it, "Don't you dare fall out when you see that man."

Bronte stood in the doorway to the bathroom with a worried look. She'd picked up on the tone of my voice and sensed my growing tension.

I stooped down to pat her. "It's okay. Just a cup of coffee, and he'll be gone from my life once again." At least, I hoped he would.

Slipping the Fox family photo into my bag, I instructed Bronte to keep out all burglars and bears. She wagged her tail as if she thought I was telling her she could join me. "Sorry, girl. Your job is here. Mine is in town. I'll be back soon."

The skies were a beautiful celestial blue, dotted with wisps of clouds. I hoped Andrew wouldn't notice the purity of the air and the luminousness of the deciduous trees as they began to leaf out. I laughed at the thought. Andrew probably didn't know the difference between a deciduous tree and a conifer. I know I didn't until I moved here.

The main street in Killdeer was weekday quiet. Weekends would be busy now through September with sportsmen fishing the lakes and later families coming for vacation. A banner stretching across the street announced the Firemen's Annual Smelt Fry. Last year, it was one of the first events I attended in town. Paper plates with deep-fried smelt, French fries, and coleslaw. Plastic cups with watery 3.2 beer. Festival food here in the Northwoods.

When I pulled up in front of Clarence's house, Joe was out front mowing. Joe worked as Clarence's assistant while he attended community college. Since I'd met him last summer, when he was one of Clarence's clients, he'd filled out. Still gangly like a teenager, his shoulders had widened. More importantly, he stood tall, and the look of defeat that had been etched in his face was gone.

He waved at me when I stepped out of the car. "Step lightly around Clarence. He's crotchety today."

I waved back. "When is he not crotchety?"

Clarence stood at the door. "I can hear you."

Inside, his house smelled of cinnamon. I pointed to the kitchen. "Lorraine must be baking."

"You're just in time."

Lorraine pulled a tray of cinnamon rolls out of the oven. She tsked, "Oh, it looks like I burned them."

Lorraine's cinnamon rolls, burned to a crisp, would be better than anything I could produce.

Clarence settled into a kitchen chair. "All the better. No one will want them, and I don't have to share."

I asked her how she was doing and how Elena and the baby were getting along. Elena, a young woman who had fled her Central American country, was working with an immigrant rights group to obtain asylum. Clarence and I had gotten involved with helping her last winter. Lorraine had volunteered to house her through the legal process. "Oh, the baby is so cute."

"And messy," Clarence added. "Never knew a human could drool like that."

"Spoken like a true childless octogenarian." I watched the icing on the cinnamon roll drip down the side and wondered if I looked like I was drooling, too.

We talked for a few minutes until Lorraine announced she needed to go home. "I'm tending to Cristina while Elena goes to her English class."

Clarence watched as she walked down the hallway. "That woman is a saint. Except when she tries to fix me brussels sprouts."

I nodded, dabbing icing off my lap. "I've started to go through Miss Nella's box." I pulled the photo from my bag and handed it to Clarence. "Do you know who these people are?"

He slipped on a pair of reading glasses from out of his front pocket and studied the photo. "Well, I recognize three of them. Dr. Fox is the tall one, Nella is the girl, and I believe the young man is Dr. Fox's brother Judd. As for the little boy...." His voice dropped off. I wasn't sure if he didn't know who he was or didn't want to say.

I pointed to Judd. "He looks like Tucker. Same smile. And I see a faint resemblance with Barrett."

Clarence handed the photo to me, leaned back in his chair, and closed his eyes. "I remember the first time I met Nella—must have been shortly after I had my fancy new law degree. I was setting up my practice in an office next to the Loonfeather." He looked at me with a glint in his eyes. "It wasn't the Loonfeather back then. They called it Mike's Tavern. Pretty scruffy place. Watering hole for the mine workers. Hell of a party when payday came."

I'd been told that downtown Killdeer had undergone a recent renaissance with the buildup of the tourist business. It went from a rowdy, hardscrabble mining town into serious decline when the mines closed. Unlike other small towns in the area, however, it survived because it was close to the bountiful and unspoiled lakes.

Clarence shifted in his chair. "She walked in looking like a scarecrow. So thin I thought the wind from a passing car might knock her over."

"How long ago was this?"

"Oh, maybe fifty years, give or take. I was a rookie lawyer at the time.

Had aspirations to defend the poor and innocent. Discovered most of my business had more to do with wills, estates, and property rights. I never did become the Killdeer version of Clarence Darrow."

Maybe he hadn't reached the heights of Clarence Darrow, but in my experience with him, he was a smart and effective defense attorney. "I'm guessing she needed advice on wills, estates, and property rights?"

Clarence laughed. "I was afraid she might keel over in my office from lack of food. To my surprise, her voice was strong and steady. No, she didn't want the ordinary estate and property advice. She needed help with a lawsuit."

"Oh?" I pictured the rundown property and wondered if someone had gotten hurt and was looking for money.

Clarence wrinkled his brow. "I can't give you details because of the settlement, but it had to do with a claim against her father."

"Malpractice?"

Once again, Clarence adjusted himself in the chair. Clearly, his hip was bothering him. "Let's say he was 'practicing' something else with a staff member. Back in those days, people didn't talk about such things like they do now."

It took me a moment to put it together. "Ah, I see. Like 'Me Too.'"

Clarence sighed. "Poor Nella. This all came about after her father had died. She adored him and devoted her life to him. I could see the physical toll it was taking on her. She saw herself as the protector of his reputation."

I leaned closer to Clarence, my curiosity piqued. "Can you tell me if it was true? What happened."

Clarence reached over and patted my hand. "That, my dear, is all confidential unless Nella chooses to put it in her memoirs. Most of the parties involved are long buried."

I pointed to the photo. "Can you at least tell me if it has anything to do with the little boy in the photo?"

He closed his eyes. "Keep sifting through that box she gave you."

Clarence wasn't telling me everything he knew. I would have pumped him for more information, except my phone pinged with a text from Andrew.

I'm here. Where are you?

I could almost hear the whine in the text.

"Sorry, gotta go."

"Hot date with that trooper of yours?"

I really didn't want to explain things to Clarence. I stood up and patted him on the shoulder. "I'll talk to you later when I've read through more of the things in the box."

Once outside, I inhaled the scent of newly mown grass. It should have lifted my spirits, but even as the sun pressed its rays through the canopy of budding oaks and maples, I felt dark clouds roiling in the background.

Andrew.

Chapter Eight: Andrew

When I walked into the Loonfeather, it was mid-afternoon quiet. Two men sat at the bar engrossed in a hockey game on the television. The bartender looked up and nodded at me. I followed his gaze to a table near the window. A server took an order from Andrew.

"I know you! I've seen you before somewhere." She giggled.

I watched as Andrew smiled. His teeth dazzled in the same way Tucker's had. I knew how expensive that smile was because I'd paid for most of it.

As if on cue, he intoned in a well-modulated voice, "ProBiolux for the Right in you."

"Oh, you're Mr. Right Digestion. I love that commercial." She turned to the bartender. "Did you see who's here?"

The two customers turned around. One looked puzzled, and the other gave Andrew a little thumbs up before going back to the game.

Andrew spotted me and stood. He touched the server on her arm. "Why don't you make that two IPAs."

As she passed me, she squinted at me as if I'd just landed from a foreign planet. Maybe she thought Mr. Right Digestion couldn't possibly know someone so ordinary. I smiled at her. "My ex." Under my breath, I added, "Definitely Mr. Wrong."

Andrew met me halfway to the table with a giant hug. I stiffened, not sure what to do. I didn't want him to feel particularly welcome.

"Oh J, it's so good to see you."

He hadn't changed much. He still had the boyish smile and the little dimple on his cheek. A friend of mine in the early days of our marriage had described him as a young Brad Pitt. I hadn't seen it then, but now I caught the resemblance. Except, Andrew had a weakness to his chin and a lack of sparkle in his blue eyes. Was that new?

He guided me back to the table. "I ordered IPAs. I know you like them."

When had he ever ordered something because I liked it?

I sat across from him willing my shoulders to relax. We were divorced. I owed him nothing. My life was good.

He leaned forward and gazed at me with soft eyes. I was vulnerable to those eyes. In the early days, I could stare at them for hours, feeling that sense of possession that only young love provides. "J, you are looking good. Country life must appeal to you."

The last time I'd seen him, I was an emotional and physical wreck and had lost so much weight my jeans had been cinched with safety pins. I was now a healthy 110 pounds, including some muscle from hauling wood, digging in the garden, and hiking through my woods. "Thank you, Andrew. You look good, too."

Except, he didn't. He had dark circles under his eyes and a slightly jaundiced hue to his skin. His normally thick blonde hair had thinned. I couldn't quite put my finger on it, but he had an air of neglect. One thing I'd learned about Andrew over the years was the vanity he carried about his looks. Something was very wrong here.

The server came with the beers. I asked her for a menu. She hardly looked at me as she gazed like a teenager with a crush at Andrew. He smiled at her. "Bring two menus, please."

She walked away with an expression of awe. Little did she know the true Andrew. He was always a good actor.

"So, how are you?" Andrew continued to smile.

"I'm good. I've been busy."

He nodded. "I know. I read your articles. Sounds wild—you know, murder and all."

I didn't want to talk about the excitement in my life with him. I wanted to find out why he was here. "Listen, Andrew, I don't mean to be impolite, but I'm curious after all this time why you are here in Minnesota and in Killdeer."

He leaned back in his chair. "Ah, J. Always one to get right to the point. I liked that about you."

No, he didn't. He let me know on many occasions that he thought I was abrupt, impolite, and far too inquisitive. A simple question like, "How did the rehearsal go?" could bring an explosion.

I waited, sipping the beer and not enjoying it.

Finally, he spoke, "Well, let's say I'm 'at liberty.' You know, between gigs."

I thought he'd signed a multi-year contract for Mr. Right Digestion. "What happened with your commercial?"

He shrugged. "You know the business…" His voice trailed off.

While I wanted to jump in with, "You got fired, didn't you?" I held back.

The server came back, "We don't get celebrities here very often." She waved her arm to indicate the room. "Though once some Hollywood guys came in. Said they were scouting locations for a television show called Fargo. They were fun. Treated the whole place to a round of drinks."

She slipped an iPhone out of her pocket. "Do you mind if I take a photo?"

He winked at her. "We actors never mind a little publicity." Pointing to me, he added, "Jamie would you mind taking the photo?"

The server, whose name tag said Mandy, handed me the phone. She leaned into him while I took a couple of pictures.

Mandy was so excited to see the photos she almost forgot to take our order.

I asked for a BLT, and Andrew had a veggie burger. He patted his flat stomach. "Got to watch my weight. Never know when I might have to wear tights again."

She giggled. "Oh, you look perfect."

He watched her take little dancing steps as she headed to the kitchen. "Nice to be recognized."

I tensed, holding back the urge to say something sarcastic. Andrew needed to be adored, and I had once been guilty of hanging on his every word.

The door opened, and a couple more men came in, settling at the bar.

Andrew toyed with his beer, moving it in little circles. When he spoke, I thought I detected genuine sadness in his face. Hard to know since he was a professional actor. "Tell me about your cabin. I hear it's pretty nice."

I took a long deep breath and let it out slowly. "Andrew, you didn't come all this way to hear about my cabin. What's going on?"

Someone at the bar clapped, pointing at the television. "Didn't I tell you he'd score?"

I waited as his silence made me more and more uncomfortable. He put his elbow on the table and rested his chin on his hand. "Uh, well, you remember Destiny?"

"Hard to forget." A little of the bitterness crept into my voice.

"Seems she had...ah...other friends in her life."

The one time I'd seen her, my impression had been of a tall, dark-haired beauty with impossibly smooth skin and a perfect body. "What do you mean?"

"She had a boyfriend the whole time she was with me."

I should have gotten some amusement out of the turn of events, but I didn't. I remembered my sense of betrayal when I found out that his week-long location shoots were actually spent at her apartment.

He raised his eyebrows, "I guess you know what it's like."

I lifted my beer and took a big swallow, nearly choking. I was filled with so many emotions at that moment—old anger, bitterness, resentment. Yet it was all tempered by an empathy for him. Apparently, he was as gullible as I was. "I'm sorry, Andrew."

My head was starting to throb. I wanted to tell him in a calm voice to please go away. I wasn't interested.

"That's not the half of it. The boyfriend. Well, I think she gave him all my information. I suspect, but can't prove it, that he stole my identity, racked up the credit cards, even tried to get into my bank account."

"Oh, my god. Are they in jail now?"

He looked down, shaking his head. For the next few minutes, he told me about discovering the theft, trying to get his credit rating fixed, and making a report to the police. "It wasn't a top priority for the NYPD."

The food came. I picked at my sandwich, feeling sorry for Andrew. A college friend had once had her identity stolen, and it took her over a year to get everything straightened out.

I tried to lighten up the conversation. "So, I guess she's out of your life now?"

Andrew hesitated a little too long before he replied. "Sure. As I said, I'm at liberty."

Somewhere in this story, Destiny lurked in the background.

Several more people entered the Loonfeather. Behind me, I heard some whispering and a high-pitched giggle. Someone else must have recognized Andrew. I stiffened, waiting for the approach, but no one came.

"Are you done with Mr. Right Digestion?" I didn't want to hear anything more about his stolen identity.

He finished his burger. "I need to move on. I'd like to try the stage again. That's why I'm here. The Guthrie Theater is a great stepping stone. Do you know some of the best Broadway actors cut their teeth at the Guthrie?"

Without letting me answer, he went into a lecture about some of the top names who'd once starred at the Guthrie. "Frank Langella and David Hyde Pierce had seasons at the Guthrie."

I nodded as if I was interested. Truth be told, I'd been very happy in the Northwoods, away from live or dead theater. Andrew had cured me of it long ago.

The server came back and asked about dessert. I passed, and Andrew ordered pie a´la mode and another beer.

"Listen, Andrew, I really have to go. You might think I spend my days enjoying the scenery and eating bonbons, but I have deadlines." I didn't mention that I also had a dog who needed to be let out.

He looked down at his lap and back at me with a troubled expression. The way his brows knit reminded me of the conversation when he told me he was leaving. "I was wondering. You know, since I haven't quite recovered from the theft…."

Warning lights flashed behind my eyes. I held up my hand, "Stop."

His eyes widened at the abruptness and firmness in my voice.

"I don't have any money. My life right now is month-to-month."

His expression relaxed into an "aw shucks" half smile. "Thought I'd ask."

Any sympathy I had for him drained away with that expression. He'd used it on me too many times before.

"You see," he continued, "this cabin of yours wasn't exactly listed in the properties in the divorce decree. I might be entitled to half."

For a moment, I sat stunned. "What? You think you're entitled to half of my cabin?" My voice rose loud enough that one of the guys at the bar turned to stare.

He still had his "aw shucks" expression. "We agreed to split everything, as you recall."

I opened my mouth, then clamped it shut. How could he? The anger, bitterness, and disappointment welled up in me. Without thinking, I picked up my half-empty beer glass. I was ready to throw it in his face when the ridiculousness of it hit me. A Hollywood drama set right here in the Loonfeather. Instead, I took a swig of the beer, set the glass down, and stood up. My face hurt from trying to maintain control. "Goodbye, Andrew. Have a safe trip back. No need to call again."

With that, I grabbed my bag and walked out. I hoped he wouldn't stiff the server.

The mid-afternoon sun warmed my face but not my heart as I slid into the driver's seat of my car. I was parked in front of the hardware store. As I fumbled with the keys, I heard two people arguing.

"I'm tired of catering to her, Tuck. We have to do something, or I'm heading back to California." Barrett Fox glared at her brother.

He stood near the door to the store with his arms folded. "Just hang on for another couple of weeks. I'm working on something. We'll see what happens."

Were they after Miss Nella's property the way Andrew was after mine?

I couldn't get out of town fast enough.

Chapter Nine: The Scrapbook

When I arrived home, several robins pecked at the grassy lawn while a flock of Canadian geese honked overhead. I stood outside the door of the cabin and took a long deep breath. The air smelled fresh and new, and I felt like I'd just emerged from a stinky dumpster. Bronte barked with impatience. I needed to give her a hug and take a long shower to wash away Andrew's words.

Later, with my hair still wet, I sat on my rock and watched the roll of the waves. "He couldn't have a claim on this place, could he?" I'd have to ask Clarence, yet I was overcome with shame. How could I have lived as long as I did with that man/boy? What was wrong with me? Unwanted tears blurred my vision.

As if my Ojibwe ancestors heard my anguish, my friend Rob arrived unexpectedly. Rob, his Native American roots etched in the deep brown of his eyes and the weathered hue of his face, walked down the slope to me.

"Heard you needed some help."

I did a double-take. "What? What did you hear?"

He laughed. "Clarence said you were doing a project at Gooseberry Acres. I can give you some history."

"You drove all the way out here to tell me about the sanatorium?"

He sat down beside me, stretching out his long legs. "Naw. I was signing paperwork at the lodge. They've commissioned me to do a mural in the dining room."

"I thought you hated working for them."

Rob had no love for the McConnells, who owned the lodge. Years ago, they had bought out his family and others from his tribe at rock-bottom prices and evicted them. Currently, due to a number of lawsuits and a criminal case, the lodge was in the midst of a transition to new ownership.

"But with the new people, you're thinking it will be okay?"

Rob peered at the lake. "The tribe is involved. I want them to succeed."

I shrugged. "Okay, as long as they don't try to take my cabin and acres from me." I'd been the subject of a scheme to buy out my land without my permission last summer. A shiver ran through me, thinking about it.

His eyes sparkled. "No worries. You have a great lawyer."

I might need one. The image of Andrew sitting at the Loonfeather crossed my vision, and I winced.

Rob wrinkled his brow. "Something wrong?"

I should have told him, explained to him about the sudden appearance of Mr. Right Digestion, but a great wall held me back. I didn't want my history to seep into my cabin by the lake and contaminate the freshness of the land and my life. I waved him away. "Old business in New York. No big deal."

"My gut says it's a bigger deal than you are letting on."

I tried to make a joke of it. "Stick with predicting the weather. Okay?"

Bronte saved me from more explanation by crashing out of the woods with a stick in her mouth. She set it down at Rob's feet and pawed at it.

He leaned down. "You want me to throw this, young pup?"

I held up my hand. "Don't toss it in the lake, please. She'll come out and shake water all over us."

Rob threw it up the hill, and Bronte bounded after it.

"Okay, Rob. Tell me about the mural."

He explained his concept. "They wanted a pictorial of Native American history. You know, tepees and birch bark canoes. I said I wanted something more abstract that brought out the essence of the earth."

Rob's paintings had an ethereal quality to them that made them come alive as if the trees quaked and the water shimmered. "You talked them into it?"

He grinned. "I promised to add an Indian lurking in the background."

We sat in comfortable silence for a few moments before I turned to him,

"You said you knew something about Gooseberry Acres?"

He folded his arms and gazed up at the sky. "My mother worked there. She used to talk about it with my aunties."

"Was it a terrible place? When I picture a sanatorium, I see a drab building with patients wandering around like zombies. Other than the house where Miss Nella lives, the only building is the main one, and it's in bad shape."

His laugh was a genuine deep in the chest rumble. "Oh my, you've been watching too many horror movies. Gooseberry wasn't an asylum. It was a private hospital for people who could afford the care and the discretion."

Bronte came down the hill with the stick. She had leaves and something greasy stuck to her coat. I smelled her before she made it to the rock.

"Phew! What did you roll in?"

Rob sniffed. "I would guess it's a little eau de dead rabbit."

"Let me hose her off, and you can tell me everything you know about Gooseberry."

A cloud obscured the sun as Rob held Bronte, and I ran the hose over her. When he let her go, she shook herself, splattering water on the two of us. Overhead the sky darkened as more clouds moved in.

"Let's go in before we get soaked." Rain pattered into the lake as I quickly toweled off my dog with an old rag.

Once inside, with the tea kettle heating, we sat at the kitchen table. I pointed to the box in the corner with Miss Nella's diaries and scrapbooks. "I'm supposed to go through that and help Miss Nella put things in order. I'm not sure it will result in a memoir. The little I've read, her diaries are filled with ordinary things like, 'I saw a flicker today.'"

I poured two mugs of mint tea and waited for him to talk.

"You've heard of the Indian schools, haven't you?"

I raised my eyebrows. "Don't tell me it was a sanatorium and Indian school."

"No. But there's a connection."

He went on to tell me about the schools. Indian children from all over were mandated to attend the schools. Families were punished if they didn't send their children. Many of them were boarding schools with deplorable conditions.

"Children from my community died of disease, starvation, and sadness. My mother was tough. She held on, and when she was fifteen, the school let her work the summer at Gooseberry. At least she was close to home."

I sipped the tea, aware of the soothing aroma of the mint, which contrasted with what I was being told. "I read that it started with the notion that the schools would make them into good citizens."

"Pah!" Rob folded his arms. "The motto was, 'Kill the Indian and make the man.' We were punished for speaking our own language or practicing our own customs. It was brutal."

"But your mother got away to work at Gooseberry?"

Rob lifted the tea to his lips, blew on it, and took a swallow. "Not exactly. In the summers, the schools would send students to work—for no pay. They called it vocational training, but it was the same as if they were indentured. My mother worked the summer in the laundry before being sent back to the Indian school."

I knew from a previous conversation that Rob's mother took her own life when Rob was a teenager. He once said he blamed the Indian school for robbing her of her spirit.

I waited for him to continue.

"The story she told my aunties was that a very handsome and kind doctor worked with Dr. Fox that summer. Where Dr. Fox was standoffish with the staff, this doctor learned their names and greeted them whenever he saw them. He once treated a burn on her arm from a hot iron. She described him as being like a movie star."

"Perhaps she had a crush on him?"

Rob smiled with a faraway expression. "It's hard to think of my mother as a teenager with a crush, but it's possible."

"I might have found something about him in Miss Nella's diary. She talked about a kind doctor. But she also talked about a handsome patient she had a crush on."

The rain pelted the roof of the cabin in a gentle rhythm.

Rob glanced at the box. "Mother also mentioned Dr. Fox's daughter."

"Was she talking about Miss Nella?"

"I think so. Of course, it was a long time ago, and I wasn't supposed to be listening."

I smiled, picturing him hiding behind a sofa to hear the women talk.

"Dr. Fox was strict with her. He didn't want her near either the staff or the patients."

"Probably scared she'd get TB."

My phone interrupted with a ping. The text was from Jim. **Passed my first test. Wanna go out for a beer?** He ended it with a smiley face.

Since when did he start using emojis? I set the phone down.

"Your trooper checking up on you?" Rob's eyes crinkled in amusement.

"Excuse me a moment." I texted Jim back. **I'll catch the next flight to DC. Don't start without me.**

"Done. Now what were you saying?"

"I think Nella was about my mother's age. She said she always dressed nice. Snooty. Stayed mostly in the residence."

I found my mind wandering back to Andrew. He always dressed well and could be snooty. Especially around my friends. Could he ruin my life here? I tuned out for a moment until Rob shifted in his chair, his expression suddenly serious.

"I know this is gossip, but my mother said she'd seen Nella sneaking around the grounds after dark once. She thought she saw her go into one of the cottages they used to have. This doctor lived in one."

"She was pretty young to be involved with the doctor." I shivered thinking about an older man luring Nella into one of the cottages.

In the distance, thunder rumbled. Bronte walked over and put her head on my lap. I stroked the smoothness of her fur. "It's okay, girl." Normally, Bronte was happy and puppylike, but she had a great fear of loud noises, especially guns and thunder.

"She said some of the other staff at the hospital called Nella loose, like she might have been messing with one of the patients, too. They had a number of young men in the hospital at the time."

I pictured Miss Nella as the dignified elderly lady and couldn't see her sneaking around with men at age fifteen. "Sounds more like downstairs gossip than reality."

"Of course, I was only ten and didn't really understand what she was talking about. But here's the important piece that struck me at the time. She said later that year, the doctor disappeared. Like he packed up in the middle of the night and was gone." Rob set down his tea and stretched his arms. "That's what I remember the most. She said, 'the doctor left, and soon after, there was a new grave in the cemetery.'"

"You mean like someone murdered him? Or he murdered someone? Was she there when it happened?"

Rob shrugged. "I don't know. Mom had friends who worked at the place year-round. She might have gotten it from one of them."

"Sounds more like the imagination of teenagers looking for intrigue."

"I agree." He stood up and stretched. Rob, in his early sixties, was tall and muscular. With his hair pulled back into a single braid, he could have been a model of the classic Native American. He glanced at his watch. "It's time for me to go. Brad has a special wild rice hot dish for me." He chuckled. "Brad seems to think I like wild rice since my family harvested it for so many years. I am not a fan. I'd give anything for a bowl of Kraft Macaroni and Cheese."

Rob and his husband Brad had a solid and loving union so, unlike my disaster with Andrew.

I saw him to the door. "I guess it's your burden to bear."

After Rob left, the rain let up, and the clouds rolled east, leaving me with a brilliant sunset over Bear Island. I watched the light disappear and wondered what the true story was about the handsome doctor and a new grave in the cemetery.

Chapter Ten: Nella's Diary

The next morning, I puttered in the cabin, sweeping, doing laundry, and cleaning the bathroom. In the last week or two, my energy had been focused on planting the garden. I pictured myself, the city girl turned vegetable gardener, raising enough produce to have a little stand on the highway. What I didn't understand about northern Minnesota gardening was the vagaries of the weather—late spring frosts, too much rain, not enough rain—and the realities of the wildlife who also wanted to share the bounty.

I walked through the dewy grass to the garden only to find something had been nibbling on the tender bean sprouts. The three fledgling tomato plants I'd bought in town were chewed down to the stem, and the soft earth was filled with deer tracks.

The image of my little vegetable stand disappeared as I surveyed the destruction. Bronte came panting to my side after chasing a squirrel up a tree. I pointed to the decimated plot. "See? Your job is to keep them out."

She wagged her tail but admitted no responsibility.

Once inside, I opened my laptop and searched for remedies. I was amazed at the number of articles on how to keep critters out of the garden. One even suggested peeing along the periphery. I tossed that one, found a recipe for deer repellent that included large amounts of cayenne pepper. The last article I read suggested simply getting an outdoor dog and training the dog to patrol the garden. I couldn't imagine Bronte spending the night outside instead of sleeping comfortably in the spot where Jim should have been.

"My next option is a high fence, I guess." I wondered where I'd get the money to buy the materials and pay Rob to build one.

With a sigh, I closed the laptop and brought Miss Nella's box over. "Where do I start?"

Bronte pricked up her ears at my voice and wandered over to me. "I think I'm wasting Miss Nella's time. I don't know what to do with all of this." I considered closing the box and calling Clarence to tell him I couldn't take this on, except Rob's words about a fresh grave in the cemetery intrigued me. Was the handsome doctor murdered?

I cleared off the kitchen table and unloaded the contents of the box. I found a total of twenty diaries, a photo album, and several scrapbooks. Thinking about the photo of Miss Nella and her family, I decided to start with the album.

"Remember, you are working on helping her with a memoir, not trying to solve a murder." I opened the album, and a musty odor wafted out. I sneezed several times. It did not appear that anyone had looked at the photos in a long time. Many had become unglued and nested between the pages.

Most of the photos from the first several pages were black-and-white group snapshots taken from too far away to get a good sense of the people. I checked the back for labels, but the only thing written was the year. In one, four women in long skirts and white pinafores stood in front of the main building. Standing to the side in a white lab coat was a younger Dr. Fox than in the photo I'd shown to Clarence. Maybe this was the nursing staff.

As I sorted through the first couple of pages, I found I was more interested in the background than the people. Even in the absence of color in the photos, I could see a well-tended flower garden in front of the main building. In with the photos was a postcard labeled Gooseberry Acres Sanatorium. It was an aerial shot showing the grounds of the hospital. In the middle was the hospital with the walkway. Dr. Fox's residence flanked one side, and several smaller buildings flanked the other. Behind the hospital was an open area that looked like a large garden. Beyond the garden, a thick forest edged the lake. I could see why developers might be interested in the land.

I peered at several more photos, but none of them gave me the sense of the place or who the people were. Going through the album reminded me of sitting in Grandmother Forest's musty parlor in Boston while she showed me old photos of Dad's side of the family. Most of them had been taken by a professional photographer, and everyone stood stiff and formal. I was too young at the time to appreciate the family history contained in the album.

Somewhere in the loft was the album, along with the paltry number of photos I had of my mother and her family. Actually, I don't think I had any pictures of Mom's family. It's as if she had needed to erase the past. It wasn't until I moved here last year that I fully understood my mother's heritage—half Ojibwe from her mother and half European from her father. I'd never met my grandparents or even heard Dad talk about them.

"Enough," I set the album down. "Time to take my coffee to the lake and figure out what comes next."

I sat on the rock, inhaling the sweetness of dewy grass mingled with the fresh water of the lake while Bronte rooted around in the woods. "Don't you dare find another dead thing to roll in," I called to her.

Out on the lake, a small fishing boat trolled the calm waters. Jim had promised me before he left for DC that when he got back, he'd teach me to fish. I had met his promise with little enthusiasm. "Don't you have to clean them after you catch them?"

He had laughed. "Well, they don't clean themselves—especially when they're dead."

God, I missed him right now.

As if the goddess of the universe had heard me, a vehicle rumbled down my road. A momentary jolt of excitement rolled through me as if Jim had miraculously flown from Washington, D.C., home to me. Except it didn't sound like Jim's truck. I slipped off the rock, ready to grab Bronte if this was a stranger. She came loping out of the woods. Judging by the way she wagged her tail, if the person in the vehicle meant harm, Bronte was not about to protect me.

The car, a white SUV with Cascade County Sheriff's Office painted on the side, pulled to a stop beside my car.

Travis Booker, sheriff of Cascade County, the next county over from mine, stepped out as Bronte squealed and pawed at his feet.

"I see she's guarding you as usual."

"Travis, what a surprise." We'd become friends last fall when he'd helped me with a writing project investigating a school shooting in Cascade, a town north of Killdeer. Since then, he'd been elected sheriff. With his new duties, I hardly saw him.

"You're looking pretty fine in your sheriff's duds." His hair was cut short, and his khaki pants were sharply creased. He'd lost some weight since his election and had more tension lines around his mouth.

I held up my mug. "Coffee?"

"Please."

We sat at the kitchen table amid the piles from Miss Nella's box. He pointed at them. "Another project, I hear."

"Are there no secrets around here?"

He laughed, "I ran into Clarence in town. He told me you were doing some work on the old Gooseberry Acres. I've been meeting with your sheriff Fowler about that camp near there."

I closed my eyes for a moment and pictured the map where Gooseberry Acres and Camp Six were located. "Oh, I see. The camp where the missing boy was from is close to your border, isn't it?"

He nodded. "Seems his parents are quite wealthy, and they are posting a substantial reward for him. Fowler and I were planning around the possibility of having a bunch of armed reward-seekers tramping through both our jurisdictions."

"I heard they haven't found anything other than a backpack."

Travis stirred milk into his coffee. "I think we are looking at a search and recovery, not a search and rescue. From what Fowler and the Camp Six people have said, the boy wasn't exactly a wilderness expert. More an expert on street drugs and video games. The parents thought Camp Six would straighten him out."

I told him what Tucker had said about seeing someone hitchhiking in the area. "It's possible he's on his way back East."

Travis shrugged. "Could be. Meanwhile, we're preparing for a zoo around here."

We were both quiet for a few moments. I felt for the kid and his family. Something must have really gone haywire for him to have been sent to Camp Six.

Travis set his coffee cup down. "I've heard things about Camp Six. It's based on the theory that if the military can straighten people out, then a military-like program can fix the problems teenagers have."

"I thought it was a wilderness camp where they taught the kids survival techniques."

Travis shook his head. "Uh, uh. Military drills, strict punishment—the whole boot camp mixture. None of it teaches the kids how to survive once they're out on the street again. Some of them end up worse off than when they went in."

"Well, I hope they find him, and Miss Nella doesn't have to contend with amateur rangers tromping all over her property. I met the caretaker, an old guy named Ed. He struck me as someone who would shoot first and maybe ask questions later."

Travis picked up one of the photos of Gooseberry and held it up to the light. "I grew up in Cascade, so this place was like a thousand miles away as far as I was concerned. But kids used to tease when we played tag, 'Gooseberry germs and no returns.' It was something passed down through the generations, I guess."

"Well, I'm not sure I can help Miss Nella with this. I don't even know where to start sorting through all these diaries." I picked up one and opened it. A little tarnished brass nametag that had been taped into it fell out. *Dr. Heller, MD.* I held it by its edges. "Like this. Who was he, and was he important to the story?"

Travis's phone rang at the same time Bronte sauntered to the door and woofed. I let her out with a stern warning, "No dead animals."

While he talked in the living room, I paged through the diary with the nametag. Miss Nella had neglected to date this one, but it started out with her writing about getting her "monthly" and hating how it made her feel. *It's like being so dirty. Or like Papa's patients who cough up blood. I wish it would go away, but Miss McEnany says it's our curse to bear. Why should we have to bear something? What was God thinking?*

Good question.

Travis finished his call and sat down to his lukewarm coffee. "I'm not sure I'm cut out for this sheriff's business. So much of it is bureaucratic paperwork. That was one of the county commissioners complaining about my request for computer upgrades. I'm tired of hearing, 'well, back when I was young, we got it done without all this internet piffle.'"

"Come on, did he really say piffle?"

Travis grinned. "I might have embellished a little."

"You have my sympathy. I have a stable of clients who want all the editing on paper. It's like, the Bronte sisters didn't have a computer. Why should we need one?"

Bronte scratched at the door, her tongue hanging out like she'd run a marathon. When I let her in, she ran directly to her water dish and slopped it all over the floor.

"Oh, the life of a dog. She doesn't have to worry about your county commissioners being stuck in the last century."

Travis's smile had a weariness to it. I leaned my elbows on the table. "So, truth now, Sheriff Booker. What really brings you here?"

He shifted in his chair. "Well, uh, I have another meeting in Killdeer this evening and thought I'd stop by and pass the time."

Stopping by meant a ten-mile drive. I shook my head. I knew if Jim wasn't in the picture, Travis would be a regular visitor. I liked him a lot—as a friend. And I worried about him because I knew he drank too much. Was he checking up on me?

He must have sensed my thought process because he sat up straighter, gazing beyond me. "Okay. I'll be honest. I'm on a fact-finding mission."

"Meaning what?"

"Rumors are circulating in the law enforcement community that Rick Fowler is stepping down for health reasons."

Sheriff Fowler and I had an uneasy relationship. I'd stumbled into a couple of situations that eventually made him look bad. I wasn't sorry to see him go.

"Hey, you just got elected to Cascade County. Are you looking for a new job already?"

Travis cleared his throat. "Uh, no. I was just wondering if Jim might be interested. Has he ever…you know…said anything?"

Wouldn't it be nice to have Jim as sheriff? A wave of guilt washed over me. He was in DC training for something he wanted to do. Even though I ached for him to be here, I'd never put that kind of pressure on him. I remembered how Andrew used to pressure me to take yet another job so he would be free to audition or enroll in more acting classes.

I worked my face into what I hoped was a smile. "Not really."

For a few moments, we lapsed into uncomfortable silence. His question touched a nerve. Jim and I hadn't talked about any kind of commitment and at this point I didn't want Travis to know how tenuous our relationship seemed to be.

I needed to move on to another topic. I told him about my gardening attempts.

He relaxed. "My mother had the same problem. She bought some godawful spray from a woman in town who claimed it was an old Ojibwe recipe. I doubt the Indians had much access to hot peppers in the olden days, but thinking back on it, the stuff she used reminded me of the pepper spray we have."

"Did it work?"

He grinned. "Sure, after she put up a six-foot fence."

At the door, as he was leaving, he turned to me. "I heard rumors that you had a tiff at the Loonfeather with some Hollywood guy yesterday."

I stiffened. "Who told you?"

"I'm a sheriff. I hear everything."

"Mandy, the server, right?"

His cheeks flushed. "Could be."

I did not feel like sharing my conversation with Andrew. "Well, it's time for me to get back to Gooseberry Acres and all the drama of a TB sanatorium." I waved at him, making it clear I was not going to talk about Andrew. Is that the reason he stopped by? Investigating rumors?

Chapter Eleven: What the Pig Knew

After Travis left, I surveyed the piles on the table and decided my heart wasn't in figuring out Miss Nella's memoir. I put all the diaries back in the box and set it in the corner. Time to concentrate on Apple Pie and the murder of Chef Mac's sous chef.

I was midway through the second chapter, in which Apple Pie is trying to figure out how to alert the human world to the dead chef. By this point, the author had told me that Chef Mac was a well-known chef and cookbook author, and Apple Pie had no love for the now-dead sous chef. Since my knowledge of cookbook authors began and ended with the movie "Julie and Julia," I found this interesting.

Perhaps the *Apple Pie a'la Murder* mystery would be a true winner. As an editor, I always held out hope a manuscript would come my way that excited me and compelled me to read it to the end without exclaiming, "Come on! You really think a reader will buy that a count during the time of Dracula would be named Troy?"

Since pigs generally couldn't call 9-1-1, I wondered how Apple Pie would handle this dilemma. To my satisfaction, he remained true to his pig-self and nosed his way out the front door in an effort to cause enough trouble for someone to find the body.

My phone rang as Apple Pie trotted after a jogger hoping she'd call 9-1-1 with a pig emergency. Caller ID said *Northern Sun Realty*.

I was used to calls from realtors wanting to list my property. Twenty acres of pristine forest on a beautiful lake? I imagined the dollar signs in their eyes when they called. I almost let it go to voicemail but decided at the last minute to answer and ask them to put my number on a "do not call" list.

"Yes," I kept my tone curt.

"Ah, is this Jamie Forest? The writer?" The female voice sounded unsure.

"Speaking."

"Ah, I'm wondering if we could talk?" The upspeak in her tone told me she was young.

I sighed. I had a pig to attend to. "I'm sorry. I have no plans to sell. I don't think we have anything to talk about."

She cleared her throat. "I, ah. Well, Jilly at the paper suggested I call you. I checked with her first because everything seemed...well...odd."

My interest was piqued. "Okay. You have my attention."

"Well, you see, this man came in today. He wanted to know how much your place might be worth. He said he was part owner and was thinking about selling his share."

"What?!" I sat down hard on the chair.

"He said he was your husband? Except Jilly from the *Times* and I are good friends, and I've read your articles, and I know you're...like you're divorced."

Many people in Jackpine County knew my story. Before I moved here from New York, I'd written an article in the New York Times Magazine about mistaken identity and being hauled off to jail in the middle of the night by a drug task force. A piece of the article talked about the raid happening the night before I was to sign my final divorce papers. After living here a year, I still got stopped every once in a while by people who'd read the article.

"What did this person look like?"

"You know that commercial that used to run with the guy in green tights—Mr. Right Digestion? He looked just like him, only a little skinnier. He had a really cool smile and all, but I still wondered. So, I told him I'd get back to him. Then I called Jilly, who gave me your number."

I took a deep breath and let it out slowly. "Thanks for letting me know. He doesn't own this property, and he has no rights to it. If he contacts you again, have him call me."

"Sure." I sensed relief in her voice. "If you ever decide to sell, though, please let me know."

When hell freezes over. Fortunately, I didn't say that out loud. What was Andrew up to?

I sat at the table for a long time. Bronte pulled herself up from her mat in the living room and trotted over to me, her nails making clicking noises on the polished wooden floor. "I think, girl, we might have trouble brewing."

After checking the time to make sure Clarence would be up from his nap, I called him.

"Engstrom." He hardly had the demeanor on the phone of someone who was trying to maintain a law business.

"Clarence, it's Jamie."

"Oh, sure. Forgot to look at caller ID. Still not quite awake."

I skipped the polite talk and plunged in. "I've got ex-husband problems." I explained to him my meeting with Andrew and the phone call from the realtor.

The line was quiet when I finished. "Clarence, are you there?"

"Just settling into a chair. So, this ex-husband thinks he might be entitled to half of your cabin?"

I looked around the room with its rustic beams and fieldstone fireplace. I didn't want Andrew anywhere near it. "That's what he said."

"Wonder if he's talked to a lawyer."

Clarence's comment made me nervous. "He didn't say anything."

"Well, here's what you need to do. First, take a deep breath and relax. He doesn't have a claim to it unless you signed a joint tenancy agreement during your marriage, and even then, it could be argued in court."

I squeezed my eyes shut. "At the time of the divorce, my dad had just died. I didn't even consider the cabin as having anything to do with the settlement. It was still in Dad's name. I think Andrew is suggesting I held that information back."

"No need to overthink it. The law is generally clear that property you specifically inherited is not considered community property."

"Even in New York?"

"It's pretty universal, but I can check with my sources to make sure."

I took a deep breath. "Okay, I'll try to relax. But something weird is up. I wouldn't be surprised if he was in deep money trouble if he's after my property."

"Don't let him bully you."

"The bullied phase of my life is over."

Before I ended the call, I told him about the box from Miss Nella. "I'm not sure I'm up to the task of trying to sort her memoirs." I described the diaries and the albums and also told him about Rob's mother and the rumors of a murder.

When Clarence spoke, he sounded like he carefully chose his words. "There are definitely some unanswered questions surrounding Gooseberry Acres, but a murder sounds too much like someone's imagination." He was silent for a moment as if gathering his thoughts. "If I recall right, the estate did have a cemetery. For some of the patients who died, the families asked that they be buried on the grounds. I'm not sure if they didn't want the expense of transporting them home or if they were afraid of getting TB."

"So, Rob's mother could have been right about a fresh grave, and it probably had nothing to do with the unnamed doctor."

"You know how rumors fly."

After we finished talking, I felt both a sense of relief that Andrew didn't have a case and a sense that something was still amiss with Gooseberry Acres. Who was the little boy in the photo? What about this kind doctor who left so abruptly? And the fresh grave?

Instead of going back to Apple Pie to find out if he was able to alert the authorities, I put on a light jacket and decided to go for a walk. "Bronte, want to check out the woods?"

She was at the door before I could zip my jacket up. Late afternoon with the cooling of the air brought out the scents of the greening pines. I took a deep breath and tried to pull a curtain on all the thoughts about Andrew and what he might be scheming.

I took the trail behind the cabin that led deeper into the forest. Eventually, it would intersect with the Lady Slipper Trail, our public trail that started in Killdeer and ended at Lake Larissa. Earlier in the spring, I'd been on a work detail fixing the muddy ruts left behind by ATVs. We hoped to clear several spots along the trail to create roundabouts to slow down the prohibited ATVs in the summer and the snowmobilers in the winter.

Carl, a grizzled old-timer and one of our hardest workers, had suggested clothesline wire across the trail at neck height. "Decapitate a few of those idiots, and maybe they'd stop tearing up the trail."

"Please tell me you're not serious." I stared at him, not knowing how to read his comment. He didn't crack a smile.

Norma, the nurse manager at the hospital, laughed. "Of course, he's not. I need those guys alive because they keep my emergency room busy. What would I do if we didn't have them to stitch up, patch up and dry out?"

I loved my work on the trail both for the comradery and the physical challenge. As I made my way through the woods, I thought about my life in New York with Andrew. The only physical challenge I had involved lugging bags of groceries up three flights of stairs when the elevator in our building broke down.

Bronte trotted ahead of me, stopping to sniff at mound of freshly dug earth. "If there's a skunk in that hole and you scare her out, you know it means another bath."

This time of late afternoon, the frogs were courting. The forest was alive with a constant chirp and trill, along with an occasional whine of mosquitoes. The big fat mosquitoes were just hatching. In another week or two, it would be time to find the Deep Woods Off mosquito repellent. Right now, though, I could walk the trail without getting eaten up. As Jim once said to me, "People look at the forest and think the danger is with the bears and wolves. In truth, the biggest danger is a man with a hunting rifle thinking you are a deer. The second biggest danger is the bugs—mosquitoes, ticks, horse flies—they'll do you in long before you'll ever confront a bear."

As I walked back, thinking about the dangers of the woods, I wondered about the boy who had gone missing so near Gooseberry Acres. If he was still alive and maybe lost in the wilderness, would he have the skills to survive?

My thoughts returned to Andrew. Maybe he was my biggest predator.

Chapter Twelve: Nanny Ninny

My phone rang at seven the next morning. When I didn't reach it in time, it rang again. I blinked the sleep out of my eyes, trying to read the caller ID. I didn't recognize it. "Hullo?"

"It would be good if you could come this morning." The female voice spoke in a low, tremulous voice.

"Miss Nella?"

"Nine o'clock would be nice."

"Um…"

"I'll see you then." Abruptly, the phone clicked off.

I sat up with a groan and a growing sense of irritation. I did not want to be at Miss Nella's beck and call. I almost called her back until I thought about Clarence. I was doing a favor for him. And it wasn't as if I was too busy to go this morning. Sighing, I shuffled to the door to let Bronte out.

The air was crisp and warm as the sun rose in a cloudless sky. It would be a perfect spring day, except I had to drive to Gooseberry Acres and explain to Miss Nella why I couldn't do her project.

While I ate my breakfast, I rehearsed my lines. Too busy. More than I could handle. Dealing with a pot-bellied pig. Not the right person for the job. In truth, a part of me wanted to take this on. I was intrigued by the Fox family and the old deteriorating sanatorium. Yet, I had no idea how to sort through the boxes and help Miss Nella with her project. I definitely didn't want to ghostwrite her memoirs.

As I shoved the box of diaries and scrapbooks into the back of the SUV, I cursed Clarence for getting me into this. Maybe Barrett or Tucker could help her. In fact, they should be the ones since it was about their family and their legacy.

I arrived a little before nine. Sunlight sparkled off the dewy grass in front of Miss Nella's house. It struck me as an island of life in the middle of a ruin. Several birds, including two robins, pecked away on the lawn. A little rabbit scampered under the lilac bush when I stepped out of the car.

Hefting the box from the car, I lugged it to the porch and dropped it by the door. My knock had a dead sound to it. I listened for footsteps but heard nothing. I knocked again, this time calling out, "Miss Nella, it's Jamie!"

The only sound came from the scolding of a blue jay on the roof of the porch.

I tried the door, and to my relief, it was unlocked. Once inside, I stood in the hallway listening for the sounds of life. "Hello! It's Jamie!"

From the sitting room where I'd met Miss Nella, I thought I heard a noise. "Miss Nella!" I approached the room bathed in darkness except for a line of sunlight coming through the closed curtain.

Miss Nella sat in her easy chair like the last time I'd seen her. Her eyes were closed and for a moment I wondered if she was dead. "Miss Nella! Are you alright?" I rushed to her in time to see her eyes open.

"What?" I heard confusion in her voice.

I knelt beside her and took her wrist, checking for a pulse. It beat in a regular rhythm. "You called me this morning. It's Jamie, the writer."

She blinked. "Oh, I must have fallen asleep. Turn on the light and hand me my glasses, will you?"

Relieved, I switched on the lamp by her chair. Miss Nella was dressed in a dark pantsuit, and her white hair was pulled back into an untidy bun. She looked at me with a bemused smile. "Thought I was dead, eh?"

"I had my phone out and ready to call 9-1-1."

"Well, let's get at it while I'm still alive. I'll ask Barrett to make us some coffee. I have things to tell you."

This would have been the perfect time to tell her I couldn't do her project. All I had to do was open my mouth and give her my excuses. I stopped, though, because I was too curious about the "things" she had to say.

"I brought your box back. I'll get it and see if Barrett is in the kitchen." I hadn't heard any sounds of activity in the house.

"They aren't early risers, those two." Miss Nella rolled her eyes. "You'd think..." She didn't finish her sentence.

I made my way down the hallway to the kitchen. Light from a bay window illuminated the room. Last time I was here, I'd hardly noticed the kitchen. Today, as I took in the empty room, I noted that it probably hadn't been updated in fifty years other than a modern stove and refrigerator. The Mr. Coffee sat empty on the counter. Clean dishes were stacked in the drainer in the sink.

"Barrett?"

No answer.

"Miss Nella would like some coffee." I was met with silence. I rooted around, finding the coffee and the filters hoping Barrett wouldn't come barreling in, demanding I get out of her kitchen.

While the coffee brewed, I lugged the box from the porch to the sitting room. "I can't seem to find Barrett, so I started the coffee."

Miss Nella adjusted herself in the chair with a shrug. "She keeps her own hours."

Back in the kitchen, I found the tray Barrett had used the other day and a package of biscotti. I poured coffee into the same mismatched mugs and brought it to Miss Nella.

"Ah," she took a biscotti. "You write, and you serve coffee. How nice."

I felt like a good little servant. I sat down with my coffee, trying to find the right words. I sounded like a fifth grader who hadn't done her homework when I finally spoke. "I...uh...went through some of your diaries and...."

She interrupted me. "And you found it to be an insurmountable task. Yes?"

The woman was astute.

"You read it on my face, didn't you?"

"Most certainly. You weren't the first person I approached on this." She had a twinkle in her eyes. "About ten years ago, I became acquainted with a graduate student in history. She thought it would be a good master's project."

62

"And what happened?"

Miss Nella waved her hand like she was trying to brush away a memory. "She wrote a nice little thesis on private TB Sanatoriums in Minnesota. It wasn't what I was looking for." She pointed to a bound book on top of her bookcase.

I set down my coffee. I'd made it too weak. It tasted like the coffee they served at the Loonfeather. "What are you looking for?"

"I want to tell the truth about Gooseberry Acres and what happened here."

"You make it sound dramatic. What is the truth you want to tell?"

Miss Nella looked beyond me. "I've learned through the years that life is complicated." She was quiet for a few moments as if she was gathering her thoughts. "I've seen too many lives cut short."

I reached in my bag and took out a notebook.

Miss Nella sipped her coffee. Her hand shook as she brought it to her lips. "Some of my memories are quite painful. But let's start at the beginning." She took a deep breath. "My mother was a nurse. That's how she met my father during World War I. By the time I was born, she was in her late thirties and in frail health. Papa never talked about her illness, but I suspect she caught TB, and he felt guilty because he couldn't cure her."

She reached for the coffee again. This time her hands were steadier.

"You were very young when she died?"

"I was a baby. I never knew her. Papa was so busy with the hospital and the patients that he brought in a nanny to care for me. Her name was Virginia McEnany. When I grew older, I called her Nanny Ninny." She laughed. "I was not an easy child to care for, and Nanny Ninny wasn't exactly maternal." She sighed. "I missed having a real mother. Papa left my mother's clothes hanging in the closet. I used to sit under them, smelling her perfume and pretending she would come back. Nanny Ninny found me in there one day, and the next day they'd all been cleared out."

A gust of wind brushed the lilac bushes against the porch as I pictured a child in the closet inhaling the scent of her mother's clothes. I shivered, remembering I did the same thing when I was little as my mother became more and more distant with her brain disease.

Miss Nella's voice pulled me back.

"Nanny Ninny stayed with me until I was ten. I remember the day I came home from school. She usually had a snack ready for me." She pointed to the coffee table. "Right here—cookies or an apple or something. I walked in to find Papa hugging her in the hallway. She was crying. I didn't sense it was a cry of sadness, but more a cry of anger. She'd gained a lot of weight that fall. Of course, I was young and innocent. I didn't understand why she was leaving."

I thought about the suddenness of her leaving and the weight gain. "She left because she was pregnant?"

Miss Nella didn't answer. "She came back later, but this time she worked as a matron in the hospital."

"Did she have a baby?"

Another gust rattled the windows. It felt like a storm was brewing. Miss Nella fidgeted with a button on her pantsuit jacket. She took a deep breath. "Now, where was I?"

"You were talking about your nanny."

"Oh posh. Enough about her."

My coffee was gone. I held up the mug. "Would you like a refill?"

"Thank you."

The kitchen remained deserted. It was well after ten, and I wondered where Barrett was. Out the kitchen window, I saw the sky had filled with slate gray clouds, muting the greens of the budding trees. The area behind the house and hospital was now an expanse of open, neglected brambles. I pictured the postcard of the grounds and how this part of the estate had once been a large garden with landscaped flower beds and walkways for the patients. Beyond the garden, the forest grew thick. If I stayed with the project, I would need to tour the grounds and find the cemetery—if one really existed.

When I returned to the sitting room, Miss Nella dozed in her chair. I set the mugs down and decided to let her sleep a little longer. I'd check out the rest of the house and see if I could rouse Barrett or Tucker. Several thoughts ran through my head. Perhaps they were late sleepers. Or perhaps they'd left—packed their bags and gone elsewhere. For one thing, Tucker's car was missing.

Across from the sitting room was a den enclosed by French doors. I peeked through the glass into the gloom of the room. Clearly, neither Barrett nor Tucker were hiding in here. I could make out a large oak desk and several old-fashioned wooden filing cabinets. Bookcases lined the walls. Even from the closed doorway, I noted an odor of mustiness. Perhaps this was Dr. Fox's private office.

I tried the doors and found they were locked. Miss Nella didn't want people in that room for some reason.

A car approached. I stepped back to Miss Nella, who snored softly in her chair. She opened her eyes when I walked in. "I've kept that room locked since Papa died. I don't allow anyone in there."

"How did you know I was looking at it?"

She chuckled. "I'm a wise old woman. Should we get back to work?"

Before we could start, the front door opened. Tucker lurched to the doorway of the sitting room. His hair was disheveled, and he hadn't shaved. He wore a long-sleeved shirt that was unbuttoned, revealing the white t-shirt underneath.

"Ah, so you are getting the story." He slurred his words.

Miss Nella picked up her coffee and set it back down. "And where might your sister be?" Her voice took on a steely tone.

"What?"

"I pay both of you to look after things. I haven't seen her this morning."

Blinking, Tucker stood up straight from his slouch. "Maybe she's sleeping in?"

Without another word, he turned to the stairs and called up. "Hey Barry, time to rise and shine." He was met with silence.

I stood up, "Maybe something is wrong."

Miss Nella touched my wrist. "Let him deal with it. I'm sure he was out partying all night, and she's still sleeping. Now, where was I?"

Tucker's footsteps creaked on the old wooden risers as he walked heavily up the stairs, still calling out to Barrett.

Miss Nella sighed. "They've been both a blessing and curse. Which reminds me. Have I told you about Uncle Judd, their father?"

Before she could say more, Tucker pounded back down the stairs. Breathless, he stumbled as he entered the sitting room. "She's not there. Bed made, nothing out of order." He peered at Miss Nella with an accusing look. "Where is she?"

Chapter Thirteen: The Back Staircase

"Well, she's not hiding in here," Miss Nella huffed, raising her eyebrows. "She's your sister. Where would she go?"

I felt like I was in the audience of a stage drama. At any moment, Barrett would enter stage right and declare that she had found her true love—or something.

Tucker sank into a chair, rubbing his face. "I don't know. I had the car, so she couldn't have gone far."

"If you want me to, I can help you look around. Maybe she's out for a walk." I offered.

Tucker shook his head. "She hates walking around here. Says the place gives her the creeps."

The longer I'd been here, the more I understood what he was talking about. "Maybe your caretaker has seen him."

"Who, Ed? He's an idiot." Tucker rocked back and forth.

This was getting us nowhere. I wouldn't be able to continue with Miss Nella's story until we found Barrett. "Miss Nella, where would I find Ed? I can give him a call and find out if he's seen her."

"No phone. He lives in a trailer down by the lake. He doesn't like to be disturbed." She spoke in a strained voice. "He's his own person."

I wondered from her response if she was a little scared of him. "No problem. I'll walk down and ask if he's seen her."

Miss Nella opened her mouth, then changed her mind. Shaking her head, she waved me away. "If you wish."

I glanced at Tucker. "Are you coming?"

"I don't like Ed." His lips curled down in a sulk.

Once I was outside, I took a long deep breath. The wind had died down, and the clouds were breaking up. A road, now little more than a track, wound around the house and back to the lake. As I followed it, the sun peeked out, shedding light on the old gardens. Despite the long weeds and the scrub trees and bushes that had overtaken the area, I could still see the cobblestone walkways through the garden. A rusted metal bench with a rotted wooden seat stood alone and abandoned along one path. I closed my eyes and pictured the old postcard of the gardens and wondered how many of the patients who walked through them lived long enough to leave Gooseberry Acres.

Shading my eyes, I surveyed the back of the hospital. A stone patio, mostly overgrown, covered an area just behind the building. I wondered if this was where they wheeled the patients out for air and sunshine. In the current neglected state, it was hard to imagine this as a healing environment.

Most of the windows in the back of the building were boarded up. Two doors, one on each end, were also boarded. A trampled narrow path led from the hospital to Miss Nella's back door. Ed must have made the path when he patrolled the property.

As I studied the hospital grounds, clouds once again covered the sun. I felt a bite of the wind rustling through the weeds. Down the drive towards the lake, Ed's old pickup truck was parked near the tree line.

I walked to the pickup and found a trailer nestled in the pines just before the land sloped to the water. The trailer was an old-fashioned silver airstream. Even without the sun, it had a shine to it as if it had been polished. Classical music wafted through an open window.

Before I knocked on the door of the trailer, I thought about Ed and his rifle. I stood in front of the door and called, "Ed, it's Jamie. I met you the other day." I hoped he wouldn't open the door and point the weapon at me.

The floor creaked inside the trailer. When Ed opened the door, I saw he wore the same clothes as the other day. His hair was greasy and flattened in the back like he'd just gotten out of bed.

"What?"

I stepped back a little at the gruffness of his tone. "I'm looking for Barrett and wondered if you'd seen her."

He peered at me as if he was trying to remember who I was. "You were with that lawyer the other day."

I tried to smile, but I think it must have looked more like a grimace. "I'm helping Miss Nella with her memoirs."

"Why does she want to do that?"

His question surprised me. I kept my voice casual, "I guess she has a story she wants to tell."

"Oh. You mean like about that doctor who disappeared?"

I could have asked him more, but at that moment, I was too concerned about Barrett. I made a mental note to follow up on this—some other time.

In the background, I heard the melodic strains of a violin. It didn't fit with the old man who stood in the doorway. I pointed inside. "The music is lovely. Is it Schubert?" My dad was a classical music buff.

He pressed his lips together. "My mother used to say it soothed the soul."

Dad would have said the same thing. As Mom got sicker with her degenerative brain disease, he found the music calmed her. Sadly, I associated it with her outbursts and fits of mania before he had to put her in a nursing home.

Ed interrupted my thoughts. "What did you want?"

"I'm looking for Barrett. She wasn't in the house, and I thought you might have seen her."

He shook his head. "Nope, she hasn't come by here. You might check the hospital. She asked about it the other day. I said, 'Don't go in there. It's not safe.'"

"Do you know why she wanted to go to the hospital?"

"Nope. Don't know and don't much care. She and that brother of hers are snoops asking too many questions. Just like their dad."

Inside, a timer dinged. "Gotta go. Time for my shows." He backed away from the door. "If you look for her in the hospital, make sure you bring a flashlight. Nella had the electricity turned off a long time ago. Not a good thing for an old building like that—no heat, no electricity. Causes the place to die a lot faster."

I thanked him and turned to walk back. The sun poked through the cloud layer, warming my face. I wished I was sitting on my rock with a cup of coffee and not walking through this place that, even in the sunshine, appeared cloaked in despair. As if the sanatorium grounds read my thoughts, a black crow descended noisily onto a dying oak tree near the edge of the abandoned garden. When I shaded my eyes to see it better, I noticed a tilted and crumbling gravestone. Scanning the area, I saw several more. This was where Gooseberry Acres buried its dead.

"Did you find her?" Tucker called from the back of the residence.

I hurried to him. "Ed hasn't seen her, but he said she was asking questions about the hospital. Could she have gone inside? He said there's no electricity. Maybe she fell or something."

The ruddy color from too much partying drained from his face. "She wouldn't..." His voice dropped off.

I needed to be done and away from this place. Without responding, I walked around the house to the hospital's main entrance.

Tucker followed me but kept his distance. "I don't think you should go inside."

The steps to the front entry were covered in leaves and debris. Before I approached the door, I looked up, half expecting to see the ghostlike presence. The second-floor windows were dark. I tried the door. To my surprise, it was unlocked. It creaked open with a squeal of rusty hinges.

Immediately, I was overcome by the odor of dust, decay, and something else—something moldy and medicinal. It was as if whatever they'd used to clean and disinfect the hospital had absorbed into the floors and walls. Sunlight filtered in through the dirty front windows. I faced an open lobby.

"Barrett, are you in here?"

My voice echoed in the emptiness. The only sound I heard was the scrape of leaves blowing across the floor behind me and a soft, almost imperceptible scrabbling sound behind the walls.

"Yuck, mice," I yelped.

Tucker had not followed me in. The door creaked and then slammed shut.

"Oh hell, now what?" I turned back to the door and tugged it open again. The last thing I needed was to be locked into this decrepit place.

"Tucker, can you find a flashlight and bring it here?"

He stood outside with his hands in his pockets, staring at me.

I tensed my jaw. "Tucker, please go find a flashlight."

As if he'd snapped out of a trance, he turned and headed for the residence.

While I waited, I surveyed the old lobby. Wainscoting covered the lower half of the walls, while the upper half was wallpapered. The peeling wallpaper revealed stained plaster underneath. At some point, water must have leaked into the room. To my right, a wooden staircase led up to the second floor. Ahead of me was a hallway with several rooms on either side.

Using the flashlight on my phone, I walked down the hallway calling out to Barrett. The floor of the old building creaked beneath my footsteps, but otherwise, the place was deadly silent. I tried the first door. It opened into an exam room complete with a rusted exam table and supply cabinets. A few hospital gowns were still stacked on one of the shelves. It appeared to me that when Dr. Fox closed the hospital, he simply locked it up, as is.

I backed out of the room. The smell, the mold, and the dust caused my eyes to water and my chest to tighten. I didn't want to stay in this building any longer than necessary.

Behind me, Tucker approached with a weak flashlight. "Sorry, I couldn't find the one in the kitchen, so got the one in the car. It needs batteries, I guess."

Quickly I checked the other closed doors. They looked similar to the first—abandoned exam rooms. At the end of the hall was an open empty room. To the left appeared to be a kitchen. The open room had several French doors opening to the garden. The doors had been boarded over, adding to the gloom of the room.

I pointed back to the lobby. "Let's take a quick look upstairs." I didn't want to climb the stairs. I wanted to run out the front door and never set foot in this place again. It surprised me how spooked I was by an old, crumbling building. The spidery feeling on the back of my neck was strong enough that I reached back as if I could flick it away.

Tucker was quiet as we made our way back to the staircase.

"Have you been in here before?"

"Once, about a month ago. Just out of curiosity. Can't be in here too long. It triggers my asthma."

Something in his voice caused me to stop for a moment. Was he lying? Had he been in here more recently?

As I moved on, I had a momentary irrational panic. I remembered the fears in the community that you could still catch TB from being in the building. "Nonsense," I uttered.

"What?" Tucker's voice was raw as he touched my arm.

I almost turned and headed straight for the door. "Let's do this as fast as we can. If we don't find her, maybe she's already back at the house."

Tucker called out, "Barry! Are you up there?" as we climbed the stairs. The risers groaned beneath our feet. I held so tightly to the phone my fingers ached. The second floor had a wide hallway with rooms on either side. I guessed they were patient rooms. When I peered into the first one, I saw an empty iron bedstead. A mattress, with a green army blanket crumpled by it, lay on the floor along with a pile of paper trash. Wan light came in through the shuttered window.

I counted ten small rooms on either side of the hallway. At the end, facing the back garden, appeared to be a nurse's station, and behind it, another room. What made the room off the nurse's station unique was the double padlock on the door.

"What do you suppose was in that room?"

"I...I don't know." Tucker wheezed and coughed. "Need to get out of here. Don't have my inhaler."

He backed up, yelling, "Barry, if you're here, come out!"

I thought I heard the soft shifting of floorboards above me. I glanced up, listening hard, but no other sound came.

"Can't breathe," Tucker gasped.

"Wait!" I held up my hand. I didn't want to be in this building by myself.

"No! I gotta get out of here." His voice boomed in the emptiness of the hallway. Before I could grab him to stay, he was fleeing down the stairs.

I steeled myself to finish looking. "Barrett? Are you up here?"

A creaking sound that seemed to come near the back staircase to the right of the nurse's station caught my attention. I hurried over. The staircase appeared to be a back way down to the main floor. Above its landing, a steeper staircase climbed to the third floor. If I remembered what Rob had told me, this was where the staff slept.

I called up the steep staircase. "Barrett?" I heard a few skittering types of noises. Rats or squirrels, probably. A kiss of damp air brushed my face from the down staircase. A door must have been open at the bottom. I aimed my phone at what felt like an abyss. "Barrett?" The only reply was the air on my cheeks.

The windowless staircase was completely dark. I picked my way down. Something skittered across the top of my shoe. I gasped and nearly dropped the phone. Gripping it even harder, I continued to a landing. I would have kept going, except when I surveyed the landing with my phone light, I picked up something shiny. Stooping to inspect and praying it wasn't some dead animal, I drew back with a sharp intake of breath.

Blood. It was blood, and it was fairly fresh. Pointing the phone down the stairs, I saw her in the shadowed lighting. She lay partly on the floor and partly on the steps.

"Oh my god! Barrett!" I nearly stumbled as I rushed to her. It was clear from the angle of her head that she wouldn't be serving Miss Nella coffee ever again.

Chapter Fourteen: Barrett Fox

Miss Nella regarded me with a frown. "I don't like all this activity. You'd think they could take her away and be done with it."

I frowned, surprised at how callous she was to the death of her helper and cousin. "They have to investigate."

"Stupid woman was where she shouldn't have been and fell. Accidents happen." She fingered a brooch pinned to her jacket. "Back then, people fell around here all the time, and it didn't cause such a fuss."

I was tired and hungry and desperate to get away from Gooseberry Acres. "Do you mean other people have fallen down those steps?"

Miss Nella was handling this like a spoiled child. "Oh, I don't know. I think one of Papa's patients got confused in the middle of the night and took a tumble. Virginia McEnany was the matron by then. I'm sure she didn't call the police. She handled it herself."

"Did the person die?"

She shrugged. "Can't remember." Turning to the window, she scowled. "How much longer do you think they'll be?"

Greg, one of the sheriff's deputies, came to the doorway. "I wonder if I could ask you some questions." He was in his late twenties, blond, with a boxy kind of body.

Miss Nella peered at him. Then, like she'd switched to a new radio station, she perked up and smiled. "Not at all, as long as I don't need my lawyer." She winked at me.

Greg frowned before he sat down with a notebook. "How long have you known Barrett Fox?"

Miss Nella looked up at the ceiling. "Hmmm. She and her brother showed up in March, I think. Yes, it was March. Came knocking on the door and told me they were my cousins."

Greg raised his eyebrows. "Did you know them?"

"Had no idea who they were. I knew their father, of course, my uncle Judd. But I hadn't seen him in years. Left in a hurry after Papa—Dr. Fox—found out what he was up to."

I leaned in, wondering what this was all about. As Miss Nella had said before, this place had secrets. I wanted to interrupt to ask about Uncle Judd's sudden departure, but clearly, this wasn't the time to talk about it.

Greg continued, his pen poised. "So, you didn't invite them to live here?"

Miss Nella sat up straighter. "Once I was sure they were my cousins, I hired them to help me out. Poor Ed, the caretaker, is getting on in years. It was time to have some help—not that they were very good at it."

Greg turned to me. "And you are here because?"

I didn't like the way his eyes narrowed when he looked at me. "Clarence Engstrom recommended me to Miss Nella to help her with a writing project." I was not in the best of standing with the Jackpine Sheriff's Department due to some problems last winter. I could understand why Greg might be a little suspicious, but I still didn't appreciate his tone.

Stay cool, Jamie.

He scribbled in his notebook and turned back to Miss Nella. "Do you know why Miss Fox was in the old building?"

She folded her arms. "Humph. Those two were always prying. It's like they thought I had hidden a treasure or something."

I remembered Ed talking about how Barrett and Tucker were "snooping" around. I made a mental note to ask him what he thought they were looking for.

"I keep that building locked ever since those damn hooligans got into it a few years back and vandalized it. If they'd gotten hurt, they probably would have sued me. Ed and I are the only ones with a key."

I interrupted. "The front door wasn't locked when I went in."

Greg raised his eyebrows. "The door wasn't locked?"

I nodded.

"Well," Miss Nella huffed, "She didn't have my key. I keep it with me." She pulled a key ring with two keys on it out of her suit coat pocket. "I don't like to leave it out of my sight."

"Perhaps Ed lent it to her?" I asked.

Miss Nella's eyes widened. "Oh, he would never do that. He didn't like those two."

While Greg asked more questions, I excused myself. My stomach gurgled, and I felt light-headed. I hoped I could find something to eat in the kitchen.

Tucker sat alone in the dining room just off the kitchen. He had a snifter with brandy in it. I joined him with a plate of cheese and crackers. "How are you doing?"

He raised the snifter. "Cheers."

I saw no evidence of grief in his expression. His eyes were reddened from lack of sleep, not from crying.

"Not a spritely day, I'd say." He took a sip of the brandy.

I knew that people took death and shock differently, but to me, his reaction was bizarre. I pushed the plate toward him. "Maybe you should get some food into you."

"Jolly good." He took a piece of cheese and nibbled on it.

"Tucker," I made my voice as firm as I could. "What *is* going on?"

He blinked as if I'd just slapped him. After a pause, the silliness left his voice. "We weren't close, you know. She was older and only a half-sister."

"Oh?"

"She came back from a bad marriage and helped me take care of Dad that last year. He was pretty far gone by then—Alzheimer's and old age."

"Must have been hard."

"She was better with him than me, I guess."

Again, he reminded me of Andrew, the ex. As I sat across from him, I wondered how much of what he was saying was true and how much was an act. "Tucker, why did you come here? What were you looking for?"

He shrugged. "We were both at loose ends, and Dad had hinted about this place." He pointed to the hospital.

"Hinted what?"

"He hinted that his brother owed him something."

I took a cracker. It was stale, but I ate it anyway. "Do you know what your father was owed?"

Tucker slowly shook his head. "He died before he could tell us. He was confused towards the end. He said his brother had buried the truth, and he was owed because of it. Repeated it many times over his last year of life. Maybe he dreamed it, but we thought it was worth a trip here."

"What did Miss Nella say when you got here?"

He leaned back. "She said she would hire us to help her out, and she'd look through her father's papers to see if she could find out what Dad was talking about. I don't think she's looked at one single paper since we came. It was an excuse to get us to stay."

"She wanted you to stay?"

Tucker drank more brandy. "Where else would she get such cheap round-the-clock help in this neck of the woods? It's not like the county is filled with people who'd want to put up with the old bat."

I cringed at his words. I knew this wasn't the full story, and I wanted to probe further, but Greg interrupted us.

He eyed Tucker. "Perhaps we could talk now."

I pushed my chair back. "I would like to leave if you don't have more questions for me."

Greg pressed his lips together. "I know how to find you."

Under other circumstances, I might have laughed. Of course, he knew how to find me. So did everyone else in the Jackpine County Sheriff's Department.

Before I left, I checked on Miss Nella. She dozed in the chair. Ed sat watching her. He'd changed into fresh clothes and combed his hair. On the coffee table was a sandwich and a glass of juice. In the background, soft classical music played on a portable CD Player.

"Is she alright?" I asked him.

"She likes classical music, too. Just like my mother." There was something childlike in his voice.

"When she wakes up, would you tell her I left?" I took several of the diaries and a photo album out of the box I'd brought in.

The image of Barrett at the bottom of the stairs flashed through my head. This would have been a perfect opportunity to flee and never come back. Yet, something bad had happened to Barrett, and I wasn't confident the sheriff would look for the truth.

There you go again. The infernal dialogue in my brain teased. *Defender of those who can't speak for themselves.* I wasn't sure Barrett needed defending, but I also knew I wouldn't let it go.

Miss Nella opened her eyes when I turned to leave the room. "Is that deputy still here?"

"He's in the dining room talking with Tucker."

"He's a nice-looking man. Too bad I'm not seventy years younger. I could go for him." I caught a hint of playfulness when she spoke.

Considering that Barrett Fox's body was being loaded into a hearse, her remark struck me as totally inappropriate. "Do you want to talk with him again?"

"Ed says he has his key to the hospital. I don't know how Barrett got the door unlocked. Maybe the deputy should know it." She held up her hand as I turned to leave. "And I want you to come back tomorrow. I have things to tell you."

Resigned to coming back, I walked to the dining room to tell Greg. Before I got to the door, I heard Tucker talking. "She might look frail, but she gets around."

I stepped in and told Greg about the key. Truly, it was time for me to leave.

As I walked down the hallway, Tucker added, "I'm sure it was an accident. Barrett could be clumsy."

I wondered if he was trying to steer Greg and the sheriff's office away from an investigation. The old hospital held too many secrets right now.

As if by a miracle, as soon as I slid into the driver's seat of the car to leave, the clouds dispersed, and the sun came out with a blinding brightness.

Chapter Fifteen: Andrew Again

The sun continued to shine as I approached Killdeer. In the last couple days, the trees had leafed out, creating a canopy of green. Next door to Clarence, the tulips were in full bloom. I'd never seen such bright reds and yellows.

Lorraine answered the door and told me Clarence was having his afternoon coffee in the kitchen. He sat with coffee and a muffin warm out of the oven. I pulled up a chair, my stomach rumbling.

"Have a muffin," he pointed to the plate. "Lorraine claims she puts kale in them, so I'll get my daily dose of green vegetables."

Lorraine laughed. "Maybe I do. Maybe sometimes I use spinach instead."

It was so refreshing to hear the patter and be in this bright, sweet-smelling kitchen away from Miss Nella, Tucker, and Gooseberry Acres.

I filled them in on the events of the morning.

Lorraine was aghast. "You mean you found the woman? Are you okay?"

I shuddered, picturing the angle of Barrett's neck, so wrong for her body. "I hope never to have another experience like that. I can't imagine what she was doing in that old hospital."

Clarence wiped a crumb from his chin. "Do they think it was an accidental fall?"

I took a bite of the muffin. It didn't have either kale or spinach in it. "I'm sure that's how it will be investigated."

"Well, it probably was."

I thought about the blood on the landing and where she'd fallen. "I'm not so sure."

"Aha. The professional investigator. Why are you skeptical, Ms. Marple?"

"I found blood on the landing above where she fell. It's possible someone hit her, and then she fell." As I said the words, I suddenly had my doubts. She could have fallen from above the landing, hit her head, and then tumbled down the rest of the stairs. "Or maybe not." I closed my eyes, picturing the scene once again. "The thing that keeps coming back to me is that I didn't find a flashlight. If she was going to explore the hospital, why wouldn't she have a flashlight?"

Lorraine stood up and brought her coffee cup to the sink. "Let the sheriff wonder about that. I'm headed back to the house. Elena and I are taking the baby for a walk on this beautiful day."

After she left, I poured more coffee for Clarence. I needed to talk about something other than Barrett Fox. "What's going to happen to Elena and Cristina? I worry about them." Elena had been brought to Killdeer in a fraudulent scheme after crossing the Mexican border. Since Cristina was born here, she was an American citizen, but Elena was undocumented.

Clarence leaned back in his chair. "I had an old law professor who said, 'the wheels of justice grind slowly.' I'm hoping slow enough that we can have a decent immigration policy before they discover her. Elena has a lot to offer this country."

I did not find his words to be reassuring. Returning to the topic of Gooseberry Acres, I related to him Miss Nella's cryptic words about secrets. "I sense she has a story to tell but can't quite get it out."

"Ah, yes."

I had hoped Clarence would be more forthcoming. "I guess I'll have to go back." I felt my shoulders slump. "Why did you talk me into this?"

He chuckled. "Thought you could use a little more income. Miss Nella can afford to pay you well."

"Are you sure? I can imagine putting hours and hours into this and then having her plead poverty."

When Clarence answered, his eyes had an amused sparkle to them. "Back in the early 1900s, Nella's grandfather invested in a little company that planned to mine a mineral called corundum in Northern Minnesota. It was used for making sandpaper and grinding wheels. Unfortunately, it turned out there wasn't any corundum. However, the company soldiered on concentrating on manufacturing. This little startup was called Minnesota Mining and Manufacturing."

"Oh?"

"Well, I'm sure you are familiar with Scotch Tape and Post-It Notes. They're a small part of the business better known now as 3M. Let's just say Miss Nella's grandfather passed on quite a legacy. It's how Dr. Fox was able to build Gooseberry Acres."

I thought about what Tucker had told me. "Interesting. Tucker said his father was owed something by Dr. Fox. Maybe it was some of the money from the estate. Reason enough to show up on Miss Nella's doorstep. He said Miss Nella promised to look into it."

"From the little Nella has told me about her uncle, she thought he was a scoundrel. A scandal years ago involving the hospital and bogus fund-raising. I doubt Dr. Fox left him any money—but I can't speak for the grandfather." He finished his coffee and set the cup down. "Speaking of money, have you heard anything more from that ex-husband?"

Groaning, I told him about the call from the realtor. "I'm sure he's in a jam. I'm hoping he's given up on getting anything from me and headed back to New York and his beloved Destiny."

Clarence stood up, wincing when he put weight on his leg. "It's nap time for the old geezer. Let my immigration lawyer friends worry about Elena. Let me worry about your ex if he becomes a pest. Your job right now is to get Nella's story down."

"And deal with a pot-bellied pig," I muttered under my breath.

Outside, a slight breeze riffled through the trees. I drove down the main street with my windows open, enjoying the freshness of the air and the scent of blooming lilacs. After talking with Clarence, I'd calmed down. All would be taken care of. The peace lasted until I passed the office of the *Killdeer Times*. I nearly slammed on my brakes when the editor walked out the door talking with Andrew. I could see by the way he was gesturing that he was speaking to her with great animation. I used to call it his oration act. It usually meant he had some great idea that would cost me money. Thank god for my signed, sealed, and filed divorce papers.

The normally morose editor, Jeanine, looked like she was hanging on every word. I wanted to stop and tell her to watch out. Instead, I rolled up my window and drove on. "Why can't he crawl back into his den?"

Once home with Bronte tended to, I sat on my rock with the phone. I had Jilly on speed dial.

"Ah, Jamie," her voice was too perky when she answered. "I was wondering when you'd call."

Since Jilly knew everything that happened in town before it happened, this was not good news. "And you say that because?"

She laughed. "Just met Mr. Right stomach or intestine or something."

"Oh god. I hoped when he found out I didn't have any money, he'd be on his way."

"Ah, no. Been in here charming our favorite newspaper editor."

Even the gentle waves of the lake and the joyous romping of my dog couldn't ease my anxiety. "What is he up to?"

"Not sure. He must have seen the expression on my face when he introduced himself as an old friend of yours because as soon as he had Jeanine's attention, he invited her to coffee and hightailed out of there. I heard something about looking into developing a summer stock playhouse."

I let out a long, weary sigh. "Please don't tell me he's trying to figure out how to stick around."

We talked a little more about Andrew before Jilly brought up Gooseberry Acres. "I hear someone fell there today. Looks like the sheriff has been busy in that part of the county—you know, with the missing camper and all."

Since I didn't think it was classified information, I told her about finding Barrett and about my project with Miss Nella.

"Ah." For a moment, her phone cut out. "...lots of rumors about that place...haunted, murder, and so on."

"I don't know about its history, but the place is a disaster waiting to happen." Or had already happened.

Jilly's phone cut out once again. "...should try talking to Grace Englund.

She was..."

I stared at the phone as it went dead. I decided I'd try calling her later. Maybe the reception would improve.

After supper, I took Bronte for a walk in the still evening. The frogs and crickets sang in the background as the air cooled around me. Above, a few stars were beginning to show. I'd read that it was harder and harder to find a place on Earth where there was no light pollution. Here in my cabin by the lake, I had a perfect view of the sky from my rock. I looked up and remembered my mother sitting on the rock during one of the summers we'd stayed in the cabin. She was humming something and swaying to the rhythm of the lake. When I approached her, she'd put her arms around me and said, "I think this must be heaven."

This evening might have been heaven, except I smelled the faint odor of a skunk. Calling Bronte, I went back into the cabin to the pile of diaries and the manuscript on the table. Instead of dealing with the mess, I took a book of poetry off the shelf and curled up on the sofa.

My phone rang before I could open the page. Jilly called back.

"Sorry, my phone ran out of juice. I think I was telling you about Grace Englund. She was a patient at Gooseberry just after the war. You might want to talk with her to get some background."

We talked a little about Gooseberry, and its past. "Jilly, people talk about a murder there. Do you know anything about it?"

She laughed. "You know the—what do they call it? Ah, urban legends? There's one about the doctor who disappeared and how some people thought he'd been murdered. Bunch of malarkey, I'm guessing—and well before my time."

Bronte sighed at my feet. She smelled fresh from romping through the grass and the woods. I reached down and patted her on the head. "Speaking of disappearing, have you heard anything more about that boy from the camp? The camp people came around the other day and showed us his photo." I didn't tell her what Tucker had said about seeing him. I wasn't sure he was telling the truth.

I heard voices in the background. Jilly must have been talking from home.

"My sources tell me they've changed from a search and rescue to a search and recover. It didn't stop the parents from posting that big reward. I figure it was a drowning. You know that little lake is darn deep. Makes me think the whole area around there is cursed."

I shivered because I'd almost drowned once in Lake Larissa. I hoped drowning wasn't the case for the boy. I remembered the panicked desperation of trying to find the surface and air. Poor kid.

Jilly continued, "We're running a story in the paper about it again. With the reward, I'm expecting more people tramping around Gooseberry. I hope Nella Fox is prepared."

"I feel for the parents, but I wonder about sending him to a boot camp. They must have been desperate."

"I heard he got into trouble with drugs. His parents caught him and offered him a deal. Go to Camp Six, or they'd turn him in. Probably they were getting pretty fed up with him at that point. The kid's name is Talbot Smithers III. Can you believe it? And the parents are loaded. Camp Six isn't cheap."

It reminded me of what I'd been told about Gooseberry Acres—a place for people who could afford it.

"The other thing about the kid," Jilly continued. "He's turning eighteen in another week. At eighteen, he's an adult and could sign himself out of the place. Why would he go AWOL before that?"

Good question. "Maybe he couldn't take it anymore?" I thought about my stay in the holding cell in Queens. I couldn't get out of there fast enough.

We ended the call with a promise to have coffee next week. Jilly said she was going to see if she could pry any information out of Jeanine about Andrew. I hoped he'd be gone by the time of our coffee date.

I checked my watch and decided it was still early enough to give Grace a call. If she'd been a patient in the late 1940s, she must be older than Miss Nella.

A woman with a strong voice answered. "Grace Englund's phone."

I introduced myself. "This is Jamie Forest. I'm an editor, and I'm working on a project that involves the Gooseberry Acres TB Sanatorium. I'm wondering if I could speak with Grace Englund."

The woman on the other line hesitated. "Grace is my mother. She...uh, goes to bed early. Could I take your number and see if she wants to get back to you tomorrow? She...uh...tires easily. But she likes company."

I left her my phone number with hopes she would call back.

That night I dreamed about being in a darkened stairway that was filling with water. Someone stood above me, holding something. When I turned to see who it was, Andrew grinned back at me.

I sat up with a start. "Damn you, Andrew! It's bad enough that I have to see you during the day. Can you not haunt me at night?"

Bronte raised her head, gave my arm a lick, and settled back to sleep.

Chapter Sixteen: TB Treatment

Grace called in the morning while I was brewing coffee and trying to shake the Andrew dream from my head. She said she would be delighted to tell me all about Gooseberry Acres. "It was quite the adventure, you know."

I arranged to visit later in the morning. Miss Nella was not happy when I told her I couldn't come out until afternoon. "Well," she grumbled. "I do my best thinking in the morning."

"I could come tomorrow, if that works better."

"No. No. We need to get started before there's more trouble."

More trouble? "Are you expecting problems?"

She snorted. "Of course. That woman died, you know. It will come back to haunt me. She probably has someone out there who will want to sue."

Grace lived five blocks from Clarence in a 1950s one-story rambler with a flowering crab apple tree in the front yard. The pink blossoms glowed in the morning dew.

I rang the doorbell expecting Grace's daughter to answer. I'd pictured Grace as a frail elderly woman wrapped in an afghan. Her daughter had said she tired easily. Inside I heard footsteps and a voice called, "I'm coming. I'll get there—pretty soon."

The door opened, and I faced a short elderly woman with pure white hair and thick glasses. She wore a sweatshirt with the Killdeer High School logo and a pair of worn blue jeans. "I hope you don't mind that I didn't dress up. After years of wearing teacher clothes, when I retired, I said I'd wear exactly what I found comfortable. And this is comfortable." She stepped back to let me in.

I introduced myself and gave her one of my business cards. She studied it. "Freelance editor, you say? I taught English for many years. Honestly, I'm still not sure about semicolons."

Grace had all the charm Miss Nella lacked.

She pointed to the doorway into the kitchen. "Do you mind sitting in the kitchen? I've got an apple crisp in the oven, and it's nice and warm and comfortable in there." She led me through a small kitchen to a table on the back wall underneath a window. Outside in the back yard, I saw a large fenced-in garden, tilled and planted.

I pointed to the garden. "I'm trying to grow some vegetables, but the deer and rabbits think it's their personal cafeteria."

"I have a secret family formula that keeps them out." Her eyes twinkled. "A fence and mothballs."

A China teapot in a knitted cozy sat on the table. "I hope you like Earl Grey tea. I always take it with milk and sugar, just like my mother. She was British, you know."

She poured the tea. "Now, you want to hear more about Gooseberry Acres."

I took out my notebook. "Miss Nella is working on her memoir and hired me to help her sort it. I thought it would be helpful to hear from someone else—to put it all in perspective." I didn't want to admit that I was curious about all the secrets Miss Nella had alluded to.

While she talked, I sipped the tea. It had a soothing taste and texture. Maybe the British did know how to make good tea.

"Oh, Gooseberry was quite a place. My parents had some means, so when I got sick, they wanted me to be in a private sanatorium. They thought the care would be better and I wouldn't be exposed to a 'rough' element." She smiled. "What they really meant was they didn't want me around poor people and minorities. Dr. Fox assured them that he only accepted 'good people.'"

Discrimination in health care was deeply rooted, I mused.

"They sent me all the way up here to the woods to recover. I thought they were sending me to Timbuktu until I saw the forests and smelled the pines."

The timer dinged on the oven. She made a motion to get up, but I stopped her. "I can take that out of the oven, if you'd like."

The apple crisp came out with a browned crust of butter, brown sugar, and cinnamon. The last time I'd tried to make one, I'd burned the crust and left the apples undone. I set it on a rack to cool. "This looks like it could go on the cover of a Betty Crocker Cookbook."

"The secret is to use a variety of apples, both tart ones and juicy ones, and add a teaspoon of coffee. My mother-in-law taught me that. She was a great baker and a strict Catholic. She thought of me as the intruder in the family because I was raised Episcopalian. Fortunately, my husband didn't listen to her."

I sat back down and picked up my pen. The room filled with the aroma of cinnamon and nutmeg. "Did you get good care at Gooseberry Acres?"

"Oh yes. I think it was the best for the times. I had my own room with a window they opened every day, even on the coldest days. They thought the cure was in fresh air and sunshine. They'd take us down to the patio outside the dining room and have us sit in the sun. Some days, it was so cold you could see your breath. They had us bundled in layers of blankets. I'm surprised some of the sicker ones didn't simply freeze to death."

I'd done a little research on TB treatment, and this fit with the known protocols. "I read they did something else called...." I had to look at my notes. "...called collapse therapy? Where they collapsed your lung to stop the growth of the TB."

Grace pointed to her chest. "First, they collapsed the right side, and then six months later, they did the left. They called it a pneumothorax."

I'd experienced a pneumothorax when I'd been hit by a bullet last summer. I shuddered, remembering how hard it was to breathe. "That must have been awful."

"The memory is very forgiving. I associate the surgery with two things. First, Dr. Fox had an assistant doctor who did all the collapse therapy. He was the nicest person." She winked at me. "And good looking. All the women who worked there thought he was a dreamboat." She wrinkled her brow. "I'm trying to think of his name. Dr. Sellars...no...Dr. Heller."

Grace gazed out the window with a faraway expression. I urged her on. "You said there was something else that helped you through."

"Oh yes. I met this very nice orderly who was working that summer to earn enough money to go back to medical school. He wasn't nearly as handsome as Dr. Heller, but he had charm."

"A little romance?"

She giggled like a young woman. "You could say that. After I got better and finished college, I married him. He was the town doctor in Killdeer for years. I never thought when my parents brought me to this wilderness that I would end up staying here."

I checked my watch. It was almost noon. I needed to grab a sandwich at the Loonfeather and drive out to see Miss Nella. "I'm sorry I can't stay and hear more. I have another appointment."

"Oh, I'm sorry you have to leave before the apple crisp is cooled. Maybe you can come back another time." Grace reached over and touched my hand. "I have plenty of time, although my daughter is strict with visitors. She thinks if I have too many, I'll break. Nonsense, of course. Young people these days..."

I laughed. Grace's daughter must have been in her sixties at least.

While I was putting my pen and notebook away, Grace thought of something else. "You know that handsome Dr. Heller. Something strange happened with him. I can't remember exactly what it was. Maybe I never knew, but suddenly he was gone. We were all so sad to find out from Dr. Fox that he was bringing in another doctor." She pressed her lips together. "The nurses gossiped, of course. They heard that he'd gotten in trouble with Dr. Fox's daughter. I never believed it because she was only sixteen or so. What grown man would mess around with a young girl like that? No. Never believed it."

Interesting. I wondered what role Dr. Heller played in Miss Nella's secrets.

"It seemed to me that the place was never the same after he left. It was almost like the soul had left the hospital. Later, after the hospital closed down and Dr. Fox died, people used to gossip that he haunted the building.

"You mean Dr. Heller?"

"Oh no, I mean Dr. Fox. I think there was a sad story somewhere in it." She stood up with a shake of her head. "Ah, well. Silly thoughts from an old lady."

I asked her to call me if she thought of anything else about Gooseberry Acres.

She accompanied me to the door. "It was a beautiful place when I was there. Now they tell me it's nothing but a ruin. I never understood why Nella stayed. She could have gone anywhere."

Maybe a secret was keeping her there all these years.

Chapter Seventeen: Uncle Judd

The clear skies and spring warmth held while I drove to Gooseberry Acres. I reviewed all the things I'd heard about Dr. Heller. Rob's mother thought something strange was going on with him. Grace confirmed his mysterious disappearance and added gossip about Dr. Heller and Miss Nella. Miss Nella had written in her diary about the good-looking doctor. She also talked about secrets. Was he one of them? Today might be the day to ask her about him.

When I arrived, the grounds appeared as deserted as before. Tucker's car was nowhere in sight. It was probably my imagination, but the hospital looked shabbier and lonelier than yesterday. Perhaps it was because the grass and weeds had been trampled by the sheriff and coroner's vehicles. I gazed up at one of the second-story windows and imagined the ghost of Dr. Fox looking out at me. With a shudder, I parked the car in front of the residence.

Knocking on the door, I called out. "Miss Nella, it's Jamie." It was unlocked. When I opened it, classical music played softly in the sitting room. Walking past the office, I noticed the door was slightly ajar. I was tempted to go inside and look around, but Miss Nella's voice stopped me.

"Come in, dear. We have lots to talk about."

The remains of lunch sat on a tray on the coffee table. Before I settled in, I offered to take the tray into the kitchen. Miss Nella waved me away. "Ed will take care of it when he comes back."

"What about Tucker? Is he helping?"

She sighed. "Oh, he's out tom-catting somewhere. Just like his dad—full of sound and fury signifying nothing."

I sat down, observing that Miss Nella wore the same pant suit as yesterday. It had stains on the front from spilled tomato soup. I wondered who was caring for her now that Barrett was gone.

"You're asking yourself if I ever get out of this chair, aren't you?" Her lips curled into a slight smile. "My dad always said I was good at reading people. That's why I never trusted Tucker and his sister."

"He told me Barrett took care of your uncle before he died."

"She was such a prune. Poor Uncle Judd probably died to get away from her."

I sensed that she stopped herself before saying goodbye and good riddance.

"Tucker also told me they came here because you owed his father."

"Nonsense again. Uncle Judd was a handsome ne'er-do-well. One of those 'change of life' babies. Twenty years younger than Papa. I'm told Grandmother Fox spoiled him rotten. He gambled away his inheritance and showed up one day wanting more." She brushed a wisp of her hair aside. "Although, to his credit, he was a charming man. When I was young, I liked him. He was more like a playmate than a grown-up." She laughed. "We used to sneak to the gazebo in the garden at night. Uncle Judd and I had a gay old time with peppermint schnapps."

I took out the photo I'd found of the family in front of the residence and showed it to her. "Is that your Uncle Judd? Tucker looks just like him."

She studied the photo, and her eyes narrowed. "That was taken before my father found out...." Her voice dropped away.

"Found out what?"

"Uncle Judd was a petty criminal. He used Gooseberry Acres and Papa's good name to solicit donations to a charity care fund. Except he was the charity. Oh, how I remember when Papa found out. He was so angry I thought he'd have a stroke. He banished Uncle Judd, and I never saw him again." The color rose on Miss Nella's cheeks. "Another reason I don't owe Tucker anything. He's a chip off the old block."

"What about the little boy in the photo?"

She waved it away. "Oh, he belonged to one of the nurses. I used to babysit him."

I tucked the photo back into my bag. It was time to put my cards on the table. "I believe you have fascinating stories to tell about your life. This place is full of history, and I'm guessing that's why you want it written down. But..."

She held up her hand. "But you don't want to write it."

I pressed my lips together. "I was under the impression you'd already written your memoirs and wanted editing help. It sounds to me like you're looking for a ghostwriter. It's too big a project for me, and I'm not sure I could do it justice." I didn't add that the abandoned hospital next door where I'd found Barrett and the ruins of the grounds gave me nightmares.

She responded with something completely unexpected. On the little table next to her chair was a pile of papers. She took the top one and handed it to me. It was a contract with my name on it to write her memoirs. I quickly scanned it, stopping where the contract listed the payment. My mouth dropped. If I completed the project to her satisfaction, she was willing to pay me enough money that I could last another year in my cabin and build a garage for the next winter. The advance she offered was also generous. No matter what happened, I could keep the advance.

"As you can see, dear. I really want my story to be told before I'm six feet under. I've read your other articles, and I know you're good."

"Clarence drew this up, didn't he?" The old devil knew I was always scraping for ways to stay in the cabin.

"I have a check already made out."

I fingered the contract with multiple voices echoing in my head. This would involve god knows how many hours and how many trips to this place that caused me to shudder when I entered the drive. Would it disrupt the tranquility I'd been striving for since I moved to Lake Larissa? Or would I be crazy to turn it down?

Again, it was as if Miss Nella read my mind. "Let's continue to talk today, and you can decide by tomorrow."

At least I had a deadline. By tomorrow I'd either be committed to the project or back to eking out my living editing the voice of a pot-bellied pig.

We were interrupted when a car pulled up to the residence. With the heavy drapes closed, I couldn't tell who had arrived.

Miss Nella sighed. "Probably Tucker. I have no idea where he goes. I hear voices in the night. Sometimes I wonder if he's hiding a girl in the hospital."

Judging by Tucker's reaction when he went into the hospital with me, I doubted he was having a tryst with anyone inside the moldy old building.

Tucker walked in looking even more haggard than yesterday. At least he'd changed his clothes. He wore a clean pair of jeans and a polo shirt. He sat down heavily in a chair across from me. Even at that distance, I smelled stale beer and a whiff of marijuana.

"How are you?" I asked.

He squeezed his eyes shut and rubbed his cheeks. "Hungover. Sad. Tired."

"Well," Miss Nella glared at him. "I'm not paying you to be hungover, sad, or tired. I'm paying you to take care of things."

His face reddened, and he opened his mouth to say something, shook his head, and closed it.

I wanted to snap at Miss Nella and point out that the poor man had just lost his sister. I turned to Tucker. "How about if you come into the kitchen with me while I make some coffee?"

Without a word, he stood up and left. I followed him to the kitchen.

"Goddamn bitch!" He paced in front of the counter. "Sits in that room like a queen. Dad said she was a spoiled child who always got her way."

I indicated the table. "Sit down and tell me what's happening."

He nearly stumbled when he sat. Tucker wasn't hungover; he was still drunk.

"Barrett didn't deserve this. I talked her into coming. She didn't want to take on another old person, but we were broke. My acting jobs had dried up, and she didn't have a job."

"Tucker, what do you think Barrett was doing in the hospital?"

He laid his head down on his arms like a little school kid. "Nella owes us. I know it. Barrett was…" He stopped and shook his head.

"Why do you think Miss Nella owes you?"

"Because."

I didn't have the patience to deal with a school kid right now. "Tucker, why does she owe you?"

Tucker lifted his head. "Dad knew something. They paid him—for years, they sent him money, and then when Nella's father died, it stopped."

"What? You think he was being paid to be quiet?"

"Maybe."

The coffee maker hissed as it filled the carafe.

"What do you think he knew?"

"Barrett said that sometimes he'd talk about 'her buried secret.'"

This was getting too far-fetched. Now we had ghosts and buried treasure along with Barrett's death. We waited in silence as the coffee brewed. As soon as it was done, I poured a cup for Tucker, who was half asleep at the table, and brought the rest into the sitting room.

Miss Nella watched me with a cynical smile. "Did you calm the boy down? He's so like his father."

"He says you sent money to your uncle up until he died."

"Nonsense. Why would I send him money?"

"Tucker thinks it was because your uncle knew something."

Miss Nella blinked, sitting up straighter. She fidgeted with the buttons on her blouse and noticed the tomato soup stain. She absently wiped at it with a sigh. "I'm going to have to call the girl who used to come out before Barrett. She'll do my hair and help me with a shower." She paused for a moment, her eyes closed. When she opened them, her voice was firm. "Now let's talk about my memoirs. I thought I'd call it 'The Gooseberry Acres Years.' What do you think?"

I think you're trying to manipulate me. I smiled in a way that made my face feel tight. "Fine."

For the next half hour, she talked about the layout of the hospital and grounds. "Dad made that walkway on the other side of the hospital to go to the cottages. Did you know we had cottages we rented to patients who were convalescing but not strong enough to go home? They loved staying here. I met a handsome boy once who lived in one of the cottages...." Her voice trailed off.

"You mean Dash?"

Her eyes widened. "How did you know that?"

I pointed to the diaries. "You wrote about him. I assumed he was one of the patients."

Miss Nella stiffened. "We won't speak of him. I was a silly, stupid girl."

Miss Nella gazed beyond me. I finished my coffee waiting for her to talk again. The room grew hot and close. I wanted to get up and open a window to let out the stale air and the smell of an old lady. Miss Nella's chin drooped to her chest, and she started to snore. I decided it was time to leave. I needed fresh air.

Chapter Eighteen: The Grounds

I stood in front of the old hospital building with my eyes closed. The sun warmed my face and crumpled, dead leaves danced in the breeze on the steps to the building. Was it only yesterday that Barrett Fox went exploring and ended up at the bottom of a dark, dank stairwell?

With Miss Nella's box of diaries stowed in the back of my car, I planned to drive home and seriously think through whether I wanted this job. The images in my brain cycled back and forth between the check Miss Nella had written out and Barrett's body in the mausoleum of a building.

Miss Nella was holding onto secrets. Perhaps she wanted to rewrite history. I remembered what she'd first told me about who she was writing her memoirs for. "The families of the people who lived and died here and the seekers of truth. That's all."

Standing here amongst the neglected grounds, I wondered about what she had said. Most of the people who were once patients were probably dead. Maybe their families would be interested, or maybe not. And what about "the seekers of the truth?"

"Too deep for me right now." Overhead, a flock of geese squawked as they flew in a V-formation. I'd once edited an article about the wisdom of birds. The author explained that geese fly in V-formation to conserve energy and as a way of keeping track of each other. He compared it to bicycle racers switching leads when the front ones tired. At the time I was doing the copyediting of the article, I hardly cared about how geese flew. Now, I could watch them with a certain amount of awe for the wisdom of Mother Nature.

As I watched the birds fly away, I decided to look at the old cemetery. Perhaps it would give me a clue as to why I would want to continue this memoir project. The cemetery was on the other side of the forgotten garden, close to where the forest thickened. I walked through the garden, picking my way through the shrubs and high grass. Green sprouts of new grass poked through the nest of tangled composting dead plants. Even in the midst of neglect, the new grass represented hope. Still, the area felt like something chill and ghostly rose from the ground.

"Imagination, Jamie. It's just old plants."

At the far end of the garden was an oak tree with its leaves beginning to bud out. I could see a number of dead and dying branches as I approached. The tree was either very, very old or diseased.

In front of the tree were the fallen remains of an old picket fence that must have encircled the cemetery. Most of the fence was gone, and what was left was bare rotting wood. I stepped around it to the first gravestone. It was small and made of a white marble, reminding me of the markers in Arlington National Cemetery. Over the years, it had tipped, as one end of it sunk deeper into the earth. I knelt to read the inscription:

Jemmy Baker 1930-1940.

No other words or sayings were inscribed. Jemmy was only ten years old. I closed my eyes, thinking about dying that young and being abandoned in this neglected place. Did she have family? Why wouldn't they take her home for burial? I guessed those were questions that would never be answered.

As I looked around at the little cemetery it occurred to me that instead of neat rows or any kind of symmetry, the stones were set in a haphazard manner as if the burials were hastily done. I'd have to ask Miss Nella about it, although I'm not sure she would tell me the real story.

I read the inscriptions on several more of the gravestones. The dead varied in age from Jemmy at ten to Isaac Peterson who was 75. The latest death looked to be around 1950. One marker had no name and no date, just a blank stone with the word "Beloved" etched into it. Unlike the others, this marker appeared to have been washed and cleaned. It stood out in its whiteness. The desiccated remains of a bouquet tied with a red ribbon lay next to the marker. Someone had recently placed those flowers.

It seemed as I stood among the old gravestones as if the world suddenly became eerily silent. The birds had stopped singing, the crickets and frogs had quit chirping, and the trees stilled. I pictured a dismal group of people standing over a grave as the coffin was lowered. Where were the grieving family members? Why did one grave have flowers, but no name? I hoped someone in the funeral group had uttered kind words to send the poor soul to the next world.

Behind the old oak, deeper in the woods, something stirred. For a moment, I half-expected to see a long-dead TB patient emerge into the sunlight. I hugged myself and my heart thumped against my chest.

Approaching footsteps crunched through the dead leaves and pine needles on the path next to the cemetery. Startled, I turned to see Ed with his rifle and an angry expression.

"You get away from there!" He pointed his rifle at the unmarked gravestone. "Nella doesn't like people causing trouble out here!"

I held up my hands. "Ed, it's Jamie. Remember, I'm helping Miss Nella?" My heart beat so hard I felt it behind my eyes. I wanted to run—to run away from this place and to run away from Ed and the rifle.

"What?" He stared at me. At least he wasn't pointing the rifle at me.

"I'm helping Miss Nella, and I wanted to tour the grounds. Maybe you can help me." I worked to keep a quaver out of my voice.

"You shouldn't be here. Nella doesn't want people here."

I pointed to the dead flowers. "Did you put them here?"

He frowned as if this was a hard question. "I take care of things."

"Do you know who's buried there? Was it a friend of Nella's?"

Ed relaxed his grip on the rifle and pointed it to the ground. "Mama said not to ask questions—just do what I'm told."

"So, you don't know why Miss Nella wanted the flowers?"

He didn't answer. He stared at his foot and kicked away a twig. "Mama said it was nobody's business."

"Maybe one of the patients who didn't want people to know he died here?"

Instead of answering my question, he mumbled, "Those kids that used to come and burn things down and break things. They stayed away from here. I made sure. It's not good to disturb the dead."

Slowly and carefully, I walked over to the blank marker and knelt down. "I wonder who this is—a person without a name."

I watched as Ed stiffened. "Babies don't always have names, you know." He gestured with his rifle. "You need to go now.

"A baby?" Maybe Miss Nella's mother had lost a baby. If so, this was a sad place to bury it.

"We don't talk about it. Mama said we shouldn't." He moved his rifle as if he was trying to sweep me back.

I stood up. "Is there a record of who's buried here?"

He shrugged. "They're dead. Mama always said to leave the dead alone."

I backed away from Ed, still holding my hands palm out. "I guess you're right."

"You go now," he grumbled. "No one should be here. Bad enough that those soldier guys trample around looking for a lost kid."

"You mean the men from Camp Six?"

Ed gripped his rifle. "Best you get going now."

I wasn't about to argue with him.

Walking back to my car, I felt that old spider tingle on the back of my neck. It was faint, as if the spider skittered across the nape of my neck and disappeared. I had so many questions for Miss Nella and a high suspicion she wouldn't answer them.

Another flock of geese passed overhead. I looked up, admiring their symmetry. At least they knew what they were doing. I wished I did.

Tucker met me outside as I was opening the door to the car. "I see you have Cousin Nella's box again. My dad had a lot of stories about this place. I might be able to help you sort some of it out." He looked back at the house. "She's getting forgetful, you know."

His demeanor had changed from a grieving, hungover brother to a curious and helpful cousin. I didn't know how to read him, but I was glad to see that he had cheered up a bit.

"Perhaps you can help me, but I haven't committed to doing this project yet."

He grinned. "It'll be a kick, I'm sure."

As I drove away, I had the distinct feeling that "a kick" wasn't the way to describe what I might be getting myself into.

Chapter Nineteen: The Secret Recipe

Once again, I found myself lugging the box of Miss Nella's diaries into my cabin. Bronte, in her enthusiasm, nearly sent me sprawling when I tripped over her. Maybe that was the omen I was looking for. I left the box in the corner and grabbed a beer. Time to wind down and chill out.

The chilling out lasted only long enough for my phone to ping with a text. **J exciting news. Possible summer gig**

I stared at it. "Just shoot me now. Why is Andrew hanging around? What did I do to deserve this?"

Ignoring the text, I took my beer out to the rock. A slight breeze rippled across the water as I took a deep breath of the lake-scented air. Andrew could do whatever he wanted as long as he stayed away from me. The little voice in my head told me he was up to something, and it involved money. Was he hoping to woo me back to get his hands on my cabin? Probably.

Bronte sat placidly at my feet. Life with her was so straightforward. If she wanted something, she let me know. If she didn't like something, she let me know. More importantly, I knew she would never walk out on me because a better-looking dog came along.

I thought about Tucker Fox, who seemed to be an older version of Andrew. Good looking, an actor without a stage, and an actor with the ability to charm. Was he scheming or was he simply fulfilling his father's wish to recover whatever was owed to him?

Time to think about something else. I called Jim, and it went directly to his voicemail. "Hey, I'm gazing at the lake, wishing you'd take me fishing.

Call me." What I really missed was not the opportunity to fish, but the long discussions in front of the fireplace and the way he could look so intense when he was working on projects that involved building and not thinking. Or the way his face softened when he talked about his son Jake. Of course, I also missed the time in the bedroom and the salty-sweet taste of his skin.

Sighing, I patted Bronte on the head and walked back to the cabin. Once inside, I considered Nella's box and the *Apple Pie* manuscript. Thinking about the neglected grounds and the forgotten cemetery, I decided I needed a slice of Apple Pie.

In the second chapter, Apple Pie revealed that Chef Mac had developed a secret recipe for a wine-infused macaroni and cheese casserole. He and the murdered sous chef were the only two who knew the ingredients. A big competition was coming up, and they planned to debut it. I wondered how you would infuse wine into macaroni. Skipping ahead to the end, where Opal, the author, had an addendum with real recipes, I searched for it. She very slyly noted at the end of the recipe section that Chef Mac was saving the mystery recipe to be revealed in book #2, *Apple Pie and a Dollop of Death*.

What I did find was an intriguing recipe for beef stew using a dry red wine. It looked like something to eat on a cold night in front of a crackling fire. I pictured it simmering on the stove with the aroma of beef mixed with sage and thyme. Clearly, the food theme of *Apple Pie* was working for me. The more I read of this book, the more I liked it.

Unfortunately, the next chapter was a jarring surprise. Instead of dwelling on the aroma of the simmering stew, *Apple Pie* took a different turn. Chef Mac took his pig with him to a local farm for fresh produce. Apple Pie turned from a fun-loving pot-bellied pet to a rage-filled pig, nudging Chef Mac and snorting at a person who threw his trash out the window of his car. "I hate people who treat the highway as their personal pig sty." He even used the F-word on two occasions. Cozy mysteries rarely used that kind of language—especially from the narrator.

As Apple Pie raged through the chapter, I wondered if Opal, the author, had some anger issues.

Jim saved me from more of the pig's ire when he returned my call. "Hey, how's life on the lake?"

"Bronte misses you."

"Hah! Bronte is happy to have my side of the bed. How are things?"

"Never a dull moment. I'm dealing with an angry pig right now."

He hesitated. "Please tell me you didn't go 'earth girl' and buy a pig."

I laughed, and it felt good. "No, my book narrator, the pot-bellied pig, has some issues." I explained where I was in the *Apple Pie* saga.

When I was done, Jim told me about the DC weather. "It's hot and muggy and crowded here. It smells like car exhaust and swamp."

"Sounds a little like New York in July and August." For a moment, I missed the way the humidity in the summer in New York held in the aromas of the little cafes in our Queens neighborhood. Then I remembered a major temper tantrum from Andrew on an oppressively hot night when the fan he was supposed to fix didn't work. He'd bellowed about how it was all my fault and stormed out of the apartment. *Apple Pie* and Andrew, two raging beasts.

I tore myself away from thoughts of my ex. "It's clean and fresh here with the bonus that the mosquitoes haven't come out yet."

He told me all was going well. "I passed my test, and now I consider myself a fledgling internet forensics nerd."

It didn't fit the picture of Jim as the athletic state trooper who skied and bicycled and enjoyed the outdoors. He sounded so pleased with himself that I restrained myself from commenting about his nerd status. I filled him in on Miss Nella and the death of her cousin Barrett. "I can't get the image out of my head of Barrett at the bottom of the stairs. Her neck was so...so twisted."

"Hey. Maybe you should beg off that project. Don't you have a manuscript already?"

"Sure. And if you're lucky, when you get back, I can make you a specialty macaroni and cheese a'la Apple Pie, the pig."

Once my brain was steered away from Miss Nella and Andrew, we had a good chat about his temporary life in Washington. He thought he'd be home in three weeks. "Still a good time to fish before all the bass are gone."

"How is Jake doing?" His five-year-old son was currently in remission from leukemia and had a good prognosis. "He sent me a picture he'd drawn of Bronte. Looked just like her if you disregard the ears, the tail, the shape, and the color."

Jim laughed. "He wants me to come home, said he's tired of seeing me on the phone. I think his grandma is ready for me to be back, too. Jake is pretty energetic."

I chose not to ask how Jake's mother was doing in rehab or what the custody arrangements would be after he returned. That was a hot mess for another day.

Our relationship was still tenuous enough that I didn't say what I really wanted to say, *I love you.* The only person I'd ever said that to had run off with a woman named Destiny. I ended the call with a cheery, "Talk to you soon."

Staring at the darkened phone screen, I reflected on why I hadn't told him about Andrew. "What's wrong with me, girl?" Bronte pricked up her ears. "I feel like I'm having an illicit affair."

In the next two chapters of *Apple Pie,* my delightful pig went back to his benign amusing narration. Apple Pie was amassing clues on who killed the sous chef. The writing was humorous enough that, at several points, I laughed out loud. It's not easy investigating when you can't talk, you're hungry all the time, and you don't have opposable thumbs. However, it was clear that Apple Pie was going to sniff out the killer. I set the manuscript down with a grin.

My good mood didn't translate into a decent night's sleep. Instead of dreaming about recipes, I found myself back in the cemetery—except it was the Forest family plot outside of Boston. I was trying to find my father's grave, and I couldn't read the gravestones. They were all blank except for the word *Beloved.* A dark presence engulfed the cemetery, and when I tried to run away, my feet were tangled in thorny rose bushes. I stumbled, and when I fell, it was to the concrete floor of the holding cell in Queens.

I woke up with a start, angry that I kept having these dreams that ended up in Queens. The incident where a drug task force mistook me for a dealer, broke into my apartment, and left me in a holding cell in Queens was two years old. Why wouldn't it stop haunting me in my sleep?

Bronte lifted her head with a questioning look. As she settled back down, I thought about the cemetery at Gooseberry Acres. What had Ed said? Something about a baby. In the middle of the night, after yet another nightmare, I knew I couldn't drop the project—too many secrets to uncover.

Chapter Twenty: The Diaries

The next morning, I paced in the kitchen, phone in hand. Did I really want to go forward with the Gooseberry project? Bronte followed me as I moved from the living room to the kitchen. Finally, she nudged me with a whine. Time to decide. With a sigh, I called Miss Nella to tell her I would accept the job. She wanted me to come right out. I declined saying I needed to read through more of the diaries so I could ask her relevant questions. I'd see her in the afternoon.

Miss Nella hung up without replying.

From the box, I arranged the diaries in chronological order. Pulling out a packet of Post-it Notes from the kitchen junk drawer, I showed them to Bronte.

"These little sticky notes are what financed Gooseberry Acres, you know." Except, back then, Post-it Notes hadn't been invented yet.

Bronte sniffed them and decided they weren't edible. She settled at my feet with a sigh.

The first diary I opened was probably written around the time Nella was ten, although she hadn't dated it. Her entries were mainly one or two sentences, and often she skipped weeks and even months. It was easy to skim through it and get a hint of the inner thoughts of a ten-year-old—friends, gifts, new shoes and a strong desire for a pet. *Oh why can't I have a kitten? Papa says no, because who would take care of it?*

She also noted that Nanny Ninny had left. *I came home, and she had her suitcase and was talking to Papa. She was crying, and he hugged her. I don't like it when he hugs her because she's so mean. I asked Papa why she was leaving, and he wouldn't say. I think it's because she got so fat and he's mad at her for eating so much.*

Miss Nella was too young and innocent to understand that Nanny Ninny was probably pregnant.

She hardly mentioned the hospital and patients except for one entry about a little girl who was a patient. It was brief and abrupt. *She died, and I asked Papa if I could have her doll. He says no to everything.*

I gleaned from her writing that after Nanny Ninny left, a succession of babysitters watched over her. She liked one named Susie and thought the one named Agnes was strict like Nanny Ninny. She decided she missed having Nanny Ninny living in the house with her. *Now I have to wait until Agnes gets here to have my breakfast. At least Nanny Ninny was always around.*

One entry was of interest, though. Almost a year after Nanny Ninny left, she came back. *Nanny Ninny is back, but she won't take care of me. Papa says she will be the new matron at the hospital. Now she can be mean to the patients like she was mean to me. Nella, do this. Nella, stand up straight. Nella, show me your arithmetic tables. Poor patients.*

In the next diary, Nanny Ninny, now called Matron McEnany, came back from a trip with a little boy she called Punky. He was going to live with her in a house close to the lake. *I asked how she got Punky, and she said he's her nephew, but he calls her Mama. I don't think it's right, especially since Agnes has to take care of him when she's taking care of me. He's ugly, and he cries a lot.*

I marked the entry with a Post-it. Maybe if this Punky was still alive, he might be able to tell me more about life on the grounds. I dug around until I found the old family photo with Uncle Judd in it. Punky must have been the child in the photo. I remembered how Miss Nella had dismissed him as a child of one of the staff members when I'd shown her the picture. I made a note to ask her again and find out if she knew where Punky might be now.

Most of the rest of this diary was preoccupied with school projects, although she had one entry talking about the war. *Papa says when the war is over, we'll be busy all the time with sick soldiers because they live so close together. That's why they get TB. I wish it was over now. My friend Carol's brother just went, and she cried at school because she doesn't want him to get killed. I'm glad I don't have a brother, so I don't have to worry about the Germans killing him.*

After an hour of going through the diaries, I set them aside. Maybe they had value to a historical society, but I didn't see how I could put this together into a memoir. This was going to be a nightmare, but I'd committed. My dad was a stickler on commitment. He'd say, "If you agreed to do it, you do it." He was an upstanding example of it with my mother. When she got so sick, he could have divorced her and left her for the state to take care of. Instead, he cared for her until he couldn't and visited her regularly in the nursing home even when she didn't know him anymore.

Thinking about this, I was ashamed of my waffling. Miss Nella would get her memoir. "I'm committed," I said aloud.

Bronte, at the sound of my voice, wagged her tail and headed for the door. She was right. It was time for a walk. I'd take her with me to the mailbox and stop in at the lodge to check in about Rob's mural project.

I grabbed Bronte's leash. She could run free for part of the trip, but as soon as she got near the lodge, I needed to rein her in. On one of our walks to the lodge last summer, she'd chased the perfectly coiffed poodle of one of the guests. The poodle reminded me of some of the dogs the professional walkers cared for in Manhattan, complete with little red sweaters and jeweled collars.

Bronte bounded ahead of me down the drive while I took in the beauty of the newly awakened forest. The brown and open forest floor was giving way to new growth. In one of the sunnier spots, little yellow and violet wildflowers bloomed. I imagined my ancestors had names for all of them and knew which ones were edible, which ones were poisonous, and which ones were good for medicine. Learning more about how the Ojibwe lived on this land was on my "to-do" list. Someday when I didn't have a damned memoir project and a charming pot-bellied pig to use up my time, I planned to study my heritage more seriously.

I stood at the edge of the drive and gazed into the woods, enjoying the quiet. As I concentrated on the sounds, I heard the rustling of leaves on the forest floor, the whispering buzz of insects, and a chittering from a gray squirrel. I wondered if my Ojibwe grandmother or great-grandmother ever stopped to breathe in the sounds and the smells. I thought about what Rob had told me of the Indian schools. Had my ancestors been forced to attend? Were they torn from their families like his mother?

My musings were interrupted by Bronte's bark as she chased a chipmunk up a tree.

"You go, girl. Protect me from the wild beasts." I laughed at her excitement.

When we approached the lodge, I clipped the leash onto Bronte. My mailbox was one of several lining the driveway to the lodge. In it were circulars, the electric bill, and a check for the last editing job I'd done.

I slipped the mail into the pocket of my windbreaker and headed toward the lodge. Tying Bronte to a bicycle rack, I instructed her to sit and be quiet. Not that she ever listened to me, but it was worth a try.

Mavis, the receptionist, looked up at me. She'd dyed her hair a deep red which emphasized the paleness of her complexion. Her reading glasses hung on a chain around her neck.

"Jamie, nice to see you."

"Hi. I stopped in because I heard a rumor about the lodge commissioning a mural."

She smiled at me. "No secrets in this town."

"What's going on?"

She set her pen down and leaned her elbows on the check-in counter. "Nothing official yet, but the new management wants to spiff the place up. I heard one of the guys say the word 'brand' like they want to do an Indian theme or something."

I gazed around at the lobby with its giant fieldstone fireplace and colorful tapestries hanging on the walls. "Seems to me it is already branded."

Mavis pursed her lips and nodded. "That's what I thought, but no one asked me. They've got big plans with remodeling the cabins and adding a casino and maybe some entertainment." She grimaced. "I like it the way it is. I've worked here since high school—it has a nice homey feel."

It occurred to me that if they expanded the resort, I would see more traffic and more noise. I sighed. "I'm not sure I like those plans. What do they mean by 'entertainment?'"

Her mouth curled into a smile. "Some Hollywood-looking guy met with the manager. I heard they talked about doing plays or musicals or something."

"You mean like summer stock?"

She shrugged. "I guess that's what they said."

Something felt like it was dropping from my chest into my stomach. I described Andrew. "Was the guy the one who plays Mr. Right Digestion on television?"

Mavis furrowed her eyebrows. "No…he was older, good looking with kind of a square jaw—more like that guy from *A Star is Born*…ah, Bradley Cooper?"

Outside, Bronte made a woofing sound. "Guess I'd better go. Good luck with the project."

The lodge phone rang as Mavis waved to me.

Bronte stood, tail wagging, as I walked out the door. My phone pinged as I untied Bronte's leash.

J, getting excited about sticking around for the summer.

"Lord save me!" I crammed the phone into my pocket.

Once we were on our way back to the cabin, I let Bronte off the leash, and she loped ahead. Behind me, a car with a broken muffler turned into the lodge parking area. I glanced back and stopped. I recognized the car as the one belonging to Tucker. Was he the Bradley Cooper guy? If so, had he somehow connected with Andrew? People talked about "gaydar," recognizing someone in a crowd who was gay. Did Tucker and Andrew have "thespian-dar?"

I shook my head. If they were teaming up, this couldn't be good. I kept walking. The peace I'd felt observing springtime in the woods vanished with the picture of Andrew and Tucker scheming together.

Chapter Twenty-One: Back to Gooseberry

That afternoon, driving out to the highway, I glanced over at the lodge parking area to see if Tucker's car was there. The only vehicles were newer looking. Had I imagined the car with the broken muffler?

"Jamie, you're seeing conspiracies where they don't exist. Spending too much time in the world of fiction," I mumbled, pulling onto the highway.

When I arrived at Gooseberry Acres, the driveway and parking area were empty. Stepping out of the car, I stretched the tension out of my shoulders. If Tucker was up to something at the lodge, it was none of my business. If he'd teamed up with Andrew, it was still none of my business—or so I told myself.

Miss Nella was in her usual chair. She wore a green pants suit with a cream-colored blouse, and her hair was pulled back into a tidy bun. She'd even put on a little makeup. A colorful afghan was neatly folded next to her chair. I pointed to the afghan, "That's a beautiful piece."

She touched it. "A patient made it for me. She was one of the last we had. With the new antibiotics, people didn't need our fresh air and sunshine anymore." She bit her lip.

"It must have been hard to close the hospital."

She slumped a little in her chair. "I was ready for it to be done. We were losing money every week—paying staff when we had no patients. But Papa..." She didn't finish her sentence.

The little sunlight that crept through the crack in the drapes showed a wetness on her cheeks. I waited a few moments before pointing to her fresh outfit, "You're looking good."

As I set several of the diaries on the coffee table, she replied, "And you're looking tired."

On the drive to Gooseberry, I'd tried to keep my thoughts on the memoir project. Except I kept going back to Andrew's text and his insinuation about having a claim to my property. He was like a storm cloud hovering over me, ready to burst. I didn't tell this to Miss Nella.

"I've got another editing project I'm working on. It's kept me up late, I guess." I lied.

I brought out my notebook and with it the old photo. "Remember I showed you this the other day? You wrote something in your early diary about a little boy named Punky. I'm wondering if that's him."

She took the photo but didn't look at it. "Could be. Sometimes the family of staff lived on the grounds. Papa had cottages for them."

"Did they mingle with the patients? It seems to me that would be dangerous."

She shook her head, handing the photo back. "Oh no. Papa was very strict about separating the patients from the staff children. From the time I was little, he lectured me about contagion. He'd talk about how a patient could give TB to you. At first, I thought he meant that they had something like a little box with TB in it. I knew I wasn't to take anything from them. Once a nice man whose wife was in the hospital tried to give me candy. I told him I couldn't take it because Papa didn't want me to get TB. Children take things so literally." She leaned back in her chair with a sigh. "I tried to stay away from the patients."

Something in her voice didn't quite ring true—a hesitation. I waited to see if she had anything more to say, but she was quiet.

We talked for a while about how she wanted her memoir structured. I suggested a couple of options, including a straight timeline. "You could start with what it was like as a young girl to be raised here and move into your adult experience. I'm sure we can pick out stories from the diaries, and you can tell me more."

Miss Nella closed her eyes as if in thought. When she spoke, her voice was so low I had to lean in to hear her. "Some of those times were so sad. I'm not sure I want to remember them."

"Maybe talking about them would be good."

She opened her eyes. "Yes. Maybe."

I waited, growing more impatient. She wanted her memoirs written, but she didn't want to remember them. I wasn't sure where to go with this. I tried again. "How about the fun times. You must have had those?"

Something in the house settled with a faint creaking sound. It reminded me that this house was close to one hundred years old, and Miss Nella wasn't that much younger. The house had a slightly mildewy odor and a feeling of neglect like the grounds. When I moved on the sofa, dust motes floated through the air. The oriental carpet had stains and worn spots. I tried to imagine how it looked in here back in the forties. Did the room always have such dark, heavy drapes? When was the last time the sun had touched this room?

Miss Nella interrupted my thoughts. She had a sad smile. "Most of the fun I had was not here." She indicated the room. "In school, my friends wouldn't come to my house to play with me. Their parents were afraid they might catch something. It was like I lived in a leper colony."

"Oh." I hadn't thought about the isolation she must have felt.

Again, Miss Nella went silent. I pulled out one of the diaries and read to her the entry about the doll. "I suppose you were lonely when you asked for the doll."

She clasped her hands together, "Oh yes, I do remember that little girl and her doll. She had the prettiest hair. That's why I noticed her when she was in the garden in a lounge chair all wrapped up in blankets. I could see her out my bedroom window. One day when Agnes was busy in the kitchen, I sneaked out to talk with her. When I got close, I saw how skinny she was and how big her eyes were." She peered at me. "That's the first time I remember understanding sickness."

"What happened?"

"She was holding this big doll that had hair like hers. Blonde and curly. I touched the doll, and the little girl grabbed my hand. 'I want to go home.' She whispered to me. 'Can't I go home to Mama?'"

I visualized the two girls together in the garden, one sick and one healthy. I saw the tenderness in the moment.

"While I stood by her, she started to cough, and when she coughed, blood came out of her mouth and down her chin. I don't know what happened to me. I should have been nice to her, but I didn't want the blood to get on her doll, so I grabbed it away. She screamed, and more blood came out, and one of the nurses took the doll back from me and told me I was a bad girl, and I should go home."

Miss Nella took a deep breath. "I've been a bad girl, but not then. All I wanted was to keep the doll from getting blood on it."

I was struck by the pain and the guilt in her words. I thought about the weedy, abandoned cemetery behind the hospital. "Do you know if the little girl was buried here?"

Miss Nella stiffened. "What?"

"I took a walk to the cemetery. There was one gravestone of a child of about ten named Jemmy. Do you know if that was her?"

She waved me away. "I wouldn't know. Papa didn't talk about the cemetery. For him, it represented his failures."

"I wonder if he kept a record of who is buried there. It might be an interesting section for the memoir." I pointed towards Dr. Fox's study.

She frowned. "The records wouldn't be in the house. Papa kept all the patient notes in the hospital. He said he didn't want the sanatorium records in the house."

I wanted to open the drapes and let the sunshine in. The darkness in this room gave me a headache.

"Do you want me to look into the cemetery? Maybe Ed could show me where your father kept the files."

Miss Nella sighed. "Perhaps you should. I don't know." Her voice dropped to almost a whisper. "Maybe the secrets are there."

I wasn't sure I'd heard her correctly. "Secrets?"

115

Miss Nella reached down for the afghan. "Could you put this on me? I'm getting chilled."

The room was warm enough that I had taken off my cardigan and sat in a short-sleeved cotton top.

I knelt beside her, unfolded the afghan, and draped it over her. She pushed it off.

"No. No. I just want it on my legs."

I was taken aback by the irritation in her voice. She directed me to cover her lap and legs. I thought about the little girl wrapped in blankets in the garden. I pointed to the afghan. "When the patients were outside, they must have kept them wrapped like this."

"They brought them out even on the coldest days. I watched a lot from my bedroom window. Papa said the fresh air was what would cure them."

At this point, I felt like I was getting nowhere. "Miss Nella, I'm not sure where to go with this. Do you want a history of Gooseberry Acres? Do you want the story of your father? Do you want the story of what it was like to grow up here? I confess to being lost."

Miss Nella turned her face from me and closed her eyes. "I want to be able to tell the truth before I die. That's all."

"Then tell me your story." My tone was filled with the exasperation I felt.

"Tomorrow. I'll tell you the truth tomorrow."

Outside, a car with a bad muffler approached. Tucker had returned.

Chapter Twenty-Two: Tucker's Story

Miss Nella seemed relieved when Tucker walked in the door. I wasn't sure I'd get any more out of her today. She looked exhausted.

He held a bag of groceries. "I should get these in the fridge."

I stood up. "Let me help you."

Miss Nella closed her eyes. "Go help him, please."

I felt like the paid help as I followed Tucker to the kitchen. As long as I had that check, I guessed I was.

"How are you doing?" I asked.

He turned to me with a sad expression. "You know, Barrett could be so annoying and so priggish. But damn if I don't miss her."

"Will you have a service?"

He shrugged. "It's only me...and Nella. I doubt it. Once they release the body, I guess she'll be cremated."

"Have they determined it was an accident?"

"They haven't said anything to me yet."

"Oh, I'm sorry. This must be hard."

He opened the refrigerator and put away a carton of milk. "It is hard. The more I think about it, the more I wonder...."

"Wonder?"

Closing the refrigerator, he stared out the window. "Barrett had a long history of depression. Nothing ever seemed to go right for her. She was married to a man who abused her, and after that, she found another who was an alcoholic. Sometimes I think she just wanted to end it."

His voice was flat and unemotional, almost like he was reading a script. "Are you saying you think it was suicide?"

He shrugged. "Actually, I'm not sure what I'm saying."

I slid into a kitchen chair and watched as he put away canned goods. He had a grace about his movements that reminded me of a dancer. Andrew had taken dance along with acting classes. He told me the lessons would be good for any sword fight scenes. The smoothness in the way he moved had helped him get the job as Mr. Right Digestion.

When Tucker finished, he sat down across from me. "Listen, I don't want to be a downer, okay?"

Out the bay window, I watched a gathering of chickadees pecking at the overgrown back lawn.

We sat in silence while the refrigerator motor started, and something inside it rattled. Tucker glanced at it. "Like lots of other things around here, that fridge is on its last legs."

He was probably referring to Miss Nella. I rested my elbows on the table. "What are you planning to do? Will you stay?"

He raised his eyebrows and shrugged. "Depends. If my agent calls with a gig, I'm out of here. If not, Nella needs me."

"What about Larissa Lodge? Weren't you trying to put together something with them?"

His eyes widened. "You know about that?"

"Andrew, my ex texted me. He seemed pretty excited."

Tucker studied me for a moment. "You and Andrew were married?"

He posed it as a question, but I could tell from the relaxed way he leaned back in the chair that he already knew about my relationship to Andrew. The last thing I wanted to do was talk about that fiasco of a marriage. I tried to keep my expression neutral. "Andrew is not a topic I like to talk about. Tell me about your summer theater ideas."

Tucker sat up a little straighter. "Okay, I get it. We'll keep Andrew offstage." He smiled, folding his arms, "I have a couple of ideas, that's all. After spending two months here, I'd love to get back to working with the living rather than the ghosts that haunt this place. I did some theater work years ago in a juvenile detention center. When the Camp Six guys came around the first time looking for that lost kid, I suggested it."

"Are you sure Camp Six would be interested in theater?"

Tucker shrugged. "Seemed worth exploring—although they haven't gotten back to me. I hear they never found the kid. I guess his parents put up a big reward. Too bad."

I shook my head, thinking about the parents and what an incredible loss this was. "And the lodge?"

"Summer stock can be a real draw."

"Kind of late, isn't it?"

He grinned, and I could see him on the big screen. He had the right kind of face, projecting a roguish charm, but something about it made me uncomfortable. I remembered seeing him with Barrett at the hardware store. It seemed at the time that the two were scheming something.

Tucker continued. "I need to stay here until I can get some things settled. It's why Barrett and I came in the first place."

Ah, maybe the answer. I probed, "Can you tell me what it's all about? Would it affect Miss Nella's memoirs?"

He whistled. "Are you looking for the truth or the fairy tale cousin Nella lives in?"

At this, I tilted my head with a slight smile. "She hired me to tell her story. I'm not an investigative journalist, but I'm sensing this place has skeletons."

Tucker glanced at his watch. "Is it late enough to have a drink? If so, I'll tell you my story."

Without waiting for my reply, he took two beers out of the refrigerator and handed one to me.

"Can I write any of this down?"

He shook his head. "Nope."

He told me about growing up in California with his father, Judd. "I admit it. Dad was a very good-looking, charming hustler. My mother once said he could sell sand to an Arab. I never really knew much about what he did. In fact, they divorced when I was still in grade school. I didn't reconnect with him until I was grown up." He paused. "I didn't know I had an older

119

half-sister until a year ago when she came to care for Dad after her second bad marriage. I was…ah…between gigs and living at his place at the time."

Thinking about Andrew's acting career, I wonder how often Tucker found himself between gigs.

He picked at the label on the beer bottle, tearing it off in little bits. "By the time she came, Dad was getting pretty demented. Sometimes he called me Alfred, and sometimes he accused me of stealing things. When Barrett came, he called her Nella even though the resemblance is…well…vague. But he had all these stories about a big cache of money that his brother owed him."

"You mean Miss Nella's father, Dr. Fox?"

"Yup. I finally did a little internet search and found out about Gooseberry Acres and the sanatorium. One night when Dad was relatively lucid, I asked him about this place. I remember how his face darkened, and he said something like, 'Alfred owes me. I saved them from ruin. I told him I'd keep his secret, and I did.'"

The word "secret" popped up a lot today. "Did you find out what he meant?"

Tucker finished his beer and set it down. "He said there were papers, and if we could get them, we would be rich."

The refrigerator clicked on again with a rattle. Tucker took another beer out. I hadn't touched mine.

"Did he ever tell you what the secret was?"

Tucker's expression was a cross between amusement and something more sinister. "Murder. He claimed he knew about a murder and something even darker. His brother paid him for his silence until suddenly it stopped."

Tucker stared at me as if to gauge my reaction. I took a sip of the beer. It was a cheap brand with a watery taste. "Do you think he was mixing up his life with a movie or television program? If he was owed money for whatever reason, wouldn't he have gone for it a long time ago?"

"Barrett and I had the same questions, but we weren't able to get any details out of Dad before he died. He left us a little money—enough to bury him and to come out here. We decided we'd meet this mysterious cousin

Nella and check it out."

I understood about pulling up stakes and trying something new, since I'd done just that when I moved here last year from New York. For me, though, I was looking for a fresh start, not a treasure.

Tucker drummed his fingers on the table. "I can see you are skeptical. I'll admit, we came on a lark. For one thing, I expected to find a large, beautiful estate, not this graveyard. When we pulled up here, I wanted to turn around and leave, but Barrett insisted we at least look into what Dad had said."

"And?"

"Something about Nella and her reaction when she answered the door made us decide to stay—at least for a while. Clearly, she needed our help—or I should say, Barrett's help. But she also didn't tell us Dad's claims were nonsense. She said she'd look through her father's papers and see if she could turn up what Dad was talking about."

It sounded like Miss Nella used this as an opportunity to get some cheap help. I didn't say it, but I think Tucker read it on my face.

"Sure, she used us. But I still think there's something to Dad's story. I've asked around town, and some of the old dogs talk about this place being haunted by someone who was murdered."

Clarence had mentioned a haunting, but he had laughed it off.

Tucker was about to say something else when the boom of a gunshot interrupted us.

"What the hell was that?" Tucker stood up.

I heard yelling from down by the lake.

Chapter Twenty-Three: Gunshots

Miss Nella called from the sitting room. "What's all the fuss? We have No Hunting signs all over. Do I have to call the sheriff?" I opened the back door to the sound of another gunshot and more yelling. "It's coming from the lake by Ed's trailer."

Tucker stood next to me. "Who's shooting, and what are they shooting at?"

"We need to find out."

Tucker raised his hands. "Oh no. I'm not going anywhere near guns. I'll check to make sure the hospital is locked up and then go sit with Nella. It's probably target practice at the camp across the lake."

I was sure the gunshots were coming from near Ed's trailer. "I'm going to make sure Ed's okay."

A little voice in my head asked me what the hell I thought I was doing. *Don't run toward the gunshots, you idiot.*

I couldn't exactly say why I didn't turn around and go back to Nella's. As I ran across the garden, I didn't feel danger—at least for me. Nearing the trailer, I made out shouts coming from the lake.

"What the hell, old man?"

"Stay away. No more burning down our things." Ed's voice was shaky.

The trailer door was wide open. I followed the voices down a well-worn path to the lake. The scene I found might have been staged in an action movie. Ed stood on the edge of the lake with his rifle pointed at two men. One was in the water up to his knees and the other sitting in a canoe. Both had their hands raised.

When Ed heard me, he turned, his rifle pointing at me. I stopped dead and raised my hands, too.

"Ed, don't shoot! It's Jamie. Remember?"

He swung the rifle back to the two men in the Camp Six camo. Slowly, with my arms still raised, I approached Ed.

"What's going on, Ed?" I kept my voice as calm as I could, considering he had a loaded weapon.

"They aren't supposed to be here," he growled. "Miss Nella doesn't like trespassers."

I stayed where Ed could see me. Both the men, despite the military outfits, looked young and scared.

Pointing to the one in the water, I asked. "What are you doing here?"

"Ma'am, we thought we might have spotted Tally in the woods. We just came for a look-see."

Ed shifted, and the man backed up a little, almost tripping into the water.

"Ed, were you shooting at them?" I stared at him.

He made a grunting sound. "Just fired in the air to scare them off."

A couple of things sped through my brain. First, Ed could be in trouble for firing his rifle. Second, the two from the camp could be in trouble for trespassing. And third, I really didn't want to be here. I stood as tall as I could and channeled Jim, the rock-solid trooper. "Ed, put the rifle down, please. These guys aren't going to set your place on fire." I spoke with as much authority as I could muster.

It worked. Ed set the rifle down, muttering, "Miss Nella isn't going to like this one bit."

Moving next to him, I addressed the guys from the camp. "I don't see what you are doing here. Your missing camper was seen hitchhiking into town. Why do you think he's here?"

The man in the water relaxed his shoulders but kept his eyes on Ed in case he decided to pick up the rifle again. "The commander says they can't find any evidence Tally went to town or headed back East. No one has seen him. He wanted us to scout out the woods in case...."

I silently finished his sentence. *In case he's dead.*

I kept my voice as stern as I could, considering I had no authority over any of these men. "Tell your commander the people here have had a lot of trouble with vandalism, so they're touchy about strangers on the property. If he wants to search, he should check with Miss Nella at the house first."

"Yes, ma'am."

At least they were polite.

We talked for a little longer, and they agreed to relay the message. After they were launched, I walked with Ed back to the trailer. "You shouldn't be firing that rifle," I told him.

"Sometimes you got to. Otherwise, they won't go away." He sounded a little scared himself.

"They're just trying to find the missing kid."

"Probably just a ghost by now," Ed muttered. "Ghost is back at the hospital."

I frowned. "What do you mean?"

"Nothing. Thought I saw something one day." He shook his head. "Don't like strangers around here." At the steps to the trailer, he paused. "Missed my afternoon shows. I always watch Family Feud."

He disappeared inside the trailer before I could ask him more about the ghost. I walked back to the house, thinking about the missing Talbot Smithers the Third. What if he hadn't hitchhiked home? What if he'd gotten to this side of the lake and died of exposure? I shivered, picking up my pace. I needed to tell Miss Nella that everything was okay. I also wanted her to talk with Ed about using his rifle. He seemed to listen to her.

Tucker sat with Miss Nella, his eyes closed. Clearly, he hadn't been as alarmed as me. Miss Nella also dozed. I shook his shoulder, and his eyes popped open with a start. "Right, oh. Everything okay?"

Maybe Tucker could play a big strong action hero, but in real life, I looked into the face of a weak man. "It's all okay."

To my surprise, he didn't ask any questions. I took this as an opportunity to go home. As I drove away, I glanced over at the hulking hospital building. I thought I saw a movement. I blinked, and it was gone. Must have been Ed's ghost.

Strange, I thought. Tucker's first reaction to the gunshots was to check to see if the hospital was locked. Did that make any sense?

Chapter Twenty-Four: Rumor of a Murder

On my way back to the cabin, I stopped in town to talk with Clarence. By now, it was mid-afternoon. The wind had picked up. Leftover leaves from last year swirled across the pavement in front of his house. Otherwise, the street was quiet.

Lorraine greeted me at the door. "He's in his study claiming to be doing legal work. I think he's playing with that new computer Joe got for him." She raised her eyebrows. "He's discovered Facebook."

"Never too old, I guess."

Clarence looked up from the laptop. "Here you are, just in time to show me how to use this Facebook thing."

I'd recently read the biggest percentage of new Facebook users were Baby Boomers and older. "If I show you how to use Facebook, you won't need me as your investigator anymore."

"Hah! Come in and sit down."

I told him about the confrontation at the lake with Ed and the Camp Six guys. "I'm not sure how safe Ed is with that rifle."

"Ah, yes. Another dilemma for Nella. She's loyal to Ed, but at some point, he might not be able to stay there."

I then filled him in on the text from Andrew and Tucker's proposal to Larissa Lodge and Camp Six. "I'm worried. Now that the two of them have somehow found each other, who knows what they'll come up with. Back in my married days, scheming like this usually cost *me* money, not Andrew.

They're both actors, and in my experience, actors tend to live in a fantasy world."

"Like your writers?"

"Probably. Although I've never met my writers in person." Perhaps someone who conjured up a pot-bellied pig sleuth did live in a fantasy world.

Lorraine brought us a tray with a carafe of coffee and two slices of banana bread. "Now, don't let it spoil your appetite. I'm making your favorite." Her eyes sparkled with amusement. "Broccoli surprise."

"You're fired," Clarence winked at me.

"Hush. You already fired me this morning." She closed the door to his study when she walked out.

I asked him if he had any news about Elena and her baby. He told me they'd finally gotten an immigration hearing scheduled—for September. "The wheels of justice sometimes grind to a halt."

At least Elena was protected for the time being from deportation.

Clarence closed the lid on the laptop and studied me. "You didn't come just to chat, did you?"

"No. I came to complain about this project you got me involved in." I filled him in on my work with Miss Nella and my frustrations with the so-called memoir. "Honestly, I don't think I can help her until she knows the story she wants to tell. She talked about secrets today but left me hanging. What do you think is going on?"

"Nella Fox is no fool. I don't doubt that when you hit on the right thing, she'll be very pleased."

"Well, I might die of old age before I figure it out," I groused.

The banana bread almost melted in my mouth. Apple Pie would have been proud. I held back the desire to groan as I ate it. My banana bread was always chewy and dry. I savored a bite before I spoke again.

"What do you know about a murder and a haunting?" I told him Tucker's story about his father believing Dr. Fox owed him for keeping quiet about a murder. Clarence leaned in, listening carefully.

"Rumors have been flying about that place ever since I was a little boy.

Dr. Fox kept the sanatorium isolated. Even though he employed some of the locals, many of his staff were from elsewhere. That's why the rumors abounded."

"What kind of rumors?"

Clarence smiled with a sigh. "Everything from how he was doing human experiments in the basement to he was a Nazi spy. You know how people prattle on about conspiracies. Look at today and the nonsense about the deep state and child pornography rings being run out of pizza parlors and butterfly sanctuaries."

"What about murder and haunting?"

Clarence finished his banana bread, licking his fingers with a satisfied smile. "I tell you, Lorraine could out-bake any of those television people."

"You're stalling. You must know something."

Wiping his hands with a napkin, he looked up at the ceiling. "Now I'm wandering into the world of rumor and innuendo. Again, remember, I was just a lad when I heard this. They said Dr. Fox had a second doctor working for him who suddenly disappeared. My mother knew someone who worked at the hospital who told her he was at work one day and never seen again."

I stirred milk into my coffee, noting Lorraine had left us a little pitcher of skim milk rather than cream. "I heard the same thing. He was nice, and good looking and kind, and suddenly he was gone."

Clarence blew on his cup of coffee. "Probably a perfectly reasonable explanation but rumor mongers don't like reason—they like conjecture. Anyway, sometime after that, people claimed to hear strange sounds in the hospital. I'm guessing it was the steam heating system, but people want to believe what they want to believe."

"I don't think Miss Nella is going to tell me any ghost stories, do you?"

"She's a practical woman. I don't think the word ghost is in her vocabulary."

I finished my coffee, feeling unsatisfied. "Miss Nella's reaction to Barrett's death bothers me, too. She's handling it like poor Barrett threw herself down those stairs just to spite her."

Clarence leaned back and rubbed his chin. "You must remember Nella is old and has spent so much of her life in isolation. I'm not surprised by her reaction."

"Oh."

We talked a bit more about what it must have been like to grow up on Gooseberry Acres. I had a gut feeling there was a lot more to Miss Nella's story, but I wasn't sure where to look or if I should look. "Maybe I'll visit Grace one more time. She seems to have a very clear recall of her time at Gooseberry."

"Ah, yes, Grace. A lovely woman. Give her another try. I'm guessing there is no great mystery within the walls of that crumbling old place—just sad memories. Lots of people died from TB in those days."

I thought of the little girl with the doll who wanted to go home. Sad indeed. "Well, Clarence, on that note, I think I'll go home and hug my dog."

"And Jim, when will we see him again?"

I tried to sound upbeat. "Soon, I hope. He says he has another couple of weeks." I didn't tell Clarence that Jim had a desk job in The Cities waiting for him.

Dark clouds rolled in from the west, blotting out the sun when I stepped into the car. A little rain spit at the windshield of the car as I drove onto the highway.

"Please don't pour. I'm not sure I closed my windows."

By the time I reached my rutted driveway, the rain was coming down in sheets. Bronte looked hurt and bewildered as I rushed by her to close the windows in the bedroom before I had puddles to clean up. "Sorry, girl. I'll get to you."

She followed me around as I dashed from window to window. Breathless, I finally knelt and gave her a good hug. She licked my face and trotted to the door. I watched from the door as she loped to the woods to do her business. Water didn't bother her. While I waited, I wondered what Bronte would think of this new cast of characters in my life. She tended to be a good judge of character. Would she like Miss Nella or Tucker? What about Andrew?

With that thought, I called her back in, praying she never had the opportunity to meet them.

An hour later, the rain let up, and the setting sun poked through the clouds.

It promised to be a magnificent sunset as the rays sparkled off the wet grass and leaves. I sat on my rock with a cup of tea and plotted out my next moves. Tomorrow I'd meet with Miss Nella again but this time with specific questions. This evening I'd find out what Apple Pie was up to in his quest to find out who killed the sous chef.

After supper, I settled at the table with the mystery manuscript to find out that Apple Pie was doggedly—or was it piggedly—stalking Chef Mac's new dishwasher/busboy during the evening dinner shift. Apple Pie observed that the busboy was particularly clumsy and that his fingernails were manicured. Also, he talked to himself in a foreign language that might have been French.

"Ah, the plot thickens along with the roux," I explained to Bronte, who was not interested.

My amusement only lasted a minute or two before the phone rang. Caller ID showed it was Jilly from the *Times.* I answered, "Aren't you working a little late?" It was after eight, and even though it was still light outside, it felt deeper into the evening.

"Sure, because I get overtime." She chuckled.

"What can I do for you? If you need a new editor, I'm not your gal. Wouldn't look good, you know, Mafia moll and all." Because of my New York accent, many in Killdeer still believed I was part of the mob.

I heard the sounds of a television in the background and boys arguing. "Excuse me a minute while I pull those two apart. If you ever have kids make sure to send them off to military school when they start popping out in pimples." She muffled the phone before she told the kids to knock it off or else. I wondered what the "or else" would be.

When she came back, she sounded a little breathless. "Better, for the moment."

"What can I do for you besides call my mobster friends to put a scare in them."

"I have a little gossip. Seems our favorite editor Jeanine is quite taken with your Mr. Right Digestion. I hear he's staying with her."

I wasn't prepared for how quickly the fury rose in me. I opened my mouth and then clamped it shut before I said something outrageous.

"Jamie? Are you still there?"

"Sorry, I had to bang my head against the wall once or twice before I could answer." My cheeks were hot, and I gripped the phone so hard my knuckles hurt. "What do you know?"

"She's pretty bouncy these days. Actually smiled at me this morning. I overheard her giggling on the phone."

I swore under my breath. Jeanine was young and vulnerable and about the age I was when I met Andrew. Again, I wondered what he was up to. "I wish he'd take his lovely dimple and Brad Pitt eyes and head back to New York." I told her about his text regarding a summer project that involved Larissa Lodge.

Jilly had heard the same thing. "Jeanine has suddenly gotten more talkative with me. She said the lodge had a Hollywood person who wanted to sponsor a theater project, and your ex would be his assistant director."

"Oh, brother." I stood up and then sat down again, willing my hand to relax. Bronte must have sensed my distress because she came over and put a paw up on my lap. I was experiencing a range of emotions, from the initial anger to anxiety and even sadness. Strange how you think you have things put neatly away, and then they pop out like this.

"Anyway, I wanted to warn you."

I thought about Tucker's involvement in this. "He's working with Tucker Fox on this scheme. Somehow the two of them connected. And just to be clear, I did not introduce them. I'd rather eat worms than see them scheming together."

Jilly laughed. She had a deep, throaty laugh, leftover, no doubt, from the years she smoked. "Point taken. Tucker has been spotted on several occasions closing down Tink's Bar—you know that place about two miles outside of Killdeer? I'm guessing your ex has spent some time there as well. I know the bartender. I'm sure he'd tell me."

In the years I'd been with Andrew, I never knew him to be a bar regular. On the other hand, I hadn't figured out he'd had Destiny on the side, either. "If that's the case, interesting that they found each other."

"It's a small town, my mobster friend."

After we ended the call, I sat staring at nothing. What was wrong with me? After all I'd been through with Andrew, I didn't understand why I felt so conflicted. Life was so much better when he was with his Destiny in New York, and I didn't have to think about him.

I scratched Bronte behind the ears. "Whatever you do, don't get involved with someone who likes to parade across the stage in green tights."

She yawned in response and let me know it was time to go to bed.

Chapter Twenty-Five: Teen Love

In the morning, I sat with Miss Nella's diaries searching for anything that might give me a hint at what she'd meant by secrets. The entries were repetitious, indicating she lived with a lot of routine. Several entries of hers talked about brushing her hair one-hundred strokes every night and brushing her teeth every morning to the count of twenty-five because "Papa insists."

It wasn't until I came to the year she turned sixteen that I started to see rebellion. It was the year Uncle Judd came to live with them after flunking out of college. Best I could tell, he was around twenty, four years older than Miss Nella. *He's so much fun. He even invited me to sneak out to one of the cottages for a party. I'm a little scared because Papa wouldn't approve, but I think I'm going to go!*

In the next entry, a week later, it's clear that young Nella had a crush on someone at the party.

His name is Dash, and Papa would kill me if he knew. I remember when he came. He was so handsome. Now he's even more gorgeous because he's getting healthy. Dash is staying in cottage #6, the best one. We shared schnapps, and he laughed when I made a face, because it burned when I drank it. He's got these heavenly green eyes. Judd says his family is rich. Dash, Dash, Dash. I love writing the name.

A couple of days later, Nella was still spinning with teenage love.

I walked in the garden and all around the grounds in hopes of seeing him. Maybe I'll drop a note under his door. I can still feel where he touched my cheek.

It sounded so innocent. I could picture Nella mooning over him, hoping to spot him. She filled one whole page of her diary with hearts.

I went to his cottage to drop off a note. I know he was inside, but I didn't dare knock in case someone saw us. I slipped the note under the door and asked him to meet me tonight in the woods where no one would see us.

Three days later, she exclaimed:

He came, and we kissed, and I didn't worry or anything about getting TB from him. He smells like spice, and his hair is slick and shiny. He said his family is rich, and someday he will take me away to New York to see Broadway. We're going to meet again.

The next page, several days later, she noted Papa was planning to take her to Minneapolis to the symphony, but she didn't want to go in case Dash wanted to meet again.

I wish I could tell Papa I was sick, but I can't lie to him. Maybe he'll have an emergency and we can't go, except he has Dr. Heller to help him. Dr. Heller is sweet.

A week later, she lamented:

Where, oh, where is Dash? It was so exciting the last time we met, and I know he wants to meet me again. Judd must have figured something out because he came to my room yesterday and said I should be careful because Dash is older and a rake. "Don't let him seduce you." I don't really know what a rake is or what seduce means. But I'm sure Dash loves me.

I could see the progression, and I found I was clenching my teeth as I read. An innocent, highly protected teenage girl and a young man who just survived a life-threatening illness. Three days after that entry, Nella wrote about seduction.

I think I got seduced last night. We kissed and touched, and then he put his hands down where he shouldn't. I told him to stop, but he said, "You want it don't you?" He wasn't sweet anymore, and I tried to get away, but he was strong. He did things that hurt and made me cry. But he said everything would be okay, and I shouldn't tell anyone, or I'd get into trouble. I don't know whether to be sad or happy. I feel kind of numb is all.

With the next entry, I took a deep breath. Nella, the sixteen-year-old, had been raped, and yet she still hung on to feelings for her rapist. How often did that happen in real life?

I haven't seen Dash in weeks. What's wrong? I've left notes at his cottage and even snuck over and hid behind a tree to get a glimpse of him. One of the aides came out of his cottage. Her hair looked all messed up and she walked kind of bent over. Could he love her more than me?

For several weeks, the entries were minimal or repetitions of *"Why? Why? Why?"*

I warmed up a cup of coffee before reading on, "Oh, Bronte, I fear what's coming." Bronte wagged her tail, hoping we'd go for a walk. The day was sunny and warm. I let her out and went back to the diary.

Don't feel good. Threw up this morning and feeling sick all the time. Dash won't respond to my notes. I asked Papa about him, and Papa said he was going home next week because he's all better. Papa wanted to know why I was asking, and I lied and said I'd seen him walking in the garden from my bedroom, and he looked so healthy. Papa said TB can be deceiving.

I sighed when I read the next entry.

Still sick and feeling funny. Didn't get my monthly. Snuck down to Papa's study and looked in one of his medical books. Can it be? Oh, I pray to God, please no.

Two days later, Nella was so angry and upset she put the pen through the page of the diary and splotched ink on it. I had to bring the page close to the reading lamp to make it out.

Told him, and he said it didn't have anything to do with him. He's leaving, and he doesn't care. I hate him, and my life is ruined!!!

I recalled fact-checking an article about teenage pregnancy before the era of birth control and abortion. The author had gotten pregnant at age sixteen and had been sent away to a home for unwed mothers. She gave up her baby for adoption because she had no other alternative. When she finally came home and went back to school, her family told people she'd spent several months visiting her aunt out of state. Single motherhood was considered a disgrace bringing shame to the girl and the family. Either the baby was put up for adoption, or a hasty marriage was arranged. The author wrote about the emotional toll on her and how later in life after she'd married, she had difficulty becoming pregnant again, "It was as if my womb couldn't go through the trauma once more."

Bronte sat at the screen door, smelling of fresh air. I realized I needed to take a break. Coffee in hand, I walked to the rock. The lake was still, with only gentle lapping of the water against the shoreline. A flock of geese made a honking ruckus flying overhead.

With a rawhide chew in her mouth, Bronte settled at my feet. I reflected on how different life was for Nella and the girls and women of her era. No birth control, no sex education, no laws on domestic abuse.

"In fact, Bronte, not all women even had the right to vote despite the 19th amendment. Can you imagine?"

Bronte thumped her tail but otherwise ignored me. I checked my watch. I needed to call Miss Nella to make sure she would see me today. I also needed to finish reading the diary. I was dragging my feet because I felt like I had stumbled upon a family secret that should stay a secret. I reminded myself that she had given me the diaries.

I stood up, faced the lake, and let the sun warm my face. It was time to find out what had happened and then decide what to ask Miss Nella.

To my disappointment, Miss Nella went back to writing about the everyday routines. When she started school in the fall, the only note she made was that she'd found a girdle in her mother's things and wore it.

It's so tight and awful, but if I wear baggy sweaters, no one knows my secret.

She wrote about going to the homecoming dance with someone named Teddy.

He's cute, I guess, but I don't want him to touch me. I'm not ever letting a boy touch me again. Can't wait to graduate and get away from here! So glad when I get home and can take the darn girdle off.

That was the last entry in the diary. The rest of the pages had been torn out. I closed the book with a great sense of sadness.

After lunch, I called Miss Nella. She answered with a raspy, "Hello, who is this?"

"Miss Nella, it's Jamie. You said yesterday you'd like to talk with me today. Can I come this afternoon?"

She hesitated for a moment as if she was trying to remember who I was.

"Oh, not today. I have a girl from town coming to do my hair. Why don't you come next week?"

I sensed her reluctance. "Miss Nella, do you really want to do this project? If not, I will tear up the check and bring back your diaries."

"Oh, my dear, of course, I want you to do it. But not today. My hair needs tending to, and without Barrett, I had to find someone else. Such a bother. We can visit next week."

Barrett Fox had caused a "bother" by falling down the stairs and dying. What a contrast between the sixteen-year-old Nella and the Miss Nella of today. After I ended the call, I felt a little lost. Instead of quitting, I went back to the place in the diary where she talked about meeting Dash. She'd said his family was wealthy but didn't give a last name. I wondered if I could track his family down.

Chapter Twenty-Six: Joshua Hawley

I called Grace. "This is Jamie. I have a few more questions about Gooseberry Acres."

She laughed. "Goodness. Suddenly all the interest in that place. Someone else called me yesterday to ask questions."

"Really?"

"A young man. At least he sounded young. He said he was doing a book on ghosts and hauntings. I told him he was talking to the wrong person because I didn't believe in either." She chuckled. "Anyway, I'm happy to talk with you again. I have a fresh apple pie just out of the oven. When would you like to stop over?"

I said I'd be there in an hour.

Setting the phone down, I patted Bronte on the head. "Guess what, girl. Real apple pie and not a fictional pig narrator."

Bronte yawned and walked away. It was time for her afternoon nap.

The sun shimmered through the budding leaves of the oak tree in front of Grace's house. It was a beautiful spring day, warm enough that I didn't need to wear a jacket or a sweater. I loved the feel of the sun on my back as I walked up to Grace's door.

She greeted me with a smile. The house smelled of apples and cinnamon. I followed her to the kitchen, noting how she breathed out through pursed lips, making a little whistling sound. I wondered if this was because of her long-ago tuberculosis and treatment.

"I have the tea ready. Have a seat." She indicated a chair at the kitchen table.

Last time I visited, I was so focused on Gooseberry Acres that I hadn't noticed the little alcove in the kitchen set up with a computer. I pointed to it as she brought the teapot to the table. "Looks like you've entered the twenty-first century."

Her eyes sparkled. "Sadly, I'm addicted to Facebook. People post the darndest things."

"I'll get you connected with Clarence. He's finally agreed to try it."

"I don't know if it's a good or a bad thing, but it sure is quicker than waiting for a letter to arrive in the mail. My daughter worries that I'll click on something and end up getting hacked." She poured the tea into delicate little teacups with a floral pattern. "I believe I'm smarter than that."

We talked about the weather and her garden and her grandchildren while she puttered at the counter, slicing the pie and adding a scoop of ice cream. "The family is scattered now. I have a grandson in Australia and another in Peru. I hope to travel to visit one of these days, but my daughter fusses so much. 'Oh, Mom, what if you get sick or fall or something.' At my age, who cares?"

I laughed. "Good point."

She finally sat down. "Now, what did you want to talk about?"

I told her I was trying to get a little more background information for Miss Nella's project. I didn't tell her about the diaries, but I did mention I'd heard the name Dash. "Does that mean anything to you? He might have been a patient about the same time you were."

She wrinkled her brow. "Oh my, I haven't thought about him in years. I think he died in the eighties. Car accident, I believe."

"You knew him, then?"

She took a forkful of pie and frowned. "Too much cinnamon. I must have measured wrong."

The pie was perfect as far as I was concerned. "I don't think so. You could win a prize with this. The crust is just right, and if I were to make it, I'd add even more cinnamon."

She set her fork down. "Thank you, my dear. Now, we were talking about Joshua Hawley at Gooseberry. Everyone called him Dash. I'm not sure why.

139

I remember he was tall and good-looking—but not as good-looking as my husband. I thought Dash used too much hair oil. What did they say in those days? 'Brylcreem a little dab'll do ya?' Well, he certainly used more than a little dab."

"I get the sense you didn't like him much?"

She patted her mouth with a linen napkin. "He had a strut about him that didn't appeal to me. Arrogance, I guess. But I can't say I didn't like him. I hardly had a word with him. I know he came from a lot of money. The Hawley family was one of the elite families in the Twin Cities. I think his father was a lawyer and a politician."

I looked out her window into the back yard. Six small brown birds pecked at the ground while a red-winged blackbird settled on a branch of her flowering crab tree like he was overseeing them. I savored another bite of the apple pie.

Grace regarded me with a slightly amused expression. "Why are you interested in him?"

I tried to sound offhand. "I have some of Miss Nella's diaries, and she mentioned him."

Grace folded her arms, her expression thoughtful. "There were rumors about him coming on to some of the young nurses. My husband didn't think much of him. Called him 'bad news.'"

While I finished my pie and had a second cup of tea, we talked more about Gooseberry Acres. She described her days as a patient. "They were very kind to me. I always wondered if it was because my parents were paying a high price for my treatment or if they were simply nice people."

"What was your day like?"

She smiled with a faraway expression. "They treated us like delicate flowers. At first when I came, I had to stay in bed all the time. I was a pretty good knitter, but they said I had to stay quiet. Imagine asking a twenty-year-old girl to lay quietly."

"I think the bed rest philosophy has changed. At least after my father had his heart attack, they had him up and moving."

Grace nodded. "When I had my hip replaced, I was out of the hospital in three days. But back when they were treating TB at Gooseberry, they were very careful. First bed rest, after that they let us up for two hours. Then it was four hours and eventually all day. By then, I was ready to go home."

"You said something about a good-looking doctor named Dr. Heller. Do you know what happened to him after he left the sanatorium?"

"I don't recall ever hearing anything. He was so nice and so good at what he did. I expected he would go on to be a great surgeon. He did many of the lobectomies at the hospital. Sometimes instead of collapsing the lung to stop the spread of the TB, they cut out part of it. One of the nurses said his patients recovered much faster than the ones Dr. Fox had operated on."

I made a note to follow up and find out more about Dr. Heller. If he practiced medicine after Gooseberry, I should be able to find a record.

"One last question, Grace. I walked the grounds the other day and found the cemetery. Do you know anything about it?"

She took a deep breath with the whistling sound as she let it out. "What a sad little place. One of the patients who was treated at the same time I was there was buried in the cemetery. She was a young woman, probably about my age. I can't remember her name, but the fresh air, the lung treatments, the lobectomy—none of it worked. The TB had spread into her spine." She shook her head. "So sad and so scary for the rest of us."

"Do you know why she was buried there instead of home?"

"I don't. I'd heard that not all families wanted to take their loved ones back. I think they were scared that somehow they'd get TB."

My phone pinged. I glanced at it and felt something drop in the pit of my stomach. **J Must talk.**

Grace raised her eyebrows. "Trouble?"

I didn't want to get into the sad tale of my marriage to Andrew. I shrugged. "Just a nuisance. Unfortunately, I need to go. This has been very helpful. And the pie was wonderful."

She insisted on cutting another slice and putting it in a plastic container. "Here, take this with you. It might help you to deal with your 'nuisance.'"

I chuckled, "Maybe so."

She walked me to the door, "Stop by any time. I don't have a lot of appointments on my calendar unless you count trips to the doctor. Never thought I'd outlive my husband, bless his heart. He's the one who could have given you all the gossip back then. He even hinted once at a possible murder."

I should have asked her more, but I was focused on the text. I thanked her and promised I'd call again. Walking to my car, I wondered what Andrew wanted. I supposed I should respond. Knowing him, he'd bother me until I did.

On the way back to the cabin, I slowed by the entrance to the lodge parking area. Tucker's car sat alongside a shiny silver SUV. I didn't like his presence so close to my cabin. I hoped he wouldn't connect this part of the county with me.

Once home, I sat on my rock, watching a fishing boat slowly trawl near Bear Island. Jim said it was a good place to catch Walleye. God, I missed him. After throwing a stick into the woods for Bronte to fetch, I texted Andrew back.

What do you need?

Ten minutes later, with no reply, I took a deep breath of relief. Maybe I wouldn't hear from him again. Time to look up Joshua "Dash" Hawley and Dr. Heller.

Dash was easy to find. He was mentioned in several articles about corporate crime. It appeared that in his late twenties, he created an investment group catering to evangelical church groups. He made friends with top ministers and elders, then promised to invest their money in Christian companies. Except, the biggest investment he made was in himself and his lifestyle. He was a lower-level Bernie Madoff preying on the prayerful.

"Wow, what a scoundrel. I wonder if Miss Nella knew about this?" Bronte didn't hear my comment because she was still outside protecting the yard from chipmunks.

I found his obituary. Grace was correct; he died in an automobile crash forty years ago. He was survived by a wife and two children. Nothing was mentioned about his indictment on fraud. The obit said he was finally at rest with his loving God. I hated to be catty about it, but it seemed like his loving God was probably himself.

In my search for Dr. Heller, I came up blank. I found several doctors named Heller, but none who would have been the right age. Nor did I find an obituary that would match his probable age.

By now, Bronte had beaten back the enemy, the chipmunks had retreated, and she was settled at my feet, chewing on a rawhide bone. "You'd think, girl, Dr. Heller would have shown up somewhere."

His disappearance left me unsettled. I knew people seemingly dropped off the face of the earth from time to time, but he was an up-and-coming surgeon. Wouldn't his family have launched a search for him? I decided I needed more information, like his full name and his birthdate. Hopefully, Miss Nella could give it to me if she wanted me to do more background work on Gooseberry during those years.

After supper, Bronte and I took a stroll into the woods. I loved the evening spring air and the sounds of the forest as the sun disappeared. The frogs in the swampy area near the lake were croaking their love songs, and in the distance, I heard the faint whoo-hoo of an owl. I leaned up against a birch tree and closed my eyes, feeling the rhythms of outdoors. It reminded me of sitting in the little park across from the apartment in Queens on a spring evening and listening to the sounds of the cars and the subway rattling as it passed over Queens Boulevard. Rural and urban, both filled with poetry.

Walking back to the cabin, I composed a poem in my head. Could I write about the contrast between the two? When was the last time I'd written a poem?

My thoughts were interrupted when Bronte stopped in front of me and started to growl.

"What is it, girl?"

She dashed ahead towards the cabin while I chased her. "Bronte! Stop!"

When I reached the cabin, Bronte stood barking in a frenzy in front of the door. A silver SUV was parked next to my car, and the cabin door was open.

Chapter Twenty-Seven: The Visitor

Creeping to Bronte, I grabbed her collar. Inside, the floorboards creaked as someone walked around. I shushed Bronte. She trembled beneath my touch. A jumble of questions ricocheted in my head. Who's here? Somebody from Camp Six? Is it Tally? Did he steal this SUV? Is it a reward seeker? Are they armed?

I considered my options. The car keys were on the kitchen counter, along with my phone. I could make a dash for them. Or Bronte and I could head down the road to the lodge.

Bronte growled a low, menacing sound as she tugged against my grip. The footsteps were nearing the door when she erupted into another barking frenzy and pulled away from me. Leaping onto the steps to the door, she crashed into the screen.

I looked up to see a man standing at the door with an amused expression. "Quite a guard dog," He shouted over the din.

"Oh, my god. Andrew! What are you doing here?" I grabbed Bronte by the collar and pulled her away from the door.

"If you call off your cavalry, I'll explain."

I knelt and whispered to Bronte, "It's okay. He won't hurt me." She had an anxious look in her eyes as she settled down.

Opening the door, I walked in, still holding Bronte. "I'll put her in the bedroom until she quiets."

Bronte bared her teeth and snarled as I tugged her into the bedroom. "I'll be fine, girl."

Once back in the kitchen, I found Andrew seated at the table with one of

Nella's diaries open to the first page. He glanced up at me. "Is this what you do?"

I pointed to the *Apple Pie* manuscript next to the diary. "I mainly edit books."

"Oh? Sounds kind of tedious." His voice had a note of disdain. "Is it worth it?"

Instead of answering, I slid into the chair across the table from him. "Andrew, what are you doing here?"

With his unshaven face, he looked like a cross between Chris Hemsworth and Chris Pratt, except he was too thin to be a superhero. He leaned back, folding his arms, "You look so good when you're irritated. Nice tint to your cheeks."

I stared at him, and slowly he broke into a grin, his eyebrows raised in amusement. It was a heart-melting expression that brought out the dimple on his chin. Neither Chris Hemsworth nor Chris Pratt could have done it better. I tried to maintain my outrage, but I'd never been good about it with Andrew. He had a way of disarming me.

Jamie, don't let your guard down.

I fought back a smile.

He laughed. "Glad you haven't lost your sense of humor."

Bronte scratched at the bedroom door, and I was quickly reminded of how she'd snarled at him.

Get a grip.

I had a retort ready about my sense of humor drying up the day he confessed his love for Destiny. I swallowed it back. "You haven't answered my question. Why are you here? If you're after my property, forget it. I have a top-notch lawyer. If you're after my money—good luck finding any."

He raised his hands in surrender. "I know I've been a jerk. I came to apologize."

Andrew, like a typical narcissist, never apologized and never admitted doing something wrong. I stared at him. "You are apologizing? Have you had a religious conversion?"

A little *sheeshing* sound escaped his lips. "What can I say? I'm a changed man." His expression turned serious. "Listen, J, since we split, I've…ah… matured. It's been hard without you."

I felt a tug deep in my chest. It was the same sensation I'd once had when he asked me to marry him. A little piece of me wanted to rejoice at his words. He missed me.

A few seconds later, the momentary charm bubble burst when he placed his elbows on the table and leaned towards me. I recognized the faux-sincere expression. He'd practiced it enough in our apartment as he prepared for auditions.

"Here's the deal. I know I was a jerk. I've been sorry ever since I signed the divorce papers. I let a jewel slip from my hands."

No, not a jewel. A financial and emotional support wife. I kept silent.

"I'm guessing you already know I've been working with a Hollywood producer. We want to create a summer theater program…."

"Enough!" I interrupted him. "And you need money to get it going."

Andrew straightened up, a slight blush rising up his neck. One thing he couldn't do as an actor was control the color of his skin when he was angry or embarrassed, or lying. "No. That's not it. I was hoping maybe we could help each other out."

The kitchen clock ticked its regular cadence as I braced myself for his proposal, "And how would we do this?"

Bronte whined in the bedroom. I wondered if she could feel the tension building through my body as Andrew spoke.

Andrew peered at me with those remarkable blue eyes. In the right light, they were the same color as the Caribbean Sea. I looked away.

He took a deep breath. "Here's what we thought. You have contacts with the magazine world. I've seen your articles, and they are amazing. Maybe you could do a feature on our project. It might bring in more funding."

What I'd written about had to do with a school shooting, human trafficking, and several deaths. What Andrew proposed seemed hardly of interest to a national magazine. "Andrew, I don't think a summer theater program would have enough originality to catch the attention of the editors I write for."

He raised his hand. "Wait, J. There's more."

For a moment, his voice sounded like the pitchman for a television ad for a pocket fishing rod for only $19.95 and shipping. I almost smiled. "What am I missing?"

"Lots. We want to focus on theater training for underprivileged kids. We've been talking with someone from the tribe who's part of the new management for the lodge remodel. The program would be for the Indian kids mainly. Don't you see? It would be a win-win."

I stifled a sigh. This could either be a genuine charitable project, or it could be a scam. "And you're working with Tucker Fox on this?"

"I always knew you were a great detective," his eyes lit with enthusiasm. "Did you know he produced a movie last year? He took it to a couple of film festivals and is in talks with a distributor."

Funny Tucker didn't mention a film project to me. I pictured the two of them at the bar drinking and making up stories. Who was scamming whom?

"Andrew, did you know Tucker is living rent-free with his cousin? Judging by his car, he doesn't have much to contribute to this. Are you even sure he did that movie?"

Andrew drummed his fingers on the table. "It's a risk, I know. But it's worthwhile. Tucker thinks he'll be getting money from a project soon. In fact, he even mentioned the place his cousin owns as a great site for the theater school. Think of it, Shakespeare in the Woods."

I wondered what Apple Pie would think of Andrew's performance. Both lived in a world of fiction. I reflected on what he'd said regarding Tucker. "Does Tucker expect to inherit Gooseberry Acres?"

Andrew shrugged. "He told me he had a claim on it. Plus, he had another thing going that should bring in money soon."

Another thing? I wondered if Tucker was planning to rob a bank. Suddenly this was no longer an amusing fairy tale. A little tingle like a spider crawling up my back caused me to sit up straighter. Behind all this theater nonsense was something dark. I was sure Andrew couldn't see it. I pictured the inside of the abandoned hospital moldy and dank, and Barrett's body splayed out at the bottom of the staircase.

"Andrew, I think the best thing you can do right now is turn around and drive your shiny SUV back to New York. Tucker might not be the person you think he is."

He frowned, and I saw the "aw shucks" expression fall from his face, replaced by narrowed eyes. "You never understood me, did you? I wasted far too many years pleasing you, trying for roles just so I could stay in New York with you. Now, when I ask for help you tell me to go back. Sorry for wasting your valuable time."

He stood up so quickly the chair nearly tipped over. With a dramatic sweep of his hand, he knocked the neatly piled *Apple Pie* manuscript off the table. "I guess this is more important to you than all those years we had together."

As the papers went flying, I instinctively bent down to grab them as they scattered. Bronte's growl escalated to a bark while I tried to retrieve the manuscript.

He stomped to the door, his lips pressed into a thin line and his eyes like slits. It was not a good look on him. "Thanks for nothing."

His exit was a dramatic slamming of the door worthy of a hammy high school play production. I sat staring at the door and listening to the sound of his SUV roar down the driveway. Bronte continued to bark until I let her out.

"What was that about, girl?"

Standing on the step, I watched the dust from the driveway settle in the sweet air of the spring night. Once back inside, I picked up the rest of *Apple Pie a'la Murder* and worked on putting them back in order. My hands shook as I stacked the pages.

Later I sat inhaling the soothing aroma of mint tea and reflected. Could this be the same man I'd once talked with about having children? I remember telling him I hoped they'd have his eyes. And he said he hoped they'd have my grit. In his bullying kind of way, he still had a hold on me.

As an antidote, I texted Jim. **Enjoying a cup of mint tea and the sounds of the love-sick frogs. Want to join me?**

I didn't hear back from him.

That night, I tossed in bed, unable to find a comfortable position. As I fluffed the pillow and turned it over to the cool side, I replayed Andrew's theatrical exit. Something about it struck me as strange. The rage had built so quickly. Andrew had his tantrums, but this felt like something else.

Pulling the covers up over my shoulders, I whispered, "Go back to your Destiny, Andrew. Please."

Chapter Twenty-Eight: The Missing Diary

A mid-May warm spell brought rising temperatures and humidity. After a winter of bone-chilling cold, I savored sitting on the rock in shorts and a T-shirt. Even though it had been a couple of days, I still felt a little off balance from Andrew's visit. Did he really want my help in publicizing his half-baked theater project? Or was it another way of showing me his contempt? After all these years, I still couldn't read him.

Jim texted while I finished my coffee and swatted the first mosquito of the season.

Passed another test. Going to the head of the class

I texted back. **Should hurry home. Felt my first mosquito. Get here before they eat me up.**

I watched the little balls waving while he texted back. **Two weeks.**

Right now, with Andrew and *Apple Pie* and Miss Nella all weighing on me, two weeks felt like forever. **I'll leave the light on for you.**

I finished reading *Apple Pie a'la Murder* later in the morning. It turned out the murderer was the rival chef who had a bistro across the street. Apple Pie solved it by following his nose as the chef prepared the wine-infused macaroni and cheese recipe he'd stolen from Chef Mac's sous chef. Cleverly, Apple Pie was able to surprise the chef, knock him over and grab the recipe in his mouth and run. The ensuing chase involved the murderous chef, a woman pushing a baby stroller with a poodle in it, and Chef Mac. I laughed out loud as I read it.

"This is a winner, girl, if I can get Opal, the author, to cut back on the tedious recipe-development scenes and tone down Apple Pie's rage against littering."

Miss Nella's phone call summoning me to Gooseberry came while I was finishing up my developmental notes on the novel.

"Hello, dear. I'd like you to come this afternoon. Make sure you bring the diaries. They will help me remember things."

I had been so involved in the pot-bellied pig saga that I'd put the Gooseberry project out of my mind. "Could we meet tomorrow instead?" I needed time to organize my questions and read through a few more diaries.

"Oh, no. I'm ready now. I will see you at two." The line went dead.

I patted Bronte on the head. "Looks like I've been called to the principal's office."

Setting *Apple Pie a'la Murder* aside, I brought over the box of diaries. In the short time I had before leaving for Gooseberry Acres, I planned to scan through a couple more diaries and make a list of questions for Miss Nella. I'd start with the dramatic diary with the torn-out pages. I wondered whether Miss Nella would talk about what looked like a very traumatic time in her life.

The diary had a blue cover and should have been at the top of the box. It wasn't there.

"What?" I thought back. Perhaps I'd picked it up and taken it into the living room to read. Somehow that didn't seem right. I searched the living room and the bedroom and could not place it.

Bronte followed me around as my search grew more frantic. "I don't understand, girl. Where did I put it?"

After a frenzied search, including taking all the diaries out of the box and placing them in chronological order, I sat down and tried to calm myself. How could I have lost it?

Bronte sat at my feet with her brow wrinkled. I stroked the top of her head and thought back. The last time I remembered seeing the diary was when Andrew had briefly looked at it.

The temper tantrum, sweeping the manuscript onto the floor and the door slamming exit. I'd known something wasn't right about it. "Andrew! Damn it!"

Grabbing my phone, I called him. No answer and no voicemail on his phone. Next, I texted him. **WHERE IS THE DIARY!?!**

No response. Andrew was working with Tucker. Of course, Tucker had expressed great interest in the diaries. They must have cooked up the scheme for Andrew to steal one of them. It would give Tucker a peek into what they contained.

"I'm so stupid!"

Bronte licked my hand in response. The gentle feel of her tongue on my skin calmed me down enough to think through a plan. First, I called Jilly.

"Hey," she answered, "it's a beautiful day. You should get out on that lake and catch a fish before they're all gone."

Fishing was the last thing on my mind. I didn't laugh. "Listen, I think my lovely ex pulled something on me. Is Jeanine there? I need to ask her about him."

"Nope, sorry. But fill me in."

I told her about his surprise visit and theatrical exit. "He's working with Tucker Fox, and I think they're looking for a smoking gun that will get Tucker money. The damned fool!"

"Boy, it looks like you snagged a carp when you married that guy. I'll admit, though, he's kind of cute."

I groaned. "When you see Jeanine, would you ask her if Andrew left a diary at her house?"

Jilly tsked. "I'm not sure she'd tell me."

"Emphasize that it's stolen property."

I considered barging over to the apartment where Jeanine lived but decided I didn't have time. I'd have to confess to Miss Nella that I'd lost the diary. "Why this on such a beautiful day?"

The humidity held in the scent of the pines as I stepped into the car. Taking one long, deep breath of the spring air, I headed down the driveway. Maybe I'd see Tucker's car, or the silver SUV Andrew was driving parked at the lodge. I slowed when I passed the turnoff. The parking lot was half-full, but none of the cars belonged to either man.

On the way to Gooseberry, I cleared my head of the anger and concentrated on what I'd read in the diary. She'd gone to a party with her Uncle Judd and met Dash. Later she and Dash had a couple of secret trysts. The second one read like a sexual assault. After that, he wouldn't see her. Later, she missed her period and wrote about being sick.

Classic. Today it would have been considered rape because she was only sixteen. Back then it would have been considered her fault for meeting him. She would have been a disgrace to the family. One of my friends in New York once told me she discovered she had an aunt when she did a DNA test. Turned out her grandmother had a baby as a teenager and gave it up. It was the big family secret. This was probably one of the secrets Miss Nella alluded to.

By the time I reached Gooseberry, I had decided I needed to find out from Miss Nella if I was right. Hormonal teenagers were known to exaggerate, but I doubted young Nella was making this up. It was written with too much pain. There was a baby somewhere in the mix here.

Chapter Twenty-Nine: Dr. Fox

I was geared up for a confrontation with Tucker about the diary and Andrew's part in stealing it. However, when I arrived, the parking area in front of the residence was empty. The leaves of the lilacs in the front yard shimmered in the breeze. Overhead the sky was a hazy blue. In the sunlight, the abandoned hospital, with its peeling paint and boarded-up windows, appeared even darker and out of place, surrounded by the greening shrubs and the encroaching forest.

I thought again about the postcard showing Gooseberry Acres in its prime and tried to imagine how Grace felt, sick and scared, as she approached the door of the hospital, not knowing whether she'd ever go home again.

"Oh, Jamie, you are morbid this afternoon. Get in there.... And stop talking to yourself."

The front door to Miss Nella's house was slightly ajar. I knocked and called out as I walked in. "Miss Nella, it's Jamie."

The double doors to the sitting room were open. Miss Nella sat in her usual chair wearing a blue pantsuit and another cream-colored blouse buttoned up to her neck. Her hair was freshly cut and styled. I wasn't sure if this was a better or a worse look for her than the bun. The haircut emphasized the paleness of her face and the papery quality of her skin.

"Hello, it's Jamie."

Miss Nella opened her eyes. For a moment, she appeared confused. "Is that you, Agnes?"

I walked over to her and knelt by her. "It's Jamie. We're working on your memoir, remember?"

She straightened in her chair. "Oh yes. I guess I was dreaming."

"You wanted me to come today?"

"I need to tell you some things. Before *they* get to it." She gestured vaguely at the door. "Too many different people around here."

"Who are you talking about? Have the Camp Six men been by again?"

She shook her head. "Never mind. This place does not belong to them."

I sat down on the sofa next to her with my notebook. "Miss Nella, first off, I have to tell you about the diary."

She blinked. "Diary?"

"You gave me a box of your diaries when I first came."

Her eyes had a glaze to them I hadn't seen before. She wrinkled her brow. "Oh, of course. Clarence said they'd be safe with you."

Now I really felt bad. "I…ah…seem to have misplaced one of them, but I'm sure I can find it." For a moment, I pictured punching Andrew in his precious nose.

She shrugged, "Never mind that. I have some things to tell you."

I waited for her to start. Although the drapes were pulled shut as usual, they were open enough to let in a crack of sunshine. A little line of light illuminated the table beside her chair. On it was a cold cup of coffee and a half-eaten pastry.

"I want to tell you about my father, Dr. Fox. He wasn't always easy to be with, but in his heart, he wanted to heal people."

"Do you want to focus your memoir on him?"

A small smile touched her lips. "Oh yes. The good and the other…." She fell silent.

What little I'd read in her diaries didn't give me much of a picture of Dr. Fox. Grace had told me the staff liked Dr. Heller better and thought patients treated by him did better than those Dr. Fox operated on. The diaries had also revealed him to be a strict father with his daughter. Of course, that was through Miss Nella's eyes.

"Well, then, let's talk about the good. Do you mind if I record this?" I took my phone out of my bag.

"Dear, at this point in my life, I hardly care. There was a time, though…"

Again, her voice trailed off.

"A time?" I cued her.

She sighed. "Papa had a temper. And he wanted things just so. His dream was to make Gooseberry Acres into a world-class TB treatment center. He was working on a cure, you know."

From what I'd read, the cure was in the antibiotics developed during the war.

"Was he part of the research on the antibiotics?"

Miss Nella ignored my question. "My mother died of TB, and he never forgave himself for not being able to help her." She paused. "Did you know that at one time, people believed a touch by a king would cure it?" She smiled, "Imagine thinking that King Henry VIII could cure TB."

I smiled. "Seems unlikely that a king had that much power."

"They called it the 'white plague.' Papa never told me how it got that name. He did a lot of research into the history of it, you know." She had a faraway gaze as she spoke.

"Can you tell me more about what he was working on?"

She folded her hands and spoke softly. "He wrote it all down. It's in his study—all his research notes."

"Perhaps they could still be useful now. I've read about the problems with treating TB today. The bacteria have become resistant to the antibiotics. It's harder and more expensive to cure."

"Humph. They should have listened to him back then. When I came back from college to help him, he spent hours in his office reading medical journals." She indicated the study. "By then, we had fewer and fewer patients to treat because of the antibiotics. I saw him become more depressed because he knew eventually what they were doing would fail." She stared at her lap. "No one would listen to him."

I wondered if Dr. Fox was a pioneer in predicting the advance of drug resistance.

"He and Dr. Heller...They were a wonderful team. It's too bad about what happened." Her voice trailed off.

"Do you know what happened to Dr. Heller? I heard he left suddenly."

"It was a mistake. All of it. Papa wouldn't listen." Miss Nella's face darkened. "He was so nice and kind. Papa had such a temper in those days."

On the roof, a flicker pecked on the metal cap to the chimney. Rata-tat-tat. I thought about Edgar Allan Poe's *The Raven* and felt a momentary chill. What was Miss Nella trying to tell me?

"Did they have a disagreement?"

Miss Nella leaned forward, peering at me. "Do you think you could find his family? I'd like to find them and tell them."

Her question took me off guard. "You mean Dr. Heller's family?"

Sighing, Miss Nella closed her eyes. "I don't like to think about those days. Dr. Heller helped me, you know—during my 'troubles.'"

Troubles could mean many things. I tried to clarify, "I'm sorry, I don't know what you mean." If she was talking about being pregnant, I wanted to approach the issue gently. "Were you sick?"

Her eyes snapped open. "What? I was never sick. He helped with the baby, of course."

The flicker started its pecking racket again, This time louder.

Miss Nella held her arms as if she was cradling an infant. "So, so tiny. Never had a chance." She began to sing in a tremulous voice. "Rockabye baby."

Pieces were falling into place. The diary about Dash, the sickness, the missed periods. "Miss Nella, did Dr. Heller deliver your baby?"

"He was kind and gentle even when I cried and screamed. I was so scared."

I was at a loss. Miss Nella had had a baby, and Dr. Heller delivered it. I took a stab at piecing it together. "Is that why Dr. Heller left? Because of the baby?"

Miss Nella hugged herself as she spoke. "I don't like to think about those times. Papa had such a temper. When he found out..."

"What happened?"

She rocked back and forth, still hugging herself. "I named the baby, even though she wasn't alive. I named her after my mother. Sarah. She was so tiny."

"Was Joshua Hawley the father?" Noting how she flinched when I said the name, I wished I had stayed quiet. I couldn't imagine the emotional pain remembering this must be causing her.

She took a deep breath and sat up straight, her hands grasping the arms of the chair. "How did you know that? Who told you? Were the staff tattling? Papa wouldn't tolerate gossip!"

I stuttered. "Um…I'm sorry. It was in your diary that you…and he…um."

She relaxed. "Oh. Of course. Maybe he was, and maybe he wasn't. It's hard to remember. It was a bad time in my life. But I got over it. Papa told me to 'buck up.' And I did."

"Would you still like me to look for Dr. Heller?"

She shook her head. "No, not Dr. Heller. I'd like you to find his family. I owe them for what happened."

Had Dr. Fox fired him for his part in delivering the baby? I wanted to ask, but I held back. "If you can give me more information about him, I can look."

Miss Nella pointed to the hospital. "Papa kept all the staff records in the hospital. Go look there." She reached into her pocket and handed me a key. "Go look tomorrow. I'm too tired today."

Outside, a car door slammed shut, and moments later, someone knocked.

"Now who could that be? I don't like to be disturbed." Miss Nella's voice rose in irritation.

I stood up. "I'll get the door if you want."

"I can't imagine who would come here. The road has a 'No Trespassing sign.'"

When I opened the door, Greg, the sheriff's deputy, waited. He stared at me through the screen. "You?"

Even with the sunshine and smell of the pines, it felt like a dark day. Behind him, two crows sat on the wires to the house, cawing.

Chapter Thirty: The Investigation

I wasn't sure what he meant. I shrugged and let him in. "Did you want to see Miss Nella?"

"I'm looking for Tucker Fox."

"I've been here about an hour, and I haven't seen him."

"It's about his sister."

I grimaced as I pictured her at the bottom of the stairs. "Oh?"

"I have more questions. Maybe you could answer some of them."

Miss Nella's voice rose from the sitting room. "Who is there?"

I motioned toward the room. "I think you'd better talk to Miss Nella first. It's her house." I didn't add "and her cousin."

I was surprised by the gentleness of his voice as Greg talked with Miss Nella. After he introduced himself, he squatted close to her. "I need to ask Jamie and Tucker a few more questions about the woman who fell."

"She was a nuisance. Wasn't even a good cook."

I was learning that it was hard to gauge Miss Nella's reactions. Sometimes she was charming, sometimes commanding, and sometimes addled.

Greg stood up. "It appears her fall might not have been an accident."

"Well, young man. Get on with it." She stared up at the ceiling. "We've been through this before. Too many deaths." She closed her eyes. "Too many deaths."

Greg looked at me with a quizzical expression. I raised my eyebrows with a little shrug. I had no idea what she was talking about.

Ushering him into the kitchen, I offered to make a pot of coffee. While the coffee brewed, we sat at the table.

He leaned toward me, tensing his jaw. "Why are you here?"

Since I had been involved with the sheriff's department in solving a murder last winter, I wasn't surprised by the question. I seemed to spend a lot of time talking to law enforcement. I was surprised by his tone of voice, though. He almost barked the question.

My policy, ever since the traumatic experience of sitting in a Queens holding cell after having been mistaken for Jamie Forester, major drug dealer, was to ask questions rather than answer them. I held my hand up. "Before we go any further, your tone tells me you suspect me of something. Can you tell me what you are looking for?"

"There were some...ah...irregularities in Barrett Fox's death."

A woman found at the bottom of a dark stairwell in an abandoned hospital might raise a red flag or two. I bit back the desire to say, "You think?" Instead, I asked the question, "Are you suspecting it wasn't an accident?"

"As I say, we need to clear up some irregularities."

I took a more conciliatory tone. "How can I help?"

He reached into his pocket and pulled out a notebook and a stubby pencil. "What was your relationship to the deceased?"

I kept my answers brief and direct to the question. "She answered the door when Clarence and I came to talk with Miss Nella. She made us coffee. I didn't talk with her."

"But you found her body?"

I pushed my hand through my hair as if that would wipe out the image of her broken neck. When I spoke, it felt like I was listing bullet points. "I came for my second visit to talk with Miss Nella. Barrett wasn't there. Ed, the caretaker, said she'd been asking questions about the hospital. Tucker and I decided to check out the hospital. When we got inside, he had trouble breathing, so he left. I went upstairs and noticed a draft from the back stairway. When I checked it out, I found her at the bottom."

I squeezed my eyes shut as I shuddered. "I don't want to ever see a sight like that again."

Greg's voice softened. "What about Tucker? How did he react when you told him?"

With my eyes closed, I tried to recreate the scene, but it was a blur of activity. "I'm not sure what to say. As soon as I found her, I called 9-1-1. After that, I ran out to tell Tucker."

Something nipped at the back of my mind, something that had struck me as odd at the time. I couldn't quite pull it out. "I remember that he just stared at me—and when he did react, he asked me if I was sure it was Barrett. I think he was in shock."

Once again, I pictured the scene, the body, the 9-1-1 call, the race to get outside and away. "When I got outside, Tucker was standing talking with Ed. I don't know when he got there, but I know Tucker had said he didn't like him."

Greg's expression told me he didn't think this was important.

"Really, that's all I know."

I stood up, took a couple of coffee cups off the shelf, and brought them to the table. Pouring the coffee, I asked, "Can you tell me what is irregular?"

Greg frowned as if trying to decide what to tell me. I noted the spot in his earlobe, indicating that it had once been pierced. Probably Sheriff Fowler wasn't too keen on his deputy sporting an earring. Acceptance of piercings and tattoos hadn't made it to Jackpine County law enforcement yet.

He cleared his throat. "Uh, her skull was fractured, like she'd been hit with something."

"Wouldn't that happen in the fall?"

"Maybe, but the coroner thought it suspicious."

I remembered the blood on the landing and told Greg about it.

He made a note. "It's also possible she fell from the top, cracked her head when she hit the landing, and then fell further."

Miss Nella called out. "Yoo-hoo. Is anybody still there? I wouldn't mind a cup of coffee now."

I set down my cup. "Is there anything else I can help you with?"

Greg closed his notebook. "I guess not. I'm just curious about why she'd be in that old building."

I wondered if she was looking for the mysterious paperwork Tucker talked about. "That might be a good question for Tucker."

As I fixed a tray with coffee and some packaged cookies, the odd thing in the back of my mind came to me.

Turning to Greg, I said, "I didn't see a flashlight on the staircase. Did you find one?"

Greg wrinkled his brow as he flipped through his notebook. "I don't remember seeing one. Why?"

"Ed told me the hospital's electricity had been turned off years ago. If I was going to explore it, I'd need a flashlight."

He shrugged. "Maybe someone picked it up."

I wanted to argue with him that it might be a clue, but better sense prevailed.

The sound of a car with a broken muffler diverted my attention. If it was Tucker, I wanted to ask him—no—accuse him of arranging to steal the diary.

Both Greg and I walked to the front. As expected, Tucker shambled up the steps. His cheeks had the ruddiness of too much to drink, and his eyes were bloodshot.

He had a slur to his words when he greeted us. "Ah, welcoming party. How nice."

Miss Nella called out from the sitting room. "Who's there? Can't you see the 'No Trespassing signs?'"

If Greg hadn't been standing behind me, I would have demanded to know where the diary was. Instead, I stepped aside and let him usher Tucker in.

As he passed me, I got a whiff of a combination of cigarette smoke, alcohol, and unwashed body. He swayed, almost stumbling into the hallway wall. Greg grabbed his arm. "Whoa, fella. It looks like you've been at it."

I wondered if Greg could arrest him for driving while intoxicated. Steadying Tucker, he guided him to the kitchen. "Let's get you some coffee."

"Right-oh and aye-aye, sir."

Much as I wanted to witness how Greg handled him, Miss Nella came first. When I entered the sitting room, she was standing. It was the first time I'd ever seen her out of her chair. "What is going on," she demanded.

I was surprised at how tall she was and how well she carried herself, considering her age. She must have been at least 5'8". With her arms akimbo, she hardly appeared to be frail. I remembered Tucker's comment about how Miss Nella was stronger than people thought.

"It's Tucker, Miss Nella. Greg, the sheriff's deputy, wants to talk with him."

"Humph! What a nuisance. I wish he'd go back to where he came from. At least I'm rid of that woman." She grabbed a polished wooden cane by her chair. "It's time for me to have a lie-down before supper." She pointed the cane in my direction. "Papa used to use this in his last days. He wasn't in his right mind, you know. All that guilt, I think."

I was curious to know about Papa's "guilt," but this was not the time to ask as Miss Nella marched to the doorway. "Do you want me to help you up the stairs?"

"Young lady, whoever you are, I can do it myself."

In the kitchen, Tucker's voice rose. "Well, you damn well better make sure it wasn't an accident before you start accusing me." The word "start" came out "shtart." Time for me to flee this mad house before I had to help Greg carry Tucker to bed, or Miss Nella took a swipe at me with her cane.

The sound of Tucker's voice must have reoriented Miss Nella. She squinted at me. "Now, where was I?"

"You were going to take a nap."

"Oh yes, dear. Why don't you come back tomorrow? This chat has been very nice."

I stood aside as she walked by me. Her left foot had a little bit of a drop, but otherwise, she appeared to be steady. She navigated the stairs by using her cane and holding onto the railing with her other hand. I waited at the bottom until I was sure she'd made it upstairs.

Before leaving, I called to Greg. "I'm on my way."

Tucker responded in a querulous voice. "Who's that? A policewoman? Can't you leave us alone?"

I silently bid Greg good luck in getting anything coherent out of Tucker. Once outside, I took a deep breath. Instead of inhaling the fresh spring air, I got a lungful of lingering exhaust from Tucker's car. It fit.

As if to add a little more chaos to the scene, Ed pulled up in his truck. He had his rifle beside him.

"Heard some noise over here. Is that the sheriff's car?"

I pointed to the house. "He's talking to Tucker right now."

"Never liked them two. Be glad when he's gone." He glowered at me. "And you, too."

This project with Miss Nella was getting harder and harder. Secrets, hauntings, unmarked graves? Could I ever sort it out? And what about Barrett? If someone shoved her down those stairs, who would speak up for her?

Topping it off, when I reached the main road, a Camp Six minibus filled with teenagers sped past. What about the missing Tally?

"Boundaries, Jamie. Boundaries," I uttered out loud. "Worry about Miss Nella and her story first."

Chapter Thirty-One: Competency

While the setting sun cast a golden glow over Lake Larissa, I sat on my rock with an IPA and rehearsed what I would say to Clarence about the Gooseberry Project. He needed to accept some responsibility for getting me into the quagmire.

"What was he thinking, girl? Getting me involved with the Fox family. Now I've got the sheriff asking me questions again. Damn!"

She dropped her stick at my feet. I picked it up and threw it into the woods. I pictured myself tearing up Miss Nella's check and throwing it into the fireplace. Except, I'd happily deposited it this afternoon. Maybe it would bounce, and I'd be off the hook.

A playful bark from Bronte brought me out of my musings and back to the rock and the lake, and the sunset. She looked at me, stick at her feet, and woofed.

Perhaps I'd spent too much time alone or in my own head, because when I peered down at her, I could swear she had an expression that said, "Don't give up on the Fox project."

"What would you know about it?" I demanded, flinging the stick up the hill.

As the sun sank behind Bear Island, the mosquitoes ventured out. After swatting several, I picked up my empty IPA bottle and went inside. At the kitchen table, I stared at my sketchy notes. Miss Nella had been raped and given birth to a baby. She'd confirmed it today. Dr. Heller was somehow involved with the birth, and she wanted me to contact the family. Other than that, I really didn't have a good grasp on her story or what she wanted told.

I needed to consult with Clarence. I sensed the old barrister was holding something back from me.

My phone binged with a text from Jim. **Might get out of class early. What are you doing next weekend?**

I replied. **Better hurry. I have other offers.**

Have your dog hold them off.

As I read his text, I wanted him here, now. I needed someone to tell me what to do about Miss Nella, Barrett, and all the secrets. Instead of continuing the thread, I turned my phone off and went to bed.

My limbs felt heavy as I forced myself out of bed the next morning. Raindrops pattered on the roof, and the cabin had a cold, wet chill about it. I almost broke down and turned on the furnace. Around here, using the furnace in late May was like admitting you were one of those citified "snowflakes." Jilly once said, "We like to suffer. That's why our Scandinavian ancestors settled here instead of California."

Knowing Clarence was not an early riser, I waited until 9:30 to call him.

"This better be good to disturb me in the wee hours of the morning," he growled.

I laughed. "I take it Lorraine hasn't poured coffee into you yet."

"She's off on some escapade with Elena and the baby."

"You're sounding a little jealous. Let me come and make you some coffee. I'll stop at the bakery for blueberry muffins if you promise to be polite to me."

"Hmmph."

He was dressed in neatly pressed slacks and a cardigan sweater when he opened the door for me. With his trimmed white hair and horn-rimmed glasses, he looked like a professor emeritus.

I smelled fresh coffee. "Did Lorraine stop by and brew the coffee for you?"

"Young lady, I am quite capable of manipulating that machine. I might be old, but I still have a wit or two."

"You are testy today, but I do apologize for stereotyping you as old and decrepit."

It turned out Clarence made a fine cup of coffee—better than Lorraine's. I complimented him.

He took a sip. "Lorraine thinks the weaker, the healthier. She doesn't know that I have a secret cache of instant coffee, and when she isn't looking, I add it to the pot."

"Ah, intrigue."

Once we were settled at the table with our coffee and muffins, I filled him in on Andrew, the diary, Miss Nella, and Greg's visit. "I admit to being completely overwhelmed by this project. Too many threads going in too many directions. Fortunately, I'd already deposited her check, or I might have torn it up."

Clarence sat back with a thoughtful expression. "Well, let's sort it out. My lawyer's suspicious instinct tells me Tucker is after money or even the estate. If so, that's more my concern than yours."

"Didn't you tell me Miss Nella wants to give the land to the state for a park? If it's in her will, he can't do anything about it, can he?"

Clarence set down his coffee cup and added more sugar. "She always has the right to change her will."

"I don't see her listening to Tucker. I get the strong feeling she'd like him to go away." I told him about Miss Nella's comments regarding Barrett. "She certainly had no love for his sister, either."

Clarence brushed a muffin crumb from his sweater. "I know Miss Nella can be...uh...taxing, but I thought this project would be good for her, and it might help keep you out of debtor's prison." He wouldn't meet my eyes.

Suddenly it became clear to me. "Oh, Clarence. You are a wily old lawyer. You wanted me to keep an eye on things after the Fox siblings showed up. Didn't you?"

He cleared his throat. "Well, perhaps. At least, I thought it might be a good idea. Now, I'm not so sure if what you are telling me is correct. The sheriff is hinting at murder?"

I told him about the suspicious head injury. "They're hedging on it, but this little tickle I get on the back of my neck says something isn't right. And on top of that, no one found a flashlight at the scene."

Clarence picked up on it right away. "If she was exploring the hospital on her own, she'd certainly take a flashlight."

I nodded.

"Hmmm...curious."

We were interrupted by my phone. Miss Nella was calling.

When I answered, her response was terse. "We need to find Dr. Heller's family and put that to right. Please come now." The call ended before I could reply.

I looked at the phone. "Miss Nella wants me, now. I feel like all she has to do is ring a bell and I'll come running."

Clarence tilted his head back and chuckled. "Ah, yes. That's our Nella Fox."

"Before I go, I need to ask, do you think she's safe? I mean, can she take care of herself? A couple of times, she's seemed confused. Right now, the only person looking after her, if you don't count Tucker showing up drunk, is Ed, the caretaker. He doesn't seem all there either."

Clarence's expression turned from amused to serious. "One of my most difficult challenges over the years when handling wills and estates has been the determination if someone is competent to make decisions. It's a complicated situation."

I hadn't thought much about competency. My experience as a teenager with my mother, as she sank deeper and deeper into her brain disease, was simply that Dad had handled all the decisions.

"Isn't it pretty straightforward? Either someone can make a decision, or they can't?"

"Oh, my dear girl, the naivety of youth. Declaring someone incompetent is a legal process that can be drawn out and messy. I've been on both ends of it. I represented a son who wanted legal guardianship after his mother remarried and the second husband was gambling away her money. On the other end, I represented a man who had some dementia but was still able to make decisions. His brother was trying to get guardianship and access to his bank accounts."

"What happened?"

168

"In the first case, we could clearly show the woman was beyond being able to make decisions, and the husband was not only using all her money but leaving her for days at a time. The son won in court and was able to put her in a good nursing home. The husband then threatened to either sue me or shoot me—I can't remember which."

"Hmmm...You aren't making much of a case for me to drop my editing business and become a lawyer. What about the second case?"

Clarence frowned. "We won, but I had to seriously dog the client to get my fee. He wasn't totally reliable, but he was still able to make decisions."

"Do you know what eventually happened to him?"

For a moment, Clarence rubbed his temples. "This is where it becomes even more complicated. He ended up in the hospital after a fall and insisted on going home even though he couldn't walk and didn't know whether it was night or day. Lots of hoo-hahs and back and forth with doctors and social workers. Other than his larcenous brother, he had no other relatives. The hospital needed to discharge him, and he refused to go to a nursing home. In his best interests, I ended up advocating for the court to assign a guardian."

I thought about Miss Nella. She didn't strike me as being unable to make reasonable decisions. "Do you think Tucker would try to have her declared incompetent to void the will?"

Clarence shrugged. "It would be a stretch. More likely, he'd try to influence her to make changes."

Toying with his empty coffee cup, he appeared lost in thought. When he finally looked at me, his eyebrows were drawn together in a frown. "Are you concerned about her safety with Tucker—or yours, for that matter?"

I took a deep breath. "I wasn't until Greg told me about Barrett. If someone pushed her, he would be the only candidate to do it."

Something niggled at me after I spoke—a snatch of a conversation. Tucker had said something about Miss Nella being stronger than she looked. Could she have pushed Barrett? I shook my head.

"What?" Clarence leaned forward.

I waved him away and stood up. "I have been summoned. I'd better go."

Clarence accompanied me to the door. Before I walked out, I had one more question for him. "Miss Nella wants me to contact Dr. Heller's family. That's why she called today. Do you know anything about him or why she would be so interested in his family?"

Clarence scratched his head. "Nella said something about him, but that's not what comes to mind. I think there was a scandal involving him."

"Scandal? Grace thought he was a good doctor."

Clarence closed his eyes. "No, not a scandal. I remember. He disappeared. Must have been in the late 40s. My parents talked about it, wondering how someone could simply go away and leave no trail."

"Well, maybe Miss Nella wants to let his family know that he was kind to her or something."

"Maybe."

When I reached my car, Clarence was still standing in the doorway. He looked either worried or puzzled. I wasn't sure which.

"On to Miss Nella and the dark estate." I tried to sound enthused, but I didn't feel it.

Chapter Thirty-Two: Finding Dr. Heller

By the time I reached Gooseberry Acres, the rain had stopped, leaving behind a cold, foggy mist. The hospital appeared even more foreboding in the subdued light. I noticed for the first time how the patchwork of boards covering up broken windows appeared to make a macabre winking face.

As I approached, I wondered if Miss Nella was strong enough to climb the stairs and push Barrett to her death. If so, why would she do that?

I shook the thought out of my head. Barrett had probably stumbled or slipped or something. The flashlight probably went flying, and if the sheriff looked hard enough for it, he'd find it somewhere along the stairway.

Once again, no cars were parked in front of the residence. I wondered where Tucker spent all his time. Had he found some vulnerable Killdeer woman to be with? Or was he at the bar with Andrew? A flush of anger swept through me, thinking about Andrew, who had not responded to my text about the missing diary. I imagined Tucker and Andrew conspiring together. For Tucker, it would be about the money. For Andrew? Money? Revenge? A way at getting back at me?

Miss Nella greeted me at the door. She appeared to be up and around more since Barrett's death. Instead of her well-appointed pantsuit, though, she was in a fluffy robe cinched tightly at her waist. Her hair, so neatly styled yesterday, stuck up in the back like she'd just gotten up and hadn't combed it yet.

Instead of asking me in, she reached into her pocket and handed me a key ring. "Papa kept all the employee records on the second floor behind the nurse's station. I want you to find the one for Dr. Heller."

I made no move to take the key. "Could I come in?"

Miss Nella frowned. In confusion, she asked. "Aren't you the one who's going to find Dr. Heller for me?"

For a moment, she had the same glaze to her eyes my mother had before the brain disease took all the light in her eyes.

"Miss Nella. I'm Jamie—remember? I'm working with you on your memoirs. You were going to tell me more about Dr. Heller today."

She turned to the hallway, leaving the door open. Her feet were bare. "If you say so."

I wished Clarence was with me right now. Maybe he could discern her ability to make competent decisions.

Miss Nella settled into her chair and slipped her glasses on. The confusion vanished. "Well, then. Let's get to it."

I decided to be direct with her. "Can you tell me why you are so anxious to contact Dr. Heller's family?"

Several files and folders were stacked on her coffee table. She reached over and took one. "I found these the other day. I think *that woman* was snooping in Papa's office. I feel bad about what happened to him. He was so nice to me when I was...." She paused. "Unwell."

"Miss Nella. You told me the other day he delivered your baby. Is that what you are talking about?"

Instead of answering, she handed me a folder. Inside were newspaper clippings from the *Killdeer Times* and several Twins Cities newspapers. "Read them."

While she watched, I scanned through the articles. They all chronicled the mysterious disappearance of Dr. Frank Heller. He was last seen working as a physician at Gooseberry Acres. Included were interviews with Dr. Heller's sister and his mother. They described him as a devout Christian and a hard-working doctor who wanted to specialize in diseases like tuberculosis in order to do missionary work in Africa. One article included a photo of him. He looked serious in his dark, round framed glasses. The glasses reminded me a bit of Harry Potter.

According to the reporting, he failed to show up at the hospital one day. They found the cottage he lived in emptied, with no indication of where he'd gone. He'd never done anything like this before.

The *St. Paul Dispatch* featured an interview with Dr. Fox. They titled him a "world renown expert" on treatment of TB. He expressed his puzzlement at the abrupt departure of his colleague and even hinted at some anger. "This was not the professional behavior of a physician caring for my patients."

The next clipping in the pile was a short article dated six months after the disappearance. A Minneapolis clairvoyant claimed she had been in touch with him. She said he spoke to her from "the other side" and told her he left the hospital because of unholy spirits.

The last article was again from the *Killdeer Times,* dated twenty years ago. Ed, the caretaker, had reported vandalism at the hospital, including someone breaking in and causing damage. The reporter went on to say, "Neighbors of the old, closed hospital have reported strange noises from the property. Some say the hospital is haunted by a doctor who disappeared in the late 1940s. Nella Fox, owner of the property, labels it non-sense and asks that the community respect the No Trespassing signs."

When I put the last article down, Miss Nella tsked, "Imagine people saying Dr. Heller haunts the hospital. He was such a nice man. No matter what happened to him, he wouldn't bother us."

"Miss Nella, do you know why he left?"

She picked at fluff on her robe. "I want his family to know he was a good man and a good doctor. Can you find them? His mother must be frantic."

I refrained from pointing out that his mother must be long dead along with his sister. "Miss Nella, I have to admit to being lost with this project. Maybe I'm not the right person for it."

She looked stricken. "Clarence told me you would be good."

I shrugged. "I don't quite know where to start."

Her eyes teared over. "I need to tell the story."

A feeling of having disappointed her crept over me. Here was an old woman who probably didn't have too many years left, and she had a story to tell. I'd edited enough stories that I knew how to put them together. "How about if I at least try to find Dr. Heller's relatives and help you write about him."

Miss Nella smiled. "That would be fine. Now, take these keys. One will open the main door, and the little ones will open the locks on the room with the files. It's behind the nurse's station."

With reluctance, I took the keys. They were on an old key ring with a small, gold medallion attached to it engraved with *Gooseberry Acres*.

Miss Nella touched the key ring. "They were special. Papa had a few made for the important people on the staff."

I fought back a shudder as I thought about going inside the old hospital with the smell of rot and decay. Since it was foggy outside, little light would filter through the boarded-up windows. This was my opportunity to back out.

Except, I was intrigued by the missing Dr. Heller. Holding the key ring in the palm of my hand, I inspected the medallion. It was dated 1930. I showed it to Miss Nella. "Is that when the hospital opened?"

"No. That's when my mother had me and when she died. He had these made as a memorial to her."

We sat in silence for a few moments before I stood up. "If I'm going to look for Dr. Heller's records, I'll need a good flashlight. Do you have one?"

"Ed keeps one with fresh batteries in the kitchen. He worries because the electricity can go out in a storm."

I checked several drawers in the kitchen but couldn't find the flashlight. Maybe Barrett had taken it. I had a flashlight on my phone, but I wanted something more substantial. When I walked back to the sitting room, Miss Nella was asleep in her chair, snoring softly. Perhaps Ed had one.

Outside, the sun poked through the fog, brightening the day. As I walked toward Ed's trailer, I decided I would do my best to track down the Heller family and help Miss Nella write to them. Beyond that, I was unsure what I could accomplish.

As I passed the little cemetery, I was drawn to it, thinking about the people who had died and about the families who buried them in such a remote, lonely place. Did they ever come to visit? Do their descendants know they've been laid to rest on these grounds?

"Jamie, I think Gooseberry Acres is getting to you." I whispered as if those who were buried might hear me.

I made my way to the grave of the little girl with the doll. Had she been buried with it? The sun broke through the fog and mist, brightening up the little plot. Something glinted on the ground near one of the graves. When I reached the headstone, it was the one that had no markings on it other than "Beloved." I knelt to inspect. Partially buried was a silver barrette.

I lifted it out and held it up. It was identical to the one I'd seen on Barrett the first day I'd come. I remembered noting it because it was so ornate and didn't fit with her plainness.

I didn't hear the footsteps approach until Ed's gruff voice caused me to startle. "What are you doing here? She doesn't like people to snoop."

Turning around, I held up the barrette. "I found this by the grave. Do you know why it's here?"

Ed squinted at me. "Sometimes the ghost leaves little things here. You should put it back."

A chill ran up my spine. "Ghost?"

Ed waved at the hospital. "Him. He haunts the place. He was quiet for a long time, but he's back now. I think those two brought him back."

"Which two?"

Ed ignored my question. "They shouldn't have done what they did. Mama said so but said I should keep quiet about it. Then she played music and gave me some tea, and I went to sleep."

My heart pounding, I tried to puzzle together what he was saying. "Ed, you've seen the ghost?"

"Only that once. Sometimes I see him in my dreams, though. Down the stairs, he went."

Ed turned abruptly. "Gotta go. Programs are on."

"Wait!" I remembered why I was on my way to his trailer. "I was coming to see you. I'm looking for a flashlight, and I couldn't find the one Miss Nella said was in the kitchen."

"Hmmph. Don't like lending things."

"Miss Nella wants me to get something for her from the hospital."

Not knowing whether he had a flashlight or not, I followed him as he marched back to the trailer. "Don't like to miss my programs," he muttered.

At the door to the trailer, he stopped me. "You bring this back right away. When it gets dark, I like to have it in case..."

I paced while I waited. From inside, I heard water running in the sink. What if he forgot about me? Did I dare knock on his door?

After a few minutes, Ed opened the door, dish towel in hand, and gave me a large flashlight. "Here, I put new batteries in it. Don't stay too long. The hospital doesn't like people to stay too long."

"I'll bring this right back as soon as I've found what I'm looking for."

He closed the door, muffling the audio from the television.

As I walked back to the hospital, I slapped at something crawling up my neck. Nothing was there. When I reached the weathered front door, I stopped, took a deep breath, and put the key in the lock. A part of me hoped I wouldn't be able to unlock the door. Another part, the brash New Yorker told me to get in there and do my job.

Chapter Thirty-Three: The File and the Staircase

The door unlocked after the third try of inserting the key and twisting. Over the years, the door had warped. It creaked as I tugged on it. I set the flashlight down and used two hands to jerk it open. When I reached down to pick of the flashlight, I noted the lens was cracked. Before entering the hospital, I switched it on to make sure it worked. The last thing I wanted was to be stuck in the dark in this mausoleum of a building. The light came on strong and white.

Once I had the door open, I left it slightly ajar.

In the darkened lobby, I stopped to get my bearings. Not much had changed since I'd found Barrett. Some of the debris on the floor had been kicked away by the ambulance attendants. A blue vinyl glove lay crumpled on the floor, along with paper packaging for medical supplies. I also saw two candy wrappers and a small potato chip bag. The EMTs must have left them behind. In their rush to get to Barrett, I'm sure they weren't thinking about litter.

I hoped to be in and out as fast as possible. Already, I felt a tightening in my chest, either from all the mold in the air or an irrational fear this place might be haunted.

In my heart, I knew I was my father's daughter—stiff, no-nonsense, Yankee stock. Still, perhaps the quarter Ojibwe that coursed through my veins sensed this was an unholy place, just like the clairvoyant had said.

"Nonsense." Yet, I couldn't control the slight tremor in my voice as I spoke aloud.

Ed's flashlight beamed brightly. I pointed it to the main stairway. I recalled the room Miss Nella described on the second floor behind the nurse's station. Marching quickly up the stairs, I ignored the mouse droppings that had accumulated over the years. At least the steps felt solid under my weight.

Why had Miss Nella insisted on keeping this building if she had no intention of maintaining it? The flashlight illuminated the peeling paint and crumbling plaster. In some places, the walls had deteriorated enough to see the lath beneath the plaster. The first thing a developer would do would be to tear it to the ground. They'd probably have to wear hazmat suits. Who knew how much lead was in the paint on the walls or asbestos in the insulation? With that thought, my chest spasmed, and I coughed. This would have been a good time to wear a mask.

Up ahead, I thought I heard the creaking of floorboards or maybe a fluttering sound like the hospital was alive with something. "Imagination, Jamie. Ghosts don't make sounds like that." I was nearly out of breath when I reached the second floor, yet I didn't want to take a deep breath. I'd read about the kinds of diseases you could get from breathing in bird droppings. In my New York days working as a fact-checker, I'd checked an article written by a building inspector. He described a disease called psittacosis caused by pigeon droppings. I gazed in the direction of the fluttering sound but saw no sign of pigeons.

How ironic if I should get a lung disease exploring an old TB hospital.

On the second floor, I aimed the flashlight at the nurse's station. It was nothing more than an enclosed counter with a desk and empty cabinets with glass doors behind it. Directly behind the desk was the locked room. When the hospital had been operational, I wondered if they would have kept the room locked. I remembered how careful the hospital was about Dad's medical records when he was so sick. He had to sign papers so the doctors could talk with me about his illness. I doubted informed consent was an issue in the days of the TB hospital.

On the other hand, TB might have been considered a disgraceful disease hidden by families. I made a mental note to research the attitudes about it if I did more with Miss Nella's project.

Before entering the nurse's station, I moved the beam of the flashlight over to the door of the back stairway where I'd found Barrett. Once I'd gotten Dr. Heller's personnel file, perhaps I could find the missing flashlight. The door was ajar and didn't look like its position had changed from when I explored it. I wondered how thorough the sheriff's investigation had been, since everybody assumed it had been an accident.

Thinking about the back of the hospital, I swept the flashlight in the direction opposite the stairway. I could see down the corridor another door that must have been the exit to the kitchen. The building probably had a dumbwaiter, but I wasn't about to look for it. Overhead I thought I heard a soft thumping from the third floor. I called out, "Hello?" and was met with silence.

"If it's the ghost, I hope it stays up there. Let's find Dr. Heller's file and get the hell out of here." My voice echoed in the vacant halls.

I thought about Grace. She had spent time in one of these rooms. Dr. Fox and Dr. Heller had taken good care of her. I shouldn't be so spooked. But then I thought of the little girl who had died. Was she all alone in a room when she passed? Would she haunt this place looking for her family—or her doll?

I didn't have to remind myself to hurry. The less I breathed the air, the better.

The padlock on the door was old and corroded. The shackle hadn't been locked in place. Someone else, maybe Barrett, had been in this room.

Gripping the flashlight, I pushed open the door. I was so tense my jaw hurt. I wasn't sure whether I thought I'd find an apparition or some creature would spring out at me. Without the beam of the flashlight, the windowless room would have been completely dark. It was no bigger than a small storeroom and had nothing in it but old wooden filing cabinets lining the walls. The air in the room, rather than smelling musty, smelled of dust and a hint of something flowery, like old rose petals. I sneezed when I walked in, and the scent disappeared. More imagination.

The cabinet's drawers had typed labels affixed to the front. I started with the cabinet nearest the door. The bottom drawer was labeled *H-K*. I squatted down, training the flashlight on the label. These were probably patient files, but it was worth a look.

When I tried to open the drawer, it wouldn't budge. Years of heat, cold, moisture, and neglect had caused it to warp. No matter how hard I tugged, I couldn't get it open.

"This was not part of the plan," I muttered.

Standing up, I tried the first drawer labeled *A-C*. It, too, was stuck, but I was able to get it partially open. The files inside were arranged in alphabetical order. I pulled out the first one. It was the medical record for a Tilda Aaronson. Scanning through it, I was surprised by the sparseness of the medical notes. Some were no more than "patient examined, temperature normal" and the date. I thought about my father's chart, an electronic record filled with notes from the doctors, nurses, and therapists. I guessed much of the patient information from the days of the TB hospital resided in Dr. Fox's or Dr. Heller's heads.

I inspected the other filing cabinets and tried a few of the drawers. I was able to pull one open, but it was empty. Perhaps most of them were empty. Perhaps years ago, Dr. Fox had archived them somewhere else.

My nose started running in the dusty room. With no air circulation, I was growing warm. As I stood in the room, I felt it was closing around me. My forehead broke out with a sheen of perspiration. It was time to leave before I was overtaken by an irrational panic.

Flashing the beam one more time around the little room, I noticed a smaller filing cabinet tucked in the far corner of the room, almost hidden from the rest. It had been shoved against the wall with little space for the drawers to open. A curling label, about to fall off, said, "Employees."

"Yes," I said aloud. The room seemed to stifle the sound of my voice.

Though the cabinet was wedged into the corner, I had enough room to partially open the drawer. I gave it a pull, and nothing happened. I tugged harder, and the cabinet scraped a little on the floor, but the drawer wouldn't open.

"Come on!" My face grew hot with effort and frustration. Using the flashlight, I inspected it up close and saw the cabinet had a lock. I stared at it, wondering how to pry it open when it occurred to me the key ring Miss Nella had given me contained two small keys. Holding the flashlight in one hand, I fumbled with the first key. It didn't fit.

Grunting in frustration, I tried the second key. "Unlock, damn it!" The key slipped in. With a twist, the drawer popped open.

Instead of employee files, however, the top drawer was filled with very old medical journals. I lifted one out to see it was an entire journal about research into tuberculosis. It was from the mid-1940s.

"Well, this is not helpful unless I want to write about TB treatment."

The bottom drawer contained several file folders labeled "research." Inside were typed papers and clippings from more medical journals. None of it provided me with any more information on Dr. Frank Heller. I was about to give up when I saw something wedged in the back of the file drawer. Because I couldn't get the drawer all the way open, I had to reach in blindly and fumble around until I could grab it. It felt like a box of some sort.

In order to retrieve it, I piled the journals and folders on the floor next to me. Once they were out, the beam from the flashlight showed an old cigar box. Inching it to the front of the drawer, I was finally able to grasp it and pull it out.

My eyes watered from all the dust from the journals and papers. I stifled a sneeze and flipped the lid open on the box. The first thing I saw was a pair of cracked and bent glasses.

I held the frames to the flashlight beam. "Harry Potter frames, like the ones Dr. Heller wore," I whispered. It appeared they'd been stepped on.

Next, I took out a wallet. The leather was cracked and brittle. I flipped it open, hoping to find identification inside. The wallet was empty, but when I folded it, I noted flaking gold embossing with the letters *FH.*

"Frank Heller?" I whispered. "Why would you leave your wallet behind?"

The rest of the box contained letters bundled in a pink ribbon. They were addressed in fading blue ink to Dr. Heller.

My brain was stuck. Why would this box be hidden at the bottom of a cabinet full of medical journals and papers?

I might have sat pondering all of this longer, except I sensed a shifting in the air in this little room. The all-hated spider, my internal warning system, crawled up my spine. Someone was in the building.

Chapter Thirty-Four: The Staircase

I froze, listening for the sound of footsteps. My heart pounded as I held my breath. Nothing. No creaking of the old floors, no skittering of rats behind the walls. No sound at all. False alarm. I'd have to have a chat with my warning spider about the boy who cried wolf.

Still, I turned off the flashlight and waited. After several moments of dead silence, I put everything back in the cigar box and closed it. I regarded the messy pile of journals and files on the floor and decided I wasn't interested in putting them back. If Miss Nella wanted them cleaned up, she could hire someone to do it. I, at least, had letters that might tell me more about how to find Dr. Heller's family.

At the door, I fumbled with the padlock and decided to leave it unlatched. I really wanted out of the building as quickly as possible.

My eyes had adjusted to the darkness in the file room. When I slipped out of the nurse's station, I could see fairly well, with gray light filtering through several windows that hadn't been broken and boarded up. I still had a little tickle between my shoulder blades, but the building remained quiet.

Resisting the urge to flee down the main staircase and out of the hospital forever, I walked softly to the back stair stopping every couple of feet to listen. If I could talk myself into going down the stairs, I might find the missing flashlight. A flapping sound stopped me cold just inside the doorway at the landing. It came from above me, and I imagined a large bat waiting to land on my head.

"Stop it, Jamie." I knew it was a myth that bats went for human hair. Still...

Pointing the flashlight up, I noted the door to the third-floor staircase was open a crack. Had it been open before I went into the file room? Something made a skittering sound at the top. I held my breath until it stopped. Probably squirrels living up there.

With the cigar box clutched in my hand, I carefully descended the back steps. On the landing where I'd found the blood, I bent down to examine the floor. I made out a partial footprint in the rust-colored stain, probably from one of the sheriff's people. With a little misgiving, I switched off the light to see if the staircase had any kind of light source. I was thrown immediately into oppressive darkness. Without the safety of the flashlight, I felt like I couldn't breathe. Barrett would never have descended these stairs without a light—unless.

Unless she was running from someone or something.

Jolted by this thought, I fumbled to turn the flashlight back on, dropping the cigar box in the process. With the flashlight on, dark spots floated in front of me for a few moments. I held back the urge to run down the rest of the steps. My lungs begged for fresh air.

Above me, I again heard a soft creaking sound. With the image of Barrett tumbling down the staircase, I picked up the box and prepared to take the rest of the steps as quickly as possible. Except, I caught a glint of something next to the wall on the step below me.

It was a key ring with a gold medallion. What had Miss Nella said? Only three of them existed. I had one, Ed had one, and here was the last one. This was the one that had belonged to Dr. Fox. Barrett must have found it in his office in the residence. That's how she got into the hospital.

Gingerly I picked it up. Barrett must have dropped it when she fell. I wondered if she was the one who opened the lock to the file room. If so, she must have had the same experience I had of not being able to open the file drawers. The thought that I was following her path sent a frigid dart through my chest. I needed to get out of here.

Once again, I felt the slight sensation of a spider on the nape of my neck. I stood still and listened. Something moved, but I couldn't pinpoint its location. Instead of waiting, I hurried down the steps. At the bottom, where Barrett's broken body had lain, the wood flooring showed through a threadbare carpet. On one side of the landing was a boarded-up door to the outdoor patio. On the other, the exit door into the day room.

I suddenly had the suffocating sensation I'd once felt locked in a holding cell in Queens with drunks and felons. My hands started to sweat, and I found I was gasping for breath. I needed to get out. I needed to be away from this hospital. Miss Nella could have her secrets. I no longer wanted any part of them.

I pushed on the exit door. It wouldn't budge. It was wedged shut. All the activity around Barrett must have caused the door to warp even more. I shook off the panic. The rational part of my brain said, slow down; go back up the stairs. The other part, the one that wasn't rational, hissed, *Get the door open!*

My fingers tingled, and I gasped for air. If I didn't calm down, I knew I'd hyperventilate and pass out. Closing my eyes, I counted to five and kicked the door. "Open up!" It creaked but wouldn't budge.

Backing up, I hurled myself at the door. It continued to be jammed.

"Get me out!" Perhaps I was yelling at a ghost, but I didn't care. I wanted to be away from this dark place, and I didn't want to go back up the stairs. I imagined a dark and evil presence waiting for me at the top of the stairs.

I tried a second time. As I propelled myself at the door, it suddenly opened. Instead of slamming into the door, I slammed into a human. We both teetered into the empty day room. The flashlight and the cigar box went flying as I landed on top of the intruder with an ooffing sound that nearly knocked the wind out of me.

For a few moments, we both lay stunned on the cracked and dirty linoleum floor. Blinking away the flashing colors floating in front of my eyes, I stared at the person beneath me. He stared back with those distinctive blue eyes.

"Andrew?" I struggled to catch my breath as I rolled off him. "What the hell are you doing here?"

He sat up, rubbing the back of his head. "Ah...looking for you. I wasn't expecting to be tackled."

"Did you wedge that door shut?"

He continued to rub his head. "No. Why would I do that?"

I stood up, feeling a bit wobbly. Near as I could tell, I hadn't broken anything, although my shoulder felt numb from hitting the door the first time. "How long have you been here?"

Andrew blinked hard. "A few minutes. I heard you yelling and came running."

I was still so stunned I couldn't sort it out. Why was Andrew in this godawful place?

He must have read my expression. "That crazy old lady said you were looking for something here."

"But why are you *here* at Gooseberry Acres?"

In the gray light of the room, I noted how carefully he adjusted his expression. "Well...ah."

At this point, I didn't care. I wanted out of the building. He could explain later.

Ed's flashlight and the cigar box had landed near the stairway door. Still a bit unsteady, I made my way to them. The contents of the box had spilled out. Besides the wallet, the glasses, and the letters, I found a small gold locket on a delicate chain. This was not the time to examine it. I put everything back in the box as Andrew walked over to me.

"What's that?" He pointed to the box.

I held it close to me. "Not your concern. Let's get the hell out of here."

"No argument from me. This place is creepier than the backstage of an old theater. I can't imagine Tucker thinking this could be converted to a theater camp."

I was ready to leave when I remembered the second key ring. I'd dropped it on the bottom landing. "Stay and hold the door open for me."

Andrew winced at my sharp tone. Back in the days of our marriage, I never commanded him to do anything.

With the flashlight switched on, I searched for the keyring. It had skidded into a corner.

"What are you doing?" Andrew asked.

I held up the key ring. "I found this. I think Barrett must have dropped it." I slid it into the cigar box. "Let's get out of here and talk. You have some explaining to do."

We made our way through the hall to the front door. I kept looking back, as though someone or something was following me. I felt like the old building was trying to hold onto us, trying to keep us within its depths.

Once outside, the first thing I did was take a deep breath of the fresh, misty air. The second thing I did was make sure the door was locked. I hoped never to set foot inside again.

"Now," I pulled myself up as tall as I could get and folded my arms. "What are you doing here?"

"I'm looking for Tucker."

"Why?"

As I asked the question, the sky darkened, and drops of rain fell. Andrew tilted his head to the sky. "Can we go inside and talk?" He pointed to the residence.

"Andrew, it's not my house. I don't know if Miss Nella wants you inside."

He grinned. "Oh, I'm sure it's okay. I charmed her."

Was he serious? I shrugged and made a dash for the porch. He followed. Once inside, I called out to Miss Nella. "It's Jamie."

"Did you bring that young man back with you?"

Unfortunately, yes.

Andrew walked beside me into the sitting room. Miss Nella had changed from her robe into a pantsuit and had combed her hair. She gazed over her glasses at him. "I've seen you somewhere before, haven't I?"

"Mr. Right Digestion at your service."

"Oh, brother," I muttered under my breath.

She smiled. "And what are you doing here?"

"Well, ma'am, I'm looking for Tucker Fox."

She raised her eyebrows. "I haven't seen him. Maybe he's gone for good."

Andrew frowned. "He said to meet him here."

Miss Nella sat up straighter. "You can't trust him, young man. He's like his father before him." She turned to me. "Did I tell you what a scoundrel Uncle Judd turned out to be? Papa had to send him away."

At this point, I wasn't interested in old scandals. I wanted to be done with the whole Fox family.

I beckoned Andrew to me. "Listen, why don't you meet me at the Loonfeather in an hour. I need to talk with her."

He didn't seem anxious to stay. Bowing to Miss Nella, he intoned, "Till we meet again."

I stiffened, holding back a desire to either laugh at him or hit him.

After he left, she remarked, "Good looking young man, but I wouldn't trust him. Too much like that other one."

Actors, I thought.

Chapter Thirty-Five: The Broken Glasses

I sat on the sofa next to Miss Nella's chair holding the cigar box.

"What have you there?" She peered at the box. "Papa used to have several of them. I don't know where they went."

"I found this in the file room behind the nurse's station." I handed it to her.

She adjusted her glasses and lifted the lid. "Oh, my…" Her voice dropped off as she pulled out the locket. "He always carried it in his pocket to remind him of his sweetheart back east." She held up the locket to the light. "He said her picture was in there."

I watched her in silence as her eyes teared up. "They would have been very happy."

She set the locket on the arm of her chair and took out the broken glasses. As she studied them, the color drained from her face. "This…this should not have happened! It was all my fault."

"Miss Nella," I kept my voice as gentle as I could. "Is this about Dr. Heller? Did something happen to him? Is this one of the secrets you talk about?"

She stared beyond me as if she was watching someone in the doorway. I glanced in that direction and saw nothing.

"I kept it a secret, you know. I wore a girdle, and in the winter, I dressed in layers. No one knew. Not my friends, not my teachers, and especially not Papa." She sighed. "I was so scared someone would find out." She fell silent.

I prompted her, "But you couldn't keep it secret forever, could you?"

"Nanny Ninny suspected. She, of all people, would know. I said I didn't want to go to a doctor." She winced. "You see, if I went to a doctor, it would be real."

I thought about the lonely sixteen-year-old keeping her secret, and it made me sad. "What happened when she found out?"

Miss Nella closed her eyes as if she wanted it to go away. I was afraid she would stop talking. When she opened them, she fingered the glasses, "She promised not to tell Papa if I would let Dr. Heller see me."

"He took care of you through your pregnancy?"

"We didn't use that word in those days. I called it my 'difficulties.'" She rested her hands in her lap. "We had a plan, you see. Nanny was going to suggest I spend the spring in Minneapolis with her sister so I could get tutoring for college. Papa was so busy and distracted that he said 'fine.' I was to go to one of those homes they had for unwed mothers. Nanny said it was a very nice one."

I was surprised they could get away with it. Dr. Fox, even distracted, didn't strike me as someone who wouldn't have noticed the change in his daughter.

As if she could read my thoughts, Miss Nella added, "I was good at keeping it secret. I hardly showed."

"Did you go to the home?"

She bit her lip, her eyes tearing over. "The baby came too soon. She came before we could go."

"You went into labor early?"

She took a deep, shuddering breath. "Papa was at a conference, and I was alone in the house when the pains started. I didn't know what to do. It was snowing and raining and blowing, and I knew they couldn't get me to Minneapolis before the baby came."

I waited, watching her face. It looked to me by the way she grimaced and clenched her fists that she was reliving what she'd gone through.

Light rain pattered on the roof, the only sound in the house. Miss Nella looked up at the ceiling. "It seemed like forever, and the pains got worse and worse. Then something happened. Something bad."

I moved closer to the edge of the sofa as her voice softened to almost a whisper.

"Blood. I was bleeding like I had my monthlies except heavier."

"Miss Nella, what did you do?"

She squeezed her eyes shut. "I wrapped myself in a blanket and went outside. The sleet was coming down fast, and the path to the hospital was icy. I fell and skinned my knee. Just like a little girl. It was so dark by then. It must have been night—I don't remember the time clearly."

I shivered thinking about her in labor, outside in the ice storm.

She picked at the fabric on the arm of her chair. Wrinkling her brow as if confused, she turned to me. "Ah...where was I?"

"You were trying to get to the hospital, and you fell."

She squeezed her eyes shut. Clearly, the memory was painful. "I don't like to think about it."

I was afraid she wouldn't tell me the rest. I waited. After a few moments, she opened her eyes and peered at me. I took it as a cue. "You said you were trying to get to the hospital, but you fell."

Shaking her head, she made a tsking sound. "I was such a foolish girl. I could have died, you know."

"Did someone find you?"

"He did. Dr. Heller was just back from town. I must have looked a sight, wrapped in my blanket in the snow."

Outside, a car with a broken muffler grunted to a stop. Of all times for Tucker to show up—I was on the verge of getting somewhere with Miss Nella's secrets. I held my breath, hoping he'd stay in the car for a few minutes while I pulled the story from her.

"Miss Nella, did Dr. Heller deliver your baby?"

"Oh my, yes. Nanny Ninny helped, of course. But they couldn't save her. She was tiny, too tiny, and I was bleeding."

The car door slammed. I reached for Miss Nella's hand. It was dry and cold. "What happened to Dr. Heller?"

She squinted at me. "That's the secret. Papa wouldn't have yelled at him if he'd understood. Papa was a good man, but he had a temper. It all wouldn't have happened if I hadn't heard Papa yelling in the staircase."

I was close. The front door opened. I squeezed Miss Nella's hand. "What

191

did Dr. Fox do?"

She opened her mouth, then pressed it shut into a thin line as Tucker walked into the room. She pointed at him. "Uncle Judd knew. Ask him. Papa paid and paid, and he shouldn't have." She turned away from me.

"What did I know?" Tucker cocked his head to one side.

I wanted to leap up and shove Tucker out of the room. This was a breakthrough moment—something I could grab onto. "Tucker," I hissed, "Could I talk with you in the kitchen?"

He didn't take the cue. Instead, he looked at Miss Nella. "Nella, what is it I'm supposed to know?"

"I forget." With a sly expression, she added, "Be careful what you wish for."

I pointed to the doorway. "Tucker, let's get Miss Nella some coffee."

He backed out with a shrug. Once he was gone, I tried to take Miss Nella's hand again. She snatched it away with a childlike cry. "I don't want to talk about it anymore."

I persisted. "Did your father do something to Dr. Heller? Did he hurt him?"

"The stairs. It was the stairs." With that, she clamped her mouth shut and turned away from me.

Frustration bubbled over when I stepped into the kitchen and found Tucker slouched at the table with an almost empty bottle of brandy. I stormed over and grabbed it away from him. "You have some explaining to do—big time!"

He sat up straighter with a "who me?" expression. It so reminded me of Andrew that I wondered if the two of them were related. He pointed toward the sitting room. "What was old cousin Nella talking about in there?" He swirled his finger near his temple to indicate he thought she was crazy.

I didn't think Miss Nella was crazy. I thought she was a little demented and confused, but not crazy. I gathered my thoughts. Before I said anything about Miss Nella, I wanted to know what he'd lured Andrew into. Instead of asking him, I told him. "You talked Andrew into coming to my cabin and swiping a diary. Why?"

He didn't deny it. "I was curious, and it didn't look like you were about to bring them back or that Nella was about to show them to me."

"And what did you find out?"

He smiled. "I haven't seen it yet, but Andrew told me it was the diary of a teenager."

"Is that what you wanted to see?"

He shrugged. When he spoke, he oozed sincerity, "My dad, in his confusion, sometimes talked about a baby and Nella."

"Baby?"

"He said it kept him in rent money for years."

I couldn't believe this. "Blackmail?"

Tucker shrugged. "Maybe, although in those last couple of years, he certainly wasn't getting any kind of regular money. He also said he was cheated out of his birthright. That's the word he used—birthright."

"You and Barrett have been after whatever this birthright might be."

His expression turned somber. "Poor Barrett. I think she found something but didn't have a chance to tell me."

He could have been sincere, and he could have been acting. Like with Andrew, I was not sure.

"How did you talk Andrew into swiping the diary?"

He grabbed for the brandy and pulled out the stopper. "Don't you know? He's desperate for money."

"You promised him money?"

He took a swig of the brandy. "Just a little, for the diary."

I stood up so abruptly the chair teetered. "My god." Definitely time to leave.

Miss Nella was snoring softly in the chair, the cigar box on her lap. I tiptoed in and lifted it up. She opened her eyes for a moment. Her voice slurred in half-sleep. "He shouldn't have lost his temper."

"Miss Nella, I'm taking the box, but I promise to bring it back. I want to look at the letters to see if I can find Dr. Heller's family."

She didn't respond.

The rain had let up, and a few rays of sunshine sparkled off the wet grass.

Even with the sun out, the air was chilly. As I was opening the car door, I was startled by Ed. He stood behind me, holding his rifle at his side.

"You said you'd bring it back."

I turned to him. "What?"

"The flashlight."

"Oh, I'm sorry. I left it in the sitting room with Miss Nella. Do you want me to get it?"

He didn't respond.

"It works fine, but the lens is cracked. I didn't break it."

He mumbled something like "I know," and walked away.

It was time to find out how Andrew fit into this weird puzzle.

Chapter Thirty-Six: Andrew's Trouble

Before I was off the estate, Andrew texted me. **J. RU coming?**
I stopped at the crumbling main gate and texted back. **On my way. Looking for explanation**

At least he'd know I was angry. Maybe he'd be forthright with me. Before pulling onto the highway, I texted Jim. **Need to talk this evening! Will call.**

For a moment, a pang of longing swept through me. I wanted to be back at my cabin with Jim sitting on my rock and enjoying the sound of the lake lapping against the shore. I wanted the peace of the wind brushing through the pines. He could help me sort out the Fox family and Andrew. As I accelerated to highway speed, though, my cheeks flushed with a sinking feeling. What would Jim say about Andrew? Why had I kept his presence a secret?

The Loonfeather was midafternoon quiet. As I walked in, my stomach growled at the smell of fried food. I'd missed lunch while I searched the old hospital.

Andrew sat at the same table as before, chatting with the same server. He was so engaged with her that he didn't notice me until I slid into the chair. His beer was half gone. I ordered one and asked for a menu even though I knew it by heart. The Loonfeather offerings didn't change much.

"Right away," Mandy smiled at Andrew but didn't make eye contact with me.

After she left, Andrew jumped in. "I'm sorry J. It seemed like a harmless stunt." He handed me a plastic bag with the diary inside. "I was going to

195

give it to Tucker. That's why I was at that place."

I put the bag on the chair next to me and tried to choose my words carefully. "Andrew, this is more than about you taking something from my cabin, isn't it?"

He frowned as if he didn't understand what I'd just said. "I don't think so."

"Let's get this out in the open. First, you tell me you think my cabin is half yours, then you try to put it on the market, and now you're after money from Tucker for the diary." I never used to challenge him like this.

Andrew blinked, his mouth slightly open. "Uh…"

Mandy interrupted us, bringing my beer and the menu. She beamed at Andrew. "The Right Thing? Right?"

"Right-oh."

My god. He sounded just like Tucker.

I glanced at the menu and ordered a BLT on whole wheat. Whole wheat at the Loonfeather was a brownish-colored white bread. Nothing like the deli down the street in Queens. For a moment, with Andrew across the table from me, I missed it. My nostalgia disappeared as soon as Andrew uttered, "J. I'm sorry." His voice oozed with sincerity.

"Andrew, what kind of trouble are you in?"

He raised his eyebrows with a shrug. "I'm not in trouble."

I glared at him.

"Okay. Okay. So besides having my identity stolen, I might have overspent a little."

I guessed he was getting excellent pay as Mr. Right Digestion, even though he'd managed to hide it from me. "You owe someone money, don't you?"

It occurred to me that if he'd hidden his assets during the divorce, I could bring a suit against him. I didn't want revenge, though. I wanted him out of my hair.

"Ah, it's complicated."

I drummed my fingers on the table. "I doubt it. You owe money, and you need to pay it back."

"Sure. Except I borrowed the money from someone Destiny knew."

I took a deep breath and blew it out. "You got messed up with a loan shark, didn't you?"

Now I understood his desperation. "You came here hoping to get money from me to pay off the debt. When I didn't have it, you got mixed up with Tucker Fox."

Andrew finished his beer and set it down with an irritated scowl. "You always have the answer. Don't you?"

What had I read about the narcissistic personality? Egocentric and never wrong. My favorite fictional character Apple Pie would have head-butted Andrew out of the bar. I fought back a smirk as I pictured the pig taking him on.

"What?" Andrew leaned onto the table. "I needed to spend that money. You know, it's an image thing. You have to look right in my line of business."

"The green tights weren't enough?"

We were saved from an escalating quarrel when Mandy brought my BLT. It was nicely toasted, even if it wasn't up to the standards of my old Queens deli. She set it in front of me, keeping her eyes on Andrew. When she turned away, I saw her wink at him. Geez.

He greeted a few people who walked in as I ate my sandwich. He'd made himself known during the short time in town. After I finished, I pushed the plate to him so he could eat the potato chips. It was an automatic gesture from our years of marriage. He always finished the chips and the French fries.

"Tell me about Tucker. How much was he going to pay you?"

Andrew ate a handful of chips before talking. "Met him at that little bar outside of town. I found out he was an actor, and we sort of clicked. He told me about how you had a box of his cousin's diaries, and he wanted to look at one."

"You schemed with him to take one from the cabin."

He pressed his hand against his chest. "Honest, I didn't think it would be a big deal. After all, it was just a diary."

"Did he tell you why it was so important? Tucker could have simply asked me to show one to him."

"He said he thought you were in cahoots with her lawyer and trying to keep something from him."

"And you believed him?"

Andrew shrugged. Of course, he believed Tucker—especially if it meant a little money. Outside, an old pickup truck rattled down the street. I glanced out the window to see if it was Ed, but I didn't recognize the truck.

Andrew finished the chips and signaled to the bartender for another beer. "Actually, he had quite a story to tell."

"I'll bet."

Andrew raised his eyebrows. "He said his father and his uncle had a falling out years ago. They were both in his grandfather's will, but his uncle, the old lady's father, was the executor and kept the money for his hospital. He said he thought he was owed. That's why he came here from California."

None of this was new to me. "I don't understand what the diaries had to do with it. What did he say?"

"He said he wanted to see if his cousin made any mention of money in them."

Mandy brought over a beer for Andrew and reached for the plate, bumping him with her hip. She giggled, "Oops, sorry."

My ex, the chick magnet.

After she bounced away, he continued. "You know, J, there was something weird going on."

I resisted the urge to say, no kidding. "What do you mean?"

"Tucker wouldn't say much, but he told me he was coming into money very soon."

"From Miss Nella?"

He shrugged. "I got the sense it was something else. Like later on, after he'd had a few to drink, he said something about 'legal age.' Then he laughed and said, 'You know, free to roam.'"

"What? That hardly makes sense. When was this?"

He tilted his head, looking up. "About a week ago."

"Did this have anything to do with the diaries? Maybe he was looking for when Miss Nella reached legal age and inherited from her grandfather?"

"I tried to push him on it. Asked him how much money and where it was coming from. He just smiled and said, 'It's a secret, but once I have it, things are going to really roll.'"

I wondered if Andrew was spinning a tale to explain why he was so entangled with Tucker. I felt a growing impatience with Andrew because I didn't believe he was telling me the whole story.

I finished my beer. By now, it was lukewarm and flat. "Anything else strike you as odd?"

Andrew sat up straighter. "Not exactly odd, but a couple days after what happened to his sister...you know...the fall, he said he thought she might have jumped. Like suicide."

"Why did you think it was odd?"

"It was the way he said it. He sounded angry, like she'd screwed up his plans. But I wondered if he was a little scared, too."

I threw my hands up in surrender. "Andrew, this is really too much for me. My advice is to stay away from Tucker. I don't trust him." *Or you.*

This was the first time I considered Tucker might be dangerous. He could have pushed Barrett down the stairs. I was ready to say more when the expression on Andrew's face stopped me.

He glared at me with a pinched expression. "You think he pushed his sister down the stairs, don't you? Well, I'm a pretty good judge of character, and I know Tucker might have lost his temper, but he wouldn't have done it!"

I was taken aback by his vehemence. I opened my mouth to retort but closed it again. It was useless to argue with him—it always had been.

As quickly as he'd escalated, he retreated. With a boyish shrug, he apologized. "Sorry, J., it's just that you always like to act superior to me. I know Tucker. We're like partners in this theater venture. He's a great guy."

My phone pinged with a text from Jim. **I'll call you in a couple hours when out of class. Save a beer for me.**

I smiled.

Andrew pointed to the phone. "A friend?"

I didn't answer his question. After I put the phone in my bag, I said, "You should sell that shiny SUV you're driving and find your way back to New

York. The theater thing is going to fall through, and Tucker is no friend of yours."

I left him a twenty-dollar bill and walked out before he could work up more indignation. When I reached the car, I glanced back at the door of the Loonfeather. "Please," I whispered aloud. "Leave before you get hurt."

Chapter Thirty-Seven: Sorting it Out

True to his text, Jim called me that evening. I was in my sad, chewed-up little garden, wondering if I should replant or give it up. Bronte watched me with concern as I inspected what was left of leaf lettuce. "Hey," I answered, walking around the cabin to get better reception.

"How's the weather?"

"Damp, but according to my weather app, it will be sunny tomorrow." I found I was irritated that the first thing he asked about was the weather. What happened to a "how are you?"

I sat on my rock and tried to shake the tension in my shoulders. I wasn't sure how to begin with Jim. I wanted his counsel on Gooseberry Acres, but I also wanted more than "how's the weather."

He told me about his classes and the work he had to do before the final exam. "It's amazing to me the cyber trail criminals can leave."

"You mean like bank records and phone records?"

"That's part of it, but some of it is simply stupidity. Like posting on your Facebook page that you just robbed a convenience store. Or like those idiots who ransacked the capitol and posted videos of what they were doing."

"You're spending weeks in DC learning how to search Facebook? Really? I could have shown you that."

He laughed. "Okay, there are far more resources than that for digging into—money transfers, fake identities. You name it. Some people are good at covering their tracks. Others, not so much."

He went on to talk about some of the online databases law enforcement has that aren't available to the general public. I only half-listened as I tried to figure out how to tell him about Andrew. I almost missed it when he asked, "So, what's new with you?"

Oh, nothing. Possible murder, ex-husband trouble—the usual. Time to stop beating around the bush.

"Jim, my ex-husband, showed up last week. He's in some kind of trouble and was looking for money."

"Oh? He came to Killdeer? Why didn't you tell me this earlier?" His voice hardened.

"I...I don't know. I think because he was part of my old life and I simply wanted him to go away." This conversation wasn't going well.

"Is he there? At your cabin?"

"What? No! As far as I know, he's in town charming all the women as Mr. Right Digestion."

"Hmmm. You should have let me know." The phone fell silent except for a hum of traffic in the background.

Suddenly, this conversation seemed more like something out of one of the romances I edited. Jim was clearly irritated. In a way, it felt good. In a way, it felt as clichéd as some of the dialogue in the last book I'd worked on. An irrational giggle rose through my chest. I couldn't fight it, and the next thing I was laughing out loud.

"What? Why are you laughing?"

Bronte danced around as if she also saw the humor in it. "Honest to god, Jim. You are sounding jealous. I love it!"

"Well," he huffed.

The ice broke when he started to laugh, "Okay. Okay. Maybe I did sound a little...ah...put out. What does Bronte think of him?"

"She and I are pretty much on the same page." Bronte pricked up her ears. I patted her on the head and sent a stick flying for her. While she was rooting around in the woods for the stick, I told him about Andrew and the stolen diary and the death of Barrett, and all the weirdness around Gooseberry Acres. It poured out of me. Jim could hardly get a word or a question in.

"Wait," he finally commanded. "This sounds far too complex for a simple

State Trooper. Let's break it down. Start with Andrew since he's my rival."

"Hah! He's no rival, and I have papers to prove it." I related Andrew's feeble ploy to get money from me, the theft of the diary, and the confrontation about his financial woes. By the time I finished, Bronte was back with her stick and contented to settle down and chew on it at my feet.

"I like it better when your biggest stresses are bad writing and comma misplacement."

I heard a muted siren in the background as he spoke and marveled at how quiet it was here by the lake. Two loons settled on the water, looking for their evening meal. I closed my eyes to their haunting cry and wished this moment would last a little longer.

Jim interrupted my thoughts. "So, what do you think of my suggestions?"

I guess I'd tuned him out for a bit. "Ah, can you run them by me again?"

"Uh huh, ignoring me, aren't you?"

"The sound of your voice lulls me."

Perhaps our talk would have grown more romantic, except Jim's phone started to cut out. "Send...away..."

"Sorry, you're breaking up."

"You...need...involve sheriff..." The phone went dead. I tried calling back but noticed I had no bars.

"Well, Bronte, I feel better. I've confessed, and I think I'm getting all this weirdness sorted out."

I went into the cabin as the sun was setting, and the mosquitoes were headed to me for dinner. Once inside, with Bronte fed, I pulled out a legal pad and began to write down everything about Gooseberry and Miss Nella on one page and everything about Andrew on another. Best to keep them separated.

When I was done, I was struck by a couple things. First, I knew Andrew had enough charm to get himself out of his scrape. He didn't need my help. Or did he? Second, I didn't regret the divorce for a moment. Third, I was still very uneasy about my relationship with Jim. Why did I become so inarticulate when it came to talking with him about love and commitment? Was it because he wasn't Mr. Right?

"Stop it, Jamie."

Bronte sauntered over and put her head on my lap. I stroked the soft fur on the top of her head. "At least I have you, dog breath and all."

I turned to the page on Gooseberry. Several things stood out. Number one was Barrett's death. If it was murder, then who did it? Tucker might have had a motive—more inheritance for him, but if so, why had he come here with her in the first place? I made a note on the paper. *Leave this to the sheriff.* I think that's what Jim was advising.

Number two was Miss Nella and her safety. How confused and how vulnerable was she? And if she was vulnerable, what did it have to do with me? *Let Clarence deal with it.*

Number three was the project itself. I still didn't know what to do with it. Maybe I needed to stick with the one specific thing Miss Nella had asked. She wanted to find Dr. Heller's family. I tried to pull the story threads together. She'd had a baby, which Dr. Heller had delivered. The baby didn't live. Shortly after that, the doctor disappeared. There were rumors of a murder—had Dr. Fox murdered Dr. Heller for some reason? Was I going down a rabbit hole with this? After all, the disappearance occurred well over seventy years ago.

I took a deep breath and stared at my scribbling. I felt a loyalty to Miss Nella to help her tell her story. I knew I wouldn't quit the project at least until I'd gotten the information she wanted to give me and until I could be assured by Clarence that she was safe.

I had a cup of tea before crawling into bed. I expected to have a restless night trying to resolve all this information. Bronte settled into her space with a sigh as I shifted in bed, trying to find a comfortable position. When I finally fell asleep, it was deep and dreamless.

The next morning the sun came out in its May glory. If I wasn't trying to get *Apple Pie* done, I would have taken Bronte for a hike along the Lady Slipper trail. When I let her out, she seemed content chasing squirrels in the yard.

I was halfway through copyediting the book. I imagined Opal Harris, the author, as an English teacher. The punctuation and sentence structure were immaculate. In fact, she put me to shame. She should be doing the copy editing, and I should be writing poetry. The problem, as I sat back and reviewed the content of the novel, was that Apple Pie, the narrator, was too perfect, other than a bad case of road rage. I wanted him to be more human.

Considering some of the other books I'd edited, this one had the marks of a best seller. And yet, the pig wasn't human enough? I laughed out loud. Time to put it away for a while.

Since the day was so pleasant, I left my phone behind and took Bronte for a walk in the woods. I stopped in the shade of a large pine, inhaling the scents and listening to the sounds of life. Jim had once said, "The forest is never silent." I wondered if this could change with global warming. Would it send the birds away and kill the forests? My Ojibwe ancestors knew the value of mother earth and knew how she sustained them. I shuddered, thinking about how man made pollution affected even the pristine Northern Minnesota lakes. I'd read a study that found traces of microplastic in some of the remote areas of the Boundary Waters, accessible only by canoe. The researchers speculated the plastic particles were carried through the air.

I thought about New York City and pictured a soggy plastic bag in the gutter in front of our apartment building. Every time I saw it, I said I'd pick it up next time when I had gloves on. As far as I knew, the bag was still there.

I called Bronte. It was time to go back to the cabin and look at the letters in the cigar box. Maybe they would tell me something useful for Miss Nella.

Chapter Thirty-Eight: The Letters

Before I took out the cigar box, I called Clarence.

He answered after several rings. "How can I help you on this beautiful day?"

I smiled, "Who is this? Where are you hiding that cantankerous old lawyer?"

He laughed. "I just had a visit with Elena and the lovely little baby. We think we've made a breakthrough with the immigration people. I'm feeling spritely."

"Well, sprite away. I'm all for it." Elena was due for some good news. With a new federal administration, we were going back to being a kinder, gentler nation. Hopefully, Elena wouldn't spend her lifetime in fear of *La Migra*. She'd had enough trauma in her young life.

We talked about the next steps in her court case and how the baby was thriving. Elena and Joe had grown into a solid couple under Lorraine's careful watch.

"And you are calling because? Let me guess, it has something to do with Nella Fox."

I told him about the cigar box and the little bundle of letters. "Miss Nella wants to find Dr. Heller's family. I'm not sure why—she won't tell me. I'm also not sure she understands they are probably all dead. Do you know why she's so adamant about finding them?"

"She hasn't told me anything, but if I dip into that chasm that's my brain, I do recall something...." He paused, making a humming sound. "I remember my parents talking about it. There were rumors from some of the Gooseberry Acres, local staff about foul play. Of course, I understood it to be fowl play—like the birds—and couldn't figure out why a doctor would be playing with the chickens." He chuckled.

"Maybe something bad happened, and Dr. Fox tried to cover it up?"

"Nella has never talked about it. My advice is to look through the letters, do as much of a search as you can, and let it go."

"She's paying me a lot to *not* let it go."

"Find out what you can, and we'll negotiate with her." Spoken like a lawyer.

Once I was off the phone, I poured another cup of coffee and took the letters out of the box. They were all addressed to Dr. Frank Heller and written on thin stationery by his sister Josie. The blue ink on the paper had faded, and the old-fashioned cursive was sometimes hard to decipher. They were postmarked from St. Paul, Minnesota.

I took note of the address on Summit Avenue. In one of my few trips to the Twin Cities since moving to Minnesota, I'd driven on Summit. It was a tree-lined street of stately old houses built during the era of the railroad barons. Living on Summit indicated money. Now that I had an address, maybe I could trace the family.

The packet held a dozen letters. I started with the oldest. Josie wrote about her studies at Macalester College and her hopes of someday going to medical school. She lamented that medical schools were only open to men and hoped she would do well enough to insist they admit her. *"I have to be 100 times better than the boys if I want to get in."* She praised Frank for his work at Gooseberry Acres. *"Frankie, I know you are going find the cure. You are so fortunate to be practicing under Dr. Fox."*

The next several letters were more of the same, with notations about the weather and hopes the war was coming to an end. *"When the boys come home, they will need you more than ever, dear brother."*

Halfway through the stack, the letters took on a more concerned tone. *"I'm so sorry you are in conflict with Dr. Fox. You are more of a scholar than he is, and he should listen to you. I've been reading the research about the new medicine for TB, too, and you are right to want to try it."*

The last three letters were hard to read. The ink was blurred from a brown stain, perhaps coffee. I could make out a few sentences. *"...How hard to lose a child...Dr. Fox should have listened...Does he know your plan?"* I wondered if she was referring to the little girl with the doll. Had Dr. Heller suggested the new antibiotic? I thought about the stack of medical journals in the file drawer.

The last letter began, *"Oh, Frankie. I'm crying as I write. That poor girl. I remember you tried to warn Dr. Fox about that rich good-for-nothing. What did he tell you? The family had money, and he was only involved in horseplay? Turns out he had his way with poor young Nella. Rest assured, Mama and I are seeing to your request. Everything will be okay."*

I checked the date on the letter and the dates in my notebook about the disappearance of Dr. Heller. Josie had written the letter several weeks before Dr. Heller's cottage emptied. Had he enlisted his sister and mother to find a home for Nella before she had the baby?

I rubbed my temples, not knowing what to do with the information. I'd have to take this to Miss Nella. It sounded like the relationship between Dr. Heller and Dr. Fox had become contentious. Nella's pregnancy and subsequent loss of the baby probably heightened it—assuming Dr. Fox knew. But what little evidence I had in the letters indicated it went much deeper—into the medical practice and care of the patients.

At least I had an address to start searching for the Heller family. Unfortunately, I didn't have access to any research tools beyond Facebook and Google. I'd have to start there and see what I could find.

Bronte whined at the door. When I let her in, the room filled with the stink of dead fish. "Oh girl, not again. Why can't you find some Chanel to roll in instead?"

I dragged her outside to scrub her down and hose her off. When I was done, her fur was shiny and sweet smelling. "I know in your little dog brain that you can't wait to get back to the dead fish, but right now, you are confined to the cabin."

On the beach, I found the offending fish, shoveled it into a bucket, and took it to the garden. I buried it near my chewed-up tomato plant with hopes the odor would keep the deer away.

Back in the cabin, Bronte watched me warily from the living room. "No, I'm not going to shampoo you again. You're safe for now."

I glanced at the last letter from Josie and wondered how to start my search. I tried Facebook and Google but found nothing fitting the age I assumed for Josie. Checking the clippings from Nella, I entered in Alma Heller, Frank Heller's mother. An obituary came up for an Alma Schweitzer Heller of St. Paul. She'd died at age ninety. Her survivors were listed as a Josephine Heller Wilson, along with a son-in-law and one grandchild. No mention was made of Frank.

"That's strange." Bronte raised her head. "If this is the right Heller, I would think Dr. Heller would be listed. Maybe it's not the right one."

Next, I tried Facebook and Google for Josephine Heller Wilson. The hits did not fit.

"Damn. I'm not a missing person's researcher." I didn't know where else to look.

Jim saved me from swearing more at my computer when he texted. **Out of class. Can you talk?**

I hated getting messages like that. Did it mean he wanted a serious talk, or did it mean he wanted to chat?

Home. Give me a call.

When the phone rang, I was ready for him to ask about the weather. Instead, he asked, "How are you?"

"Uh..." I stuttered. "Fine, I guess."

"What's wrong?"

The muscles in my stomach tightened. "You caught me off guard. You always ask about the weather before you ask how I'm doing. I was ready to tell you about the perfection of the day."

Jim paused. "Do I really?"

"Yes."

Bronte sauntered over to me with a worried wrinkle to her brow. She sensed the tension.

Jim sounded contrite. "I'm sorry. I care more about you than whether it's raining, or the sun is shining."

This was the first time since he'd gone off to Washington, D.C., that he'd said anything about caring. Perhaps something bad was up.

"Jim, what's wrong? Why are you calling in the middle of the day?"

He cleared his throat. "Well...uh...I guess I missed you."

I clearly remembered Andrew saying something similar. Except he was trying to cover for the guilt he felt after the first time he'd slept with Destiny. I held back from blurting out, "Did you just cheat on me?" Instead, I replied. "I miss you too." *Every day and every night.*

Bronte sat next to me and lifted her paw as if to give me comfort. I heard the long sigh on the other end of the phone. "Jamie, I called because I've made a big decision."

I held my breath while the nasty voice inside my head told me, *here it comes. The break-up.*

"I...um." He paused. When he spoke, it came out in a rapid burst. "I don't want to spend the next many years behind a desk staring at a computer. I don't want to live in a city. I...I want to live in your snug little cabin by the lake."

My jaw dropped. "What? What are you saying?" I stared out the window, my heart racing, unable to speak. Two robins with bright orange chests landed in the yard and started pecking at the ground.

"Jamie? Are you there?"

"Sorry. You took me totally by surprise. What are you saying?"

The pause was so long, I checked to make sure we were still connected.

"Jamie, I'm saying I want us to be together, and now isn't soon enough."

I found I'd been holding my breath. "Wow...I mean...uh...wow."

Bronte relaxed and settled at my feet. We talked for a long time about his plans. He told me the classes had gone well, and the more he learned, the more he thought what he was learning could be useful in local law enforcement. "I heard Rick Fowler is retiring as sheriff. I thought I'd make a run for it."

I grinned, thinking about Jim as the sheriff of Jackpine County. "You know I have a reputation around here for making the sheriff look bad."

"How about if you stay out of trouble at least until I get back?"

His question reminded me of the letters on the table. "If I promise to stay out of trouble, could you do something for me while you're still there?" I told him about Miss Nella's request to find Dr. Heller's family. "I have an old, old address and possibly the married name of his sister. Do you think you could find her?"

Voices rose in the background as Jim talked. A woman called out, "Hey Jim, coffee break is over." Jim covered the phone and said something I couldn't hear. When he got back to me, he spoke in a low tone. "Let me look into it. They've mainly been training us on how to follow money trails and how to extract information stored on hard drives. I've got some good resources here, but it might be a little touchy to use them for personal reasons."

I desperately wanted to be done with Miss Nella, Tucker, and all of Gooseberry Acres. "If you get caught, tell them it's for an old lady. I'm sure they'll understand."

Before we ended the call, I said the words I'd had so much trouble saying in the past. "I love you, Jim."

I expected him to say "Ditto," but he came back with, "And I love you, Ms. Forest. Can't wait to say it in person."

After the call ended, I felt like I was floating. "What do you think, Bronte? Is there room for another person here?"

Bronte walked to the back door and scratched at it. I guess that was the only answer I could expect from her.

My euphoria lasted about twenty minutes before my phone rang.

When I answered, Miss Nella spoke in a tremulous voice, "You must come now and bring those letters. I don't have much time."

Chapter Thirty-Nine: Nella's Story

I stared with apprehension at the dead phone. The tremor in Miss Nella's voice alarmed me. What did she mean, she didn't have much time? Was she ill? Or worse, was Tucker threatening her? I almost called Clarence to alert him, but decided I was overreacting on this warm, sunny spring day.

As I drove to Gooseberry Acres, I observed how quickly everything was greening up and preparing for summer. The aspen and birch were leafing out into a brilliant canopy. How could anything bad happen on a beautiful day like this?

When I arrived at Gooseberry Acres, I saw that Nella's lawn had been newly mown. Ed must have been round to tend to it. The parking area in front of the house was empty of both Tucker's car and Ed's rusted pickup. The air filled with the smells of new grass and the sweetness of the blooming lilac bushes in front of the house.

I stood on the porch for a moment to take in the scents of the fresh air. Miss Nella called out. "Are you coming in? I don't have all day." She hardly sounded like she was in trouble.

I found her in the sitting room wearing a bathrobe and slippers. Her hair wasn't combed, and the red lipstick she wore was smeared. Thinking about the dignified woman I'd first met, I decided she wasn't well.

"Miss Nella, are you okay?"

"Humph. It took you long enough to get here."

"You...uh...don't look well."

She squinted at me. "What do you mean?"

I searched for kind words to describe her state of disarray but couldn't come up with any. "Miss Nella, you're not dressed even though it's afternoon. It doesn't look like you've combed your hair, and your appearance worries me. Is anyone caring for you?"

She glared at me. "Young lady, I won't be spoken to like that. There's nothing wrong with the way I look!"

I needed to talk with Clarence about her. Without Barrett tending to her and Tucker missing in action, I worried about her.

As if my words sank in, the glare disappeared as she blinked away tears. "You are right. I've been so confused lately. I need to get that girl from town to start coming out here again. Poor Ed. He tries, but he's just a simple soul."

I took out my phone. "Do you want me to call the girl?"

She waved me away. "Oh no. I'll see to it. Right now, we need to talk before that man comes back." She pointed upstairs, "He's pestering and pestering, just like his sister. Why did they have to come and disturb everything?"

"Are you afraid of Tucker?"

"What? No. He's like a horsefly buzzing around my head. And he's eating me out of house and home. Always asking for grocery money. You'd think we were feeding an army."

I pictured all the cans he'd unloaded the other day. Most were convenience foods, like Hormel Chili and SpaghettiOs. He'd also purchased snack foods—the kind that are either too salty or too sweet. Tucker was clearly not much of a cook. But was he a threat to Miss Nella?

I asked her again, "Does Tucker scare you?"

She shook her head. "Posh! No. He's not the one to be feared."

I sat down on the sofa next to her and leaned close. She smelled of old skin, talcum powder, and unwashed hair. "Miss Nella, who are you afraid of?"

She stared beyond me as if someone was at the door. "Ghosts, my dear. Ghosts of all the bad things I have done. I think those two woke up the ghosts." She waved her hand at the hospital. "Sometimes I hear noises, and sometimes I think I see the ghosts."

My phone dinged with a text. Miss Nella pointed to it. "Better see who that is. These phones are such a nuisance, aren't they? I remember when we had to call the operator to get connected. In fact, our home phone was on a party line. Imagine that! We could listen in on other's conversations."

I checked the text. It was from Andrew. **Wanna have supper J. Call me.**

I slipped the phone back in my bag and smiled at Miss Nella. "It's nothing important. Maybe we should get to work."

Handing her the cigar box, I told her I had some questions.

Miss Nella took it from me. "I remember Nanny Ninny kept that box for a long time. I didn't know what was in it until you showed me yesterday. Have you read the letters?"

"They're from Dr. Heller's sister, Josie."

Miss Nella reached in and took an envelope. "She was such a nice person. Dr. Heller used to talk about her—his little sister. He said she wanted to be a doctor. I wonder if she did." She was silent for a moment. "He haunts me, sometimes. He had the nicest smile and the gentlest hands. In a way, I was in love with him."

"Miss Nella, why does he haunt you? Did something bad happen to him?"

She furrowed her brow. "I suppose it's time to tell someone. I killed him, of course." She took off her glasses and dabbed at her eyes.

It felt like the house shuddered with her words. In the kitchen, the refrigerator snapped on and began to hum. Outside, a flock of crows created a cacophony of noise.

She must have meant metaphorically. I couldn't see Miss Nella murdering anyone. "What do you mean, you killed him?"

I set my phone on record and took out my notebook.

Her eyes widened, and she dropped the envelope. "Down the stairs. I pushed him down the stairs. They all knew, but they kept it quiet. It was wrong…." She lapsed into silence as I tried to make sense of her words.

"You mean here?" I pointed to the doorway.

She scowled, pointing in the direction of the hospital. "No. No. No. There! I need to tell them he was a good man and a good doctor. He didn't disappear. We buried him."

With a few prompts from me, the story—the grave secret—finally came

214

out. According to Miss Nella, the relationship between Dr. Fox and Dr. Heller deteriorated prior to when he died. As she put it, "Papa was old school. He felt the surgeries, the fresh air, and good nutrition was the key to curing TB. Dr. Heller was keen on trying this new drug called Streptomycin. Papa would have none of it."

She shifted in her chair and took a deep breath. "By the time I had my troubles, Dr. Heller was talking about leaving—except he'd signed a contract. He was also complaining to Papa about the laxness of supervision with some of the patients who were convalescing." She turned to me. "He was right, you know. But Papa was worried about money and didn't want to chase patients away."

I thought we were finally getting to the heart of the secrets. "I didn't know money was an issue."

"Oh yes. You see, Papa wasn't a good businessman. He trusted Uncle Judd and Uncle Judd...well, he had his hand in the till. No doubt about it."

Money, professional disagreements, and now a pregnant daughter. No wonder Dr. Heller's sister Josie picked up on the tension here.

"Papa was gone, you know, when I had the baby. He said he was at a medical conference, but he was really meeting with bankers, I think. I was so sick after the baby came that Dr. Heller and Nanny Ninny, now Matron McEnany, took care of me in the hospital."

She took a deep breath, and when she spoke again, her voice had a tremor to it. "They wouldn't let me see the baby or hold her. Said she was born dead. They swept her away from me." She looked up at the ceiling as if in prayer. "Sometimes I imagine her as a little girl in a pink dress. And then I look down at my arms, and they're empty."

She folded her arms as if she was holding a baby. "You see, I wasn't well that night." She relaxed her arms. "When I heard them arguing in the back stairway, it was as if my bed was trying to swallow me up. I was cold and hot, and the shadows danced around me. I even saw the little girl with the doll—except she had no eyes." She shivered. "She walked right into my room holding her doll."

"I wanted Papa to make her go away. I even called out to him, but he didn't hear me. He never listened to me. They kept arguing and arguing. I didn't know what they were saying at first. I was so scared."

I pictured her at sixteen, alone in the hospital room, and held back a desire to grab her hand. Miss Nella's voice had taken on a singsong quality to it, as if she was trying to ward off the images in her head.

"I...I don't really remember doing it. Suddenly I was there, on the landing, and I wanted the voices to stop. I didn't want Papa to accuse Dr. Heller of being the father. I didn't want Dr. Heller to accuse Papa of being a bad father and a bad doctor. I just wanted it to stop!"

She clutched her hands to her chest. A sheen of perspiration had broken out on her forehead. I reached over and touched her arm. "Miss Nella, are you okay? You don't have to go on."

She squinted at me as if she'd forgotten I was in the room. An odd little smile crossed her lips. "I stopped them all right. I must have. I remember screaming and pushing at them, and I remember some crashing sounds and some cries, but that was all. When I woke up later, I was in bed, and Papa was holding my hand, telling me it was all right and they'd taken care of it."

I closed my eyes, trying to piece this all together. "Miss Nella, did you push Dr. Heller down the stairs?"

She didn't reply. Instead, she closed her eyes, and her hands relaxed and fell to her lap.

It made sense now. Dr. Fox would do anything to protect his daughter. I thought about the unmarked grave with the dried flowers. They'd kept this secret all these years from the Heller family. They must have buried Dr. Heller in the cemetery. I recalled what Rob had told me about his mother's experience here. She'd talked about a fresh grave. Others must have suspected. That's where the ghost stories came from.

I rubbed my forehead. I needed to talk with Clarence as soon as possible. Could Miss Nella be charged with murder after all these years? In that moment, I felt the blood draining from my head. Barrett had died after falling down the stairs. Did Miss Nella have the capacity to find her and shove her?

"Oh man," I whispered as I turned off my phone recorder. "What have I gotten into?"

As if to make it worse, Tucker's car pulled up with a roar. I needed to escape and consult with Clarence. More than anything, I wanted off this property.

Chapter Forty: Consultation with Clarence

Tucker swayed as he approached the porch. He wore a sloppy grin and carried a bag of groceries. "Hey ho, how are you?"

I was not interested in talking with him. I brushed by with a curt, "Tucker. Looks like you could use some sleep."

"Right-oh."

Before I could drive away, Ed came walking down the road from his trailer. He carried his hunting rifle and a paper bag. I should have told him to watch over Miss Nella. I should have told him Tucker was drunk. Instead, I started the car, put it in gear and drove away. My hands trembled as they gripped the steering wheel. Miss Nella's story and the image of Dr. Heller in his Harry Potter glasses tumbling down the stairs morphed into the image of Barrett at the bottom of the stairs.

I took several deep breaths before pulling out onto the highway and considered my options. I could write up what Miss Nella had said, find a descendant of Dr. Heller, and be done with it. Yet, Barrett's broken body kept interfering with my plans to make the memoir short and not-so-sweet.

When I parked in front of Clarence's house, the sun poured through the trees, dappling the lawn. It was newly mowed like Miss Nella's, but the scent of the cut grass seemed purer and crisper.

Lorraine answered the door. She had on an old-fashioned apron and was wiping her hands when she let me in. "This is a surprise. He just got up from his nap, so he's still a bit of a grump."

I asked how she was doing with Elena and the baby. Her cheeks glowed when she answered. "They are both beautiful. I'll be so sad when she and Joe get married. I love the smell of new baby in the house."

My mind wasn't on new baby smells and young couples in love. I forced a smile and pointed to the kitchen. "Is he in there?"

"He finished his coffee, so he should be presentable."

Clarence wrinkled his brow when I sat down. "You seem rather bothered."

"I'm on the verge of turning in my resignation from any assignment coming from you." I took out my phone. "You need to listen to this."

Without further explanation, I played the recording of Miss Nella. Her voice was more childlike than I had noticed when I'd recorded her.

Lorraine leaned against the counter, arms folded and her eyes narrowed. When Miss Nella got to the point where she described the little girl with no eyes, she slipped into a kitchen chair.

When it was finished, we all sat in silence. Lorraine had a stunned expression while Clarence simply looked thoughtful. Hearing it the second time again brought another chill down my back.

I broke the silence. "Clarence, I don't know what to do with this."

He stroked his chin. "Hmmm..."

Lorraine fidgeted with the dish towel in her hands. "So sad." She stood up abruptly. "I think I will leave this up to you two. I need to get home. Just pop the hotdish in the oven for supper tonight."

Clarence watched as she hurried out of the room. After she left, he commented, "Lorraine doesn't like stories with sad endings. Her marriage was that way—a sad ending."

I realized I didn't know much about Lorraine other than her amazing cooking and her generosity in taking Elena and the baby in last winter. This was not the time to ask, however.

The kitchen clock ticked away, punctuating the eerie quiet that had settled into the kitchen. Finally, Clarence leaned back. "Well, that explains some things."

"You knew something like this had happened?"

He raised his eyebrows. "I'm not that smart. I always wondered why she wouldn't sell the place. I'm guessing she didn't want to risk having that grave dug up."

I pictured her as a sixteen-year-old, alone and ill, having lost her baby. Was it possible, in her confusion, she thought these things happened when they didn't? I'd once fact-checked an article about postpartum depression and post-partum psychosis. What Miss Nella thought was real might not have been. I explained it to Clarence.

"Maybe it's not that simple. Maybe she dreamed it all up. Maybe Dr. Heller left in a huff over disagreements with Dr. Fox about the treatment, and Miss Nella made it into a story that wasn't real." Yet, the cigar box had contained the broken glasses. I remembered the expression on Miss Nella's face when she'd held the twisted frames up.

Clarence frowned. "I think what she said was real. What I wonder is if she accidentally pushed the wrong man down the stairs."

"Oh my. Are we talking a botched patricide?"

Shaking his head, Clarence picked at the blueberry muffin on the plate in front of him. "I've seen a lot of things in my practice. From what I've heard, Dr. Fox was not an easy man to get along with. He was of an old-fashioned authoritarian background."

Again, the room fell still as I thought about motivations for murder. In *Apple Pie a´la Murder,* the wise pot-bellied pig had said murder happened for money, love, jealousy, or power. Thinking about Miss Nella, I added insanity. Or did it happen because of money?

"Miss Nella said in the recording that her father was talking with bankers about finances. I thought you said he was well-off."

Clarence brushed a pile of crumbs from his lap. "Miss Nella is in good financial shape, but her father was not—at least when he died. She'd inherited 3M stock from her grandfather and managed it wisely. Dr. Fox, on the other hand, put all his inheritance into the hospital."

"Maybe a source of conflict? Would he ask for her money?"

He shook his head. "From what Nella has told me, her money was held in a trust until she reached the age of twenty-five. If she was sixteen when it happened, I doubt she was involved in any financial conflict."

"Maybe he took his brother Judd's inheritance. Tucker thought he was owed."

Clarence shrugged. "I guess it's possible. Since I was a youngster when all of this supposedly happened, I wasn't privy to the arrangements." He paused, "Although I do vaguely recall something my father said—something about a financial scandal related to Gooseberry Acres. I wasn't much interested at the time, especially since I didn't know what the word scandal meant. Plus, my mother once again caught me with my ear to the keyhole, as they say."

I finished my coffee and gazed up at the ceiling. "I don't know what to do with this information. Are we talking about an old, unsolved murder?"

Clarence's expression grew thoughtful. "Right now, all we have are the ramblings of an elderly lady and no body. I think at this point, you need to let Nella decide what she wants to do."

"That would mean going back to Gooseberry Acres. I'm not one to believe in spirits, but that place is haunted."

"Maybe haunted by bad memories."

I didn't say the words that floated through my head. *Not bad memories. Evil.* Although I loved and respected Clarence, I wasn't totally comfortable with his advice to let Miss Nella decide. It didn't seem right to ask the alleged murderer whether she wanted her own crime investigated. However, I did agree these were simply ramblings at this point.

Clarence glanced up at the clock. "Looks like it's time for me to do that Facebook thing. Did you know I found a law school classmate who's still alive and practicing—or malpracticing. We're doing that messaging thing."

I pictured Clarence hunched over the computer typing with two fingers. "Oh, that reminds me, I asked Jim to check into the Heller family and see if he can trace them."

Clarence's eyes had an extra little glint to them. "And how is your Jim? Still stuck in DC?"

"Home soon." I didn't want to elaborate. If I said it out loud, I might jinx his plans to come back here and run for sheriff.

Clarence groaned as he got out of the chair. "I'm going to see if anyone likes me on Facebook."

I walked beside him as he limped down the hallway. "Clarence, I sense you know something about Miss Nella that you aren't telling me. Am I wrong?"

He kept walking. "I have some things to muse upon before I answer your question."

"You mean lawyer-client privilege?"

He looked at me with a grim smile. "Perhaps you should take a little break from Gooseberry Acres until I review my files."

The tone of his voice sent that little spider crawling up the back of my neck.

"I'm not sure I want to abandon Miss Nella after she revealed her haunting secret—especially with Tucker still hanging around."

Clarence replied, "Now, onto the netherworld of the internet."

I was dismissed.

Once home, I grabbed a beer and walked out to my rock. I had a lot to think about, including Jim's phone call. While I was imagining what it would be like to have him around all the time, my phone pinged with a text. It was from Andrew. I'd completely forgotten his text from the afternoon.

R U there?

Sighing, I texted back. **Sorry busy.**

Wanna have dinner?

I took another swallow of the beer. It felt fizzy and refreshing going down. **No.** With that, I switched off the phone. Andrew was not my concern right now. Or so I thought.

Chapter Forty-One: Distress Call from Andrew

As if the goddess of the skies sensed my sour mood regarding Gooseberry Acres, the next day dawned gray and rainy. I was learning that spring in Northern Minnesota was a fickle season. One day, it was sunny, and I considered going for a swim off my beach. The next, I had to fight with myself not to turn the furnace back on.

Huddled in the kitchen wearing a t-shirt, a turtleneck, and a hoodie, I gave up and turned up the thermostat. Despite what Jilly had said about being Minnesota-tough, I decided to be a New York City girl who hated the cold.

"I can turn the furnace on when it's below sixty-two degrees, even if it's the Fourth of July. To heck with conserving propane and being a Northwoods pioneer." Bronte must have agreed because she settled in front of the heat duct in the living room.

I decided I would spend the gray, foggy morning reading Miss Nella's diaries. I arranged them in chronological order after the one with the torn-out pages. I was surprised, considering the trauma she'd gone through after she lost the baby, by how superficial they were. I thought she'd refer to it or the horror of Dr. Heller's death. It caused me to wonder once again if what she'd told me was her imagination and not the true story.

She chronicled leaving Gooseberry for college and coming back after her four years. Her notes about college were sketchy and mainly talked about the weather, the shabbiness of the dorms, and her classes. She made no mention of a boyfriend or of having any interest in men. If she did the usual college partying, she didn't talk about it. I sensed a careful reserve in her writing, a need to keep her day-to-day life superficial.

The only thing that stood out was the interest she took in business. She was one of only three women in her economics class. She complained when she tried to enroll in a business finance class, and her advisor, described as a large, sweaty man with acne scars, told her, *"I don't think this is the right class for you. If you want to study business, you should go to secretarial school and learn dictation." I came as close as I ever had to throwing the paperweight on his desk at him!*

She also followed the stock market. I found it strange for a young coed to be so concerned with the ups and downs of the New York Stock Exchange. Perhaps this had to do with worry about her father and his financial situation.

At one point, she lamented, *I can't find any friends to talk with about economics and finance. All the girls go on and on about the boys, and all the boys look at me as if I am crazy when I bring it up.*

Times had certainly changed, but I guessed Miss Nella was stuck in a culture that still had women staying home as housewives and mothers. In fact, she did write in her junior year, *"they expect me to finish college and either get married or become a teacher. I'm not interested in marriage, and I don't like children! Little Punky cured me of that!"*

By noon, my eyes ached from reading her cursive. My notebook was blank. It was clear Miss Nella didn't fit in. Perhaps if I continued with this project, we could talk about what it was like to try to be an independent woman in the 1950s and 1960s before the advent of women's liberation. In truth, I didn't think that's what Miss Nella was looking for. Her story about the stairway was an opening to something deeper.

Outside it continued to drizzle. I stood up, stretched, and decided despite the rain, I needed fresh air. Bronte raised her head from where she was napping.

"Want to go for a walk, girl?"

She trotted to the door with enthusiasm until I opened it, and she saw the drizzly mist.

"Listen, you're a lab of some sort. You like water, right?" She gazed back at me as if to say, "It's cold, it's wet, and you're crazy."

I pulled on my rain boots and a yellow slicker. Once out in the fresh air, Bronte leapt off the back step and dashed to her place in the woods. The rain released even more of the spring fragrance. I inhaled through my nose, enjoying the aroma of fresh lake water, greening trees, moss, and pine. If I could capture it, I might have a fragrance more bracing than Christian Dior's Ambre Nuit.

We walked all the way to the mailboxes. Another manuscript was crammed in, along with the loan bill for my new furnace and my property tax statement. I tucked them all under my raincoat. As we walked back, the misty rain turned into actual raindrops. Halfway back to the cabin, it began to pour. Bronte dashed ahead, abandoning me in her haste to get to the door. As I splashed through the puddles, it occurred to me that whatever had happened to Miss Nella when Dr. Heller disappeared, she'd buried it deep. What had triggered her desire to unbury it now? Maybe the latest diaries held a clue.

I had no experience in psychology or psychoanalysis, but it seemed to me her need to tell the story was related to Tucker and Barrett showing up. Why? Did it have to do with inheritance? Or perhaps a fear they would discover something before she had a chance to tell her version?

At the door, I grabbed Bronte's collar. I didn't want her tracking mud all over the floor. "Whoa, girl. You can come in, but you need your muddy paws wiped first." Once inside, I commanded her to sit on the door mat while I grabbed a towel and wiped her down. We were both drenched.

In the midst of taking off my wet raincoat and boots, my phone pinged with a text. I ignored it until I was dry enough to not drip water into the kitchen. The text was from Jim.

Found your Heller family.

I replied, **wow that was quick!**

Will email information. Now back to class Can't wait to graduate!

I pictured him at 6'2" with his rugged, outdoor complexion wearing a

225

graduation gown and nothing underneath. Oh dear, it really had been too long.

I unwrapped the manuscript to find a letter from the author. This was her first historical romance, and she'd worked on it for ten years. She needed help with the plot development and the steamy scenes. My mind went back to Jim and what might be under his graduation gown. I shook my head and set the manuscript aside.

"I think I need a cold shower."

Bronte settled on her rug in the living room, ignored me.

After lunch, I sorted through the last of the pile of diaries and picked up the newest. It was written in the late 1960s. If she had more, she hadn't chosen to share them with me.

She was nearing forty years old by then. It started in January with her usual description of the weather. *Below zero for New Year's Day. Worried about the water pipes in the hospital since Papa doesn't want to heat the building much. Maybe Ed should drain them.*

It told me Ed, the caretaker, was around back then.

My resolution for this year is to entirely close the place down and stop listening to Papa's dreams about turning it into a resort/spa. What nonsense! It's been five years since we had a patient, and Papa sits looking out the window as if waiting for them to return. I can't tell him this, but I'm glad to have it over with.

I jotted down a question about when the hospital closed. Checking the previous diaries, I found the one from 1962. Maybe that would tell me about the closure.

She hadn't written anything until March, when she noted a huge snowstorm that blocked them in for several days. *It's too hard to keep this place going with so few patients. Papa and Nanny Ninny insist more will come, but treatment for TB is now in the community. Sanatoriums all over are closing or turning into nursing homes. What we have here isn't needed anymore. They won't listen to me! Thank goodness we were finally plowed out. The three patients we have were scared, especially when the electricity went out, and the generator couldn't keep the building warm enough. Tired of this and their fantasies!*

I read several more pages of entries talking about the weather and the spring thaw that brought mud and potholes to the drive. In June, she wrote about the disaster. *They must have come in the middle of the night—the hooligans! Set four of the cottages on fire. Thank God they were all empty. Burned them to the ground. Now that Nanny Ninny and Punky live in our house, they didn't hear anything either. I worry about what Halloween might bring. Good thing Punky has his rifle.*

In the rest of the journal, Miss Nella was preoccupied with assessing the damage, working with insurance, and trying to convince her father not to look at rebuilding. In late September, she wrote about saying goodbye to the last patient. *At last, I watched as Papa shook the hand of Mr. Turner when he bid him goodbye. I think he had a tear in his eye, knowing the hospital was now closed. I'm so relieved. After all of this, I'd like to burn the place down. Maybe one of the vandals will do it for me!*

I set the diary aside and sat quietly, thinking about Miss Nella and a lifetime of living on the grounds of a hospital. It was clear she wanted out of it, yet here she was now, more than fifty years later, still living by the wreck of the old sanatorium. Why had she stayed?

I searched the final diary for an answer but found nothing. It appeared Doctor Fox had suffered several strokes, and Virginia McEnany was still living in the residence and caring for him. Her last entry was dated mid-November. *Papa laid to rest. Now I have to deal with the McEnany problem. Will it never end?*

McEnany problem? I made a note to ask Miss Nella, although I wasn't sure she'd tell me.

I gathered the diaries and put them back in the box. Tomorrow, I would take them to Gooseberry Acres.

In the meantime, I needed to finish *Apple Pie* and send it off. I'd neglected my favorite pot-bellied pig long enough.

The text from Andrew came in the early evening as the sun was dropping behind Bear Island. The clouds had cleared, and the sunset had a reddish brilliance to it. Red sky in the evening, sailor's delight. Tomorrow should be a better day.

Stranded. Things weird. Can you come get me? Tucker not

answering.

What? I stared at the message. Was this some kind of a joke? Was he that desperate to see me? Enough of this texting. I called him. When he answered, there was so much noise in the background I had to yell into the phone.

"Andrew, wherever you are, step outside."

It took a few moments as he moved to the door. "Oh, J. Sorry. It's just that Tucker was supposed to bring my car back, and he hasn't come, and I can't reach him. I'm stranded."

"Where are you?" My voice rose in irritation.

"Tink's Bar. You know, outside of town."

I silently swore. "You want me to pick you up at Tink's?"

"I need to get my car back. Tucker has it at that Gooseberry Place."

He sounded desperate. I restrained myself from either ending the call or demanding he call one of his local women to help him out. With a long, whistling sigh, I replied. "Okay, I'll come."

"J, you are a lifesaver."

I ended the call without responding.

How could it be that I'd end up haunted by an abandoned hospital and an ex-husband? Where were all the women he was charming? Why pick on me? Of course, I knew why. I always rescued him. It seemed like it was in my blood.

Chapter Forty-Two: Missing Tucker

Bronte paced in the kitchen as I grabbed my bag and phone. I threw in a small flashlight, because the battery on my phone was low, and I didn't have a charger that worked in my twenty-year-old Escape. I remembered how Jim had suggested I get one and how I'd decided it was a luxury I didn't need. Not a good decision.

At the last minute, I knelt by Bronte. "I know you're worried. Would you like to come along?" The thought of driving after dark to Tink's Bar, quite frankly, gave me goosebumps. I'd never been there, but my state trooper friends referred to it as the place for stupid, drunk, and armed idiots. Jilly once told me she could always tell when the unemployment checks came in by how full the parking lot was at Tink's.

Bronte sat watching me as I walked to the door. "Well, then. Come on!" She pricked up her ears and nearly bowled me over as she scrambled to get out. It was dark by now, with the stars twinkling in a bright array. I had my dog and the beautiful nightfall. What could possibly go wrong?

My phone pinged before I made it down the driveway. **Plz hurry. Not a good vibe!**

When I stopped to get on the highway, I answered. **Coming**

Thinking back on the years we'd been married, I could count a number of instances where I had to hurry to the subway at some ridiculous hour to rescue Andrew. Once, a strange woman called me to say that he'd asked her to call because he'd been mugged after a performance at an obscure little theater in the Meatpacking District. When I arrived, I found him sitting outside the stage door so drunk he could hardly walk. It took what seemed like hours to find a taxi to take us home. Meantime, he'd thrown up all over his pants and kept mumbling, "J. J., you are so wunnerful. So sorry." His phone and wallet were still in his jacket, and the strange woman was nowhere to be found. Later, after the divorce, I found out from a fellow cast member that he'd been drinking with the stage manager, had sex with her, and had gotten stupidly drunk.

"I hope he isn't drunk again." Bronte pawed my thigh at the sound of my voice. Such an adventure for her.

The fog started to roll in, obscuring the beauty of the night as soon as we turned onto the highway. It thickened with every mile. Once I was through Killdeer, I had to slow down so I wouldn't miss the bar. I knew it was just outside of town. I kept an eye on the odometer to make sure I didn't drive past it. Bronte sensed my growing tension, letting out a whimper when I had to brake suddenly as something crossed my path.

I reached over and patted her. "It's okay. Just some creature of the night." I sounded more assured than I felt. As careful as I was, I almost missed the place because the neon sign was so obscured by the fog. Several lights were out, and Tink's Bar became Ink Bar. As a writer, I should have appreciated the irony, but I wasn't in the mood.

The rutted gravel parking lot was about half full. Tucker's car sat partway out of a parking spot as if it had died just as he'd backed it out. I pulled in next to it and sat for a moment. I wasn't excited about walking into the bar. Several motorcycles were lined up near the entrance, and most of the rest of the vehicles were pickup trucks. Definitely not a yuppie hangout.

Bronte pawed at my lap. "Okay, girl, you stay here. If I'm not out in five minutes, go get the cavalry." She licked the back of my hand as if she understood.

Even before I reached the door, I felt the thumping of the bass from the music inside. I hoped Andrew was waiting right by the door. If my phone hadn't been so low on battery, I would have texted him to meet me outside. As it was, at least I had enough juice to call 9-1-1 if necessary.

A bulletin board outside the door was filled with fliers about fishing contests, cars for sale, and a few real estate listings for trailers. Tacked up next to a photo of a rusted pickup truck was the poster for the missing Talbot Smithers from Camp Six. I glanced at it. His birthday was next week. Those poor parents, their child turning eighteen and probably at the bottom of the lake. That part of the county was cursed. I wondered if the sheriff's office had been contending with people trampling all over trying to find him and claim the reward. At least they'd left Miss Nella and Gooseberry Acres alone.

I pushed the battered wooden door open. Once inside, I was assaulted by a wall of noise. Scanning the crowd of mostly men, I recognized several who had attended a county commissioner meeting last summer when we were trying to stop a mining operation from destroying the lakes. They'd spoken up about the need for jobs. It had not been a friendly encounter. One of them glowered at me and quickly turned to his friend.

Under my breath, I muttered, "Andrew, damn it, where are you?"

As more of the men looked at me, I took a deep breath and pushed my way to the bartender. He had to lean over the bar to hear me. "Have you seen the guy who plays 'Mr. Right Digestion?'"

He nodded toward the bathroom. "In there."

I was torn between waiting at the bar and fleeing. How long before someone sidled up to me? I felt like I was in the middle of a badly written Western, and soon the fights would break out, and the chairs would go flying. Instead, the men who had been staring at me returned to their beer and their buddies. No one was particularly interested. Minnesota Nice, I guess.

Andrew emerged from the bathroom with a grim set to his mouth. When he reached me, he leaned close to my ear. I smelled the beer on his breath. "Let's get the hell out of here. I've got a bad vibe about this place."

I almost laughed as we made our way out. No one was paying any attention to us. We were hardly a blip on their radar.

Bronte growled when Andrew opened the door. I shooed her into the backseat. After I started the car, I sat with it in park. Turning to Andrew, I demanded, "What was all the drama? I thought you were being held up or about to be beaten up. Looked to me like no one even noticed you were there."

He shrugged. "I guess I just got spooked. You know, stuck with no car and all."

As we drove back to town and caught the highway north to Gooseberry, he explained. "Last night Tucker and I met here. When his car wouldn't start, I offered to drive him back to that hospital place. He talked me into dropping me off where I was staying and taking the car. I know I shouldn't have let him, but I was…uh…probably not real fit to drive."

"You were drunk."

He shrugged like a little kid. "I guess. Anyway, the plan was for him to bring it back here to Tink's, except he never showed up when he was supposed to. And he isn't answering his phone or texts."

"Andrew, this sounds like an amazingly hair-brained plan, even for you." I shook my head. "How did you get to Tink's today?"

Andrew mumbled. "I have my resources."

"Then why didn't you call your 'resources' now?"

"Ah…I guess they were busy."

I didn't say it out loud, but I speculated that Jeanine had finally had enough of Mr. Right Digestion.

"Do you know why Tucker hasn't been answering?" I kept the car at forty because of the dense fog.

Andrew peered ahead, slow to answer.

A number of scenarios raced through my head. Tucker was still sleeping it off. Tucker had absconded with Andrew's car and was on his way back to California. Or…something had actually happened to him. I didn't see Tucker leaving until he got his hands on whatever he thought Nella owed him and whatever other scheme he was involved in.

When he spoke, he sounded puzzled. "J, something was off about him yesterday."

"What do you mean?"

"He was, like, antsy to get back to that place. He said he discovered a voicemail message from his sister and needed to check it out."

"Voicemail? But she died over a week ago."

"I guess he hadn't checked his messages."

With the darkness and the fog, the trees that lined the highway looked like giant walls, holding us in. "Do you know what it was that Tucker found out?"

"He wasn't specific, but he said his sister was in the old hospital when she called and that she'd found something."

"Was he going to look for it?"

Andrew let out a weary sigh. "I don't know. I just want my car back. It's the only thing I own right now. I hope he didn't crash it or something. Then I wouldn't have anything."

"Hmmm…" As usual, Andrew brought the conversation back to himself.

With the fog, it was hard to tell where I was. I didn't realize I'd driven past the entrance to Gooseberry until truck coming the other direction lit up the road. Maybe it was a message that I should keep on driving. I slowed to a stop, put the car in reverse, and backed up. When I turned onto the rutted drive, Bronte yipped once and then sat very still. "What do you sense, girl?"

Through the blanket of fog, the old hospital stood like a dark monolith in the landscape. I made out a dim light from the residence, and as I neared, I saw Andrew's silver SUV parked in front of the house.

"Looks like he's still here."

Andrew grunted in disgust. "At least he could have returned my calls."

Tucker was probably in the house, sound asleep in bed. Once I parked next to the SUV, Andrew sat with a stony expression. He made no effort to get out of the car when I unbuckled my seat belt. "I'll wait here. I don't want to scare the old lady."

Typical of him to let me do all the work. At this point, I didn't care. I simply wanted out of this estate. I didn't reply.

Bronte scrambled over the seat on the driver's side and followed me to the porch. I pointed to her, "You stay."

Inside, the house was quiet. A soft light shown in the hallway from Miss Nella's sitting room. I walked in, calling, "Miss Nella, it's Jamie. I'm looking for Tucker."

Miss Nella's chin was on her chest. As I neared, I saw the gentle rise and fall of her chest as she slept. I gently shook her. "Miss Nella. I'm looking for Tucker."

Slowly she opened her eyes. "Nanny, is that you? I've had a bad dream. I can't find my baby doll."

"It's Jamie. Remember? I'm working on your memoirs?"

Her head snapped up. "What? What are you doing here?"

I squatted close to her. "I'm looking for Tucker."

She blinked. "Oh, that bothersome man. Just like the woman. I told her all the papers were in the hospital. Papa gave what he could to Judd for years. I had to put a stop to it after Papa died. I wish he'd stop asking for more." She pointed towards the door. "I told Ed I wanted him gone. Has he left yet?"

I had no idea what she was talking about. "Miss Nella, did he go over to the hospital?"

She folded her arms. "I don't know, and I don't care. There's nothing more for him."

I knew I didn't have time to sort out what she was telling me. "Miss Nella, can I check upstairs to see if Tucker is there?"

"Go. Do what you have to do."

I quickly ran up the stairs flipping on lights. Miss Nella's fluffy robe was folded over an easy chair in the first bedroom. The bed was made, and the room had an air of military tidiness. In contrast, the next room looked like someone had gone through the drawers. Several were half-open with clothes spilling out. A scrap of paper lay on the bed.

I picked it up. The writing appeared to be feminine. *Need to find the other Fox.*

"What?"

Outside, Bronte began to bark. I left the paper on the bed, and I hurried to the last room. It smelled of dirty sheets and unwashed clothes. Tucker's bed was unmade, an open suitcase on top. A flier about the missing Talbot was next to the suitcase.

I stared at it, wondering how the missing boy was connected to Tucker. Shaking my head, I turned to the dresser. Andrew's key fob was on the dresser, along with Tucker's wallet. It looked like he was getting ready to leave. I grabbed the fob.

"Tucker? Where are you?" My stomach roiled, and for a moment, I felt light-headed. The spider on the back of my neck was back.

Chapter Forty-Three: The Fire

I knew. *I knew* Tucker was in trouble. I didn't know why or how, but the voice inside my head told me I needed to go back to that dreaded hospital.

Once I was outside, I hurried to my car. Andrew sat in the passenger seat, his head tilted back, and his eyes closed. I opened the door and shook him. "I'm going after Tucker." I pointed to the hospital. "I think he's in trouble. You can come or not." I grabbed the flashlight and phone from my bag.

He responded with a groan. I didn't wait to see if he would come. Bronte chased after me as I ran to the hospital. The front door was open.

"Stay, girl. This isn't a place for you." She ignored me and followed. Once inside the building, I stopped to listen. Bronte paced next to me as I stood in the inky darkness. As my eyes adjusted, I thought I saw moving shadows. Bronte was the first to hear it—a haunting low moan. I stiffened, remembering all the talk about the ghosts that roamed the old hospital. Bronte growled and headed into the midnight black of the corridor towards the back staircase.

I turned on the flashlight and followed her. Near the door to the staircase, I stopped and swept the room with the flashlight. In the silence, nothing appeared different than before, but something felt wrong. The exit door was partway open, the way I'd left it the last time I was here. Bronte barked and slipped in.

"Bronte," I called. "Stay with me." Her nails clicked on the staircase as she scrambled up. Her barking grew more frantic.

"Bronte!" I ran to the door. Pointing the flashlight up, I saw she had stopped on the landing—the same landing where I'd found the blood. The hair was up on the back of her neck as she pawed at something on the landing. I rushed up, missing a step and almost falling. *Slow down, Jamie. Slow down.*

Tucker lay on the bare wood, his leg splayed at a funny angle. Congealed blood covered the side of his face. An old medical file lay next to him.

"Tucker, can you hear me?"

He groaned and pointed up. "He's there. Scared me... like a ghost. Thought he'd gone... before I could collect...Someone else, too."

Bronte lifted her head and bared her teeth. I pointed the flashlight to the top of the stairs but saw nothing. This was not the time to figure out what Tucker was trying to say.

"I'm calling 9-1-1 now, Tucker. It looks like your leg might be broken."

His eyes widened. "Get me out. Please. This...this...a bad place."

Scrabbling noises came from upstairs. They might have been footsteps, or they might have been the noises of an animal like a squirrel. Bronte let out a deep bark and dashed up the stairs.

"Bronte! No!"

I fumbled with the phone. The signal was weak, and when I hit the emergency button, it wouldn't ring. "Please answer!"

I tried again, and nothing happened. Where was Andrew when I needed him? I heard Bronte's bark coming from the second floor. I might have also heard a cry. For a moment, I felt paralyzed. Go up the stairs and find my dog or down the stairs to get help? I snapped out of it when her bark grew louder. Bronte would have to take care of herself. I needed to get help. Tucker was in trouble, and I smelled a faint odor of smoke. What had Tucker said? He's there? I hoped I wasn't leaving Bronte to deal with a ghost.

"Bronte, forgive me," I whispered, running back down the stairs. Racing through the darkness of the old building, I felt a sting in my eyes. Smoke or fear? I couldn't tell which. When I emerged out the front door, the fog had grown so thick, I was immediately disoriented. Without lights, the grounds were nearly as dark as the inside of the hospital. Where was the car?

"Andrew, for god's sake, where are you?" I stumbled in the direction of the car. The cold, moist air wrapped its icy fingers around me. In that moment, I could understand how people panicked underwater when they couldn't tell whether they were moving to the surface or the bottom.

Slow down, Jamie. Think! I stopped and listened, peering through the murk to see the faint glimmer of a light from the house.

"Andrew! Help me!"

"I'm here."

I couldn't see him. "Call 9-1-1! Tucker is on the back landing. We need an ambulance!"

Bronte barked inside the hospital. I turned back. I needed to get her. Who knew what lurked in the old hospital? Ghosts or a real person or maybe a rabid animal?

Behind me, Andrew yelled. "I can't get a signal."

"Go inside and use the phone in the house. Hurry!"

When I turned back to the hulking presence of the hospital, I thought I saw a flicker of light. Not a flicker, but flames. "Oh my god!" Inside, the acrid smell of smoke hit me. The hospital was on fire.

Who did this? I ran back to the stairway. As I did, the smell grew stronger. I had to get to my dog and get Tucker out. As I rushed into the stairway, the smoke hit me, stinging my eyes. With the flashlight pointed up the staircase, I saw it rolling in from the second floor.

"Bronte!" I called. "Come."

The only sound I heard in response was a low groan from Tucker. I didn't know a lot about fire, but I did know it needed oxygen. It would suck up the air from the staircase to feed its appetite. I had to get to the top of the stairs and close the door. It would buy us a little time.

I took the stairs two at a time. At the landing, I stopped long enough to kneel down to Tucker. "It's on fire up there. I'm going to close the door and figure out how to get you out."

At the top, I heard the crackling sound of the fire as it caught on the old wooden frame of the building. I kept low, crawling to the doorway. "Bronte!" I coughed and gasped. The smoke was filling my lungs. I peered through the doorway but saw nothing but smoke. No dog, no ghost just smoke. With all the strength I had, I pushed at the heavy exit door. The floor was warped, and for a moment, it stuck. I stood and heaved myself at it. It gave, and with one more thrust, shut.

I had just shut the door on Bronte and perhaps delivered her a death sentence. I prayed she had already found her way to the main stairway or the stairway to the kitchen.

The fire grew from a crackling sound to a low roar. No time to worry about my dog. I needed to get Tucker out.

At the landing, I yelled at him. "Tucker, wake up! You need to sit up so I can get you down these stairs."

"Wha?"

I squatted down and glanced at the file next to him.

"File," his voice slurred. "Need the file."

I grabbed it and handed it to him. "Here, hold on to it."

Grunting, I got my arm around his shoulder. "Sit up!" My voice grew louder as I fought off the panic that was telling me to leave him and flee. If I couldn't get him up, I would have to somehow drag him out.

I must have gotten through to him because he made a weak attempt to sit. When he moved, he howled, "Oh shit, my leg! My leg!"

Right now, I didn't care about his leg. I was in a battle for his life and mine. "Listen. We're going to bump down the stairs like little kids, okay? Take it one at a time."

Still clutching the file, he screamed with the first movement. I kept steady pressure on his shoulders. "Down one at a time." I worked to keep the shrillness out of my voice. My heart pounded, and my eyes watered from the smoke. How long would it take us?

We'd only made it down two steps when a light showed from below.

"J? I'm here."

"Andrew, hurry. We have to get him out!" *And I have to find Bronte.*

He ran up the stairs. "My god, we're going to die."

Not a good time to be dramatic. "Grab him on your side." I spoke into Tucker's ear, "We're going to get you down."

It was clumsy and slow-going—or at least it felt that way. Tucker was nearly dead weight, and after two steps, I wasn't sure I could hold him anymore. I might have collapsed at that point, except I thought I heard Bronte barking through the din. I had to get Tucker out and go back for her.

One step, then another, as the smoke grew thicker. I didn't want my life to end here in this haunted wreck of a place where people had suffered, and people had died. I wanted my dog, and I wanted my cabin, and I wanted Jim. Even though my body screamed with fatigue, we kept going.

At the bottom of the stairs, I came close to caving in. I didn't think I could support Tucker long enough to get out the door. No one would be there for the rescue, not this soon. I knew it would take time for the ambulance to get here and the volunteer fire department to round up enough men to man the rig.

Somehow, Andrew and I managed to drag Tucker to the front lobby one agonizing step at a time. We stopped for a moment near the front door so I could catch my breath. Behind us, a piece of the ceiling collapsed.

"Go!" Andrew shouted. "We need to get back away from the building!" We dragged Tucker out into the weedy front garden and laid him down in the wet grass. We both gulped the smoky, foggy air. My heart thumped so hard I wondered if it could escape my chest.

Tucker lay in the weeds, barely conscious but still holding the file. I checked his carotid pulse and found it was steady.

I looked at the hospital to see flames leaping out the roof. "Oh, my god. I need to get Bronte!" I gasped. All the weariness left me as I jumped to my feet and ran.

Andrew shouted something at me. I couldn't understand it above the crackling and roar of the fire. *I needed to get my dog.*

"Bronte!" As I scrambled back toward the hospital, I heard distant sirens. Help was on the way. At that point, I didn't care. I was too intent on getting back into the building to find Bronte. I didn't hear the sound from behind me until someone's arms were around my waist, and I was tackled to the ground. I hit chest first, and all the breath went out of me.

Chapter Forty-Four: Ghost

I gasped at the smoke-filled air, trying to catch my breath. Someone was on top of me. It was as if the oppressiveness of this place was concentrated on holding me down. The sirens approached, and I heard the first sounds of the old building collapsing. I tried to push myself up when a familiar voice commanded, "Oh no, you don't."

Andrew straddled me. I tried to shake him off. "I have to get my dog." The words came out in a half-sob as I pictured Bronte trapped and confused.

He pointed to the building. "No one is going inside. It's totally in flames."

The ambulance arrived, followed shortly by the firetruck. Andrew moved off me and pointed to the flashing lights. "We need to get them to Tucker. Now!"

Pushing myself to a stand, I watched in horror as glass exploded from the side of the building, sending a spray of shards. The wind had picked up, and sparks and debris started landing on the roof of Nella's house. I *knew* it was too late for Bronte.

"Miss Nella!" She was probably asleep in her chair.

I was up and stumbling to the house when a fireman in a yellow jacket grabbed my arm. I pointed to the house. "Miss Nella is inside."

He stopped me. "Jamie, we'll take care of it."

"Oh my god, Rob." I stared at him through the fog, and the smoke and tears rolled down my cheeks. "Bronte followed me into the hospital and ran upstairs. I can't find her." I was having a hard time catching my breath.

"Jamie, sit down over there. We'll look for Bronte."

I knew he was trying to reassure me, and I knew there was no way we could get my dog out of the burning building. He studied me, wiping away one of the tears before giving me a quick hug. I watched his graceful lope as he ran to the house. I sat almost in a trance, watching the firemen do their work. Ill-equipped with no water source other than what they had brought, and water from the house, they worked to save the residence and stop the dead grass and bushes on the grounds from igniting.

The hospital wouldn't be saved, and the ashes of this cursed building would be Bronte's burial ground. Why had she run away from me? Why had I taken her along? I vowed I wouldn't cry.

The flames continued to lick at the fog-encased sky as I walked numbly toward the ambulance. I felt like I was observing all of this in the third person. As I neared where they were tending to Tucker, I stopped, suddenly lightheaded. Little dark blobs floated in front of my eyes, and my knees weakened. Sinking to the ground away from all the flashing vehicles, I rested my head on my knees. In the distance, above the roar of the fire and the shouts of the firefighters, I thought I heard Bronte's bark. I knew it would haunt me forever. I lifted my head and turned to the imagined sound. There it was again—Bronte's "I'm in distress" bark.

"Bronte?" I lurched to my feet. Taking a deep breath, I concentrated on listening for her. I was straining so hard, I didn't hear Rob come up to me.

"We got her."

"What?" For a moment, I was totally confused.

"The old lady. Miss Fox."

"Oh, good." Dazed, I started to shiver. Everything around me seemed unreal. I held up my finger. "Shhh…"

"Jamie, are you all right?"

Again, I heard my dog's bark. I stumbled towards it.

"Jamie! Where are you going?"

"My dog. She's barking for me."

Rob grabbed my arm. "You're in shock, Jamie. You need to come with me."

I shook him off. "I heard her. She was in the hospital with me, and I couldn't find her. But I hear her now."

I'm sure Rob thought I'd gone completely off the deep end. How could I hear anything above the roar of the fire and the noise of the fire crew?

"She's calling to me, Rob. I hear her." I pointed in the direction I thought I'd detected the bark. It was somewhere behind the house and the hospital, maybe in the weedy, forgotten garden. I stumbled in that direction stopping every few feet to listen.

If it had been anyone else but Rob, who had an inner sense when it came to animals, he might have dragged me back to the ambulance.

I was behind the house when I heard it again. Perhaps the ghost of my lovable mutt.

"It's Bronte. I'm sure of it." I picked up my speed.

"Wait." He grabbed my arm. I tried to pull away, and as I did, I heard her again. This time Rob straightened. "My god."

We both ran together. I tripped on a tangle of old rose bushes and nearly pitched head-first onto the old stone walk. Behind me, a wall of the old building collapsed. The air was choked with smoke and fog. "Bronte!" I gasped as Rob grabbed my arm to keep me from falling.

And there she was, bounding through the old garden, yipping and barking. I knelt while she licked my face. I wanted to hug her, and I wanted to scold her at the same time. We might have continued this reunion, except Rob's voice rose above the din.

"Jamie, help me!"

He was kneeling about ten feet from me. I pushed myself up and ran to him. Rob was slipping out of his yellow fireman's jacket and wrapping it around someone. Bronte joined him, wagging her tail.

When I got to the person on the ground, I half-expected to see a ghostly Dr. Heller. Instead, it was the boy from the flier. We had found the real ghost.

His eyes were open and appeared so white on his sooty face. He coughed, gasping for breath.

"We'll get you help," Rob talked to him in a gentle voice before he pulled out his radio and called.

I squatted by him. When he tried to talk, it came out in a croak. I wondered how badly his lungs had been damaged by the fire.

"Nice doggy," he rasped. "Saved me."

"Don't talk. Help is coming."

"We were going to split the reward." His voice trailed off.

With the flickering light of the fire, I saw something shiny near him. I picked it up—a flashlight. Suddenly, things started to clear in my fogged brain.

"Did you take the flashlight?" I kept my voice as gentle as possible.

The boy coughed, tears running down his face leaving streaks. "I didn't know she was there. Startled her, and she fell." His voice dropped off.

"Shhh…We'll get it sorted out."

"The old guy. He started the fire. He was mumbling something about 'Mama said no one should have the file.'"

Bronte sat next to me, watching over the boy who was shivering so hard his teeth rattled.

Rob whispered, "He's going into shock." He turned away and talked on his radio again.

"Please," the boy whispered. "Don't send me back to the camp. Please?"

"You're safe here. It's okay."

Except I wasn't sure it would be okay. I knew how serious the damage to his lungs could be. Ironic that it happened in a TB sanatorium.

He closed his eyes.

The EMTs came running with a stretcher. As soon as they arrived, I whispered to Rob, "I need to find Ed. I think he started the fire. He might be hurt."

Rob grabbed my arm. "No. You need to get checked out."

"I'm fine, really."

I wasn't fine, but I needed to be away from all the chaos. I stood up, feeling wobbly, and walked slowly through the ruined garden. Bronte stayed close. By the little cemetery, I looked back. The old hospital spewed flames and black smoke like some CGI-created monster. I tore my gaze away from it.

As I neared the trailer, the smoke lessened. A slight breeze blew off the lake. I stopped to take deep breaths of the fresh air. Bronte stayed close, and when something exploded inside the hospital, she whimpered. I reached down and gave her a hug. "You're a hero, you know. How did you ever save that kid?"

She licked my face. She had a story to tell that I would never hear.

Chapter Forty-Five: The Story of Punky

A light was on in the trailer, and soft classical music wafted out the front door.

"Ed? It's Jamie. Can I come in?"

"Too much trouble out there. Mama never liked trouble."

"I'm coming in."

I smelled the odor of gasoline as soon as I stepped inside. Ed sat on the sofa in the little front room of the trailer. He stared straight ahead with a dazed expression. His hands rested on his lap. They had clearly gotten burned.

"Are you hurt? It looks like your hands got singed."

Bronte trotted over to him and sat next to him. He tried to reach over to pet her but stopped. "Mama would be angry. She didn't like me to be around fire."

"It's okay, Ed. We'll get you help."

I took my phone out only to see that the battery was dead. I'd have to run back to get the paramedics.

"Ed, why did you start the fire? Did you know the boy was hiding there?"

He slowly shook his head. "Didn't know, but Nella said she was tired of all the snooping and wanted it to stop. I tried to help her make it stop."

I looked around at the neatness of the trailer. For Ed, everything had a place, and I guessed Tucker and Barrett had disturbed it. The counter top in the tiny kitchen was bare and scrubbed. The only disarray was on the kitchen table. Several files were spread out.

A piece of me wanted to read the files and find out if they told more of the story about the secrets of this place. Bronte barked as Ed leaned back against the sofa. His sooty face was bathed in sweat, and his teeth rattled from shivering. I needed to get him help.

A crocheted afghan, similar to the one Miss Nella had, was folded on the arm of the sofa. I draped it over Ed and propped his feet up on the coffee table. "I'm going for help. I won't be gone long."

The air was sooty and acrid as I ran back to the fire truck. The ambulance with Tucker and the boy had left. I yelled to anyone who could hear me. "Help! I need help down by the lake!"

In the chaos and the roar of the fire, my voice didn't carry. I spotted Rob by Andrew's car. Miss Nella sat in the passenger seat, wrapped in a blanket. Rob was speaking to her in soothing tones.

"No, ma'am, you can't go back into your house. It's not safe. We're waiting for a second ambulance. You might have inhaled smoke. We have to take you to the hospital."

Breathless, I ran up to him and tugged him away. "Ed's in the trailer by the lake. He got burned and isn't looking good."

Miss Nella stared at me. "Who are you? Is little Punky okay?"

Of course! Ed was Punky. How could I have not seen it? The little boy who was slow grew up to be Ed, the caretaker.

Ten minutes later, the ambulance arrived at the trailer.

While they tended to him, I slid onto the kitchen chair and picked up a file. The first one I looked at was labeled in neat handwriting, "Birth Certificate, Confirmation Certificate, Diploma."

I opened it to the birth certificate. What had the note in Barrett's bedroom said, something about another Fox? Well, here it was—Edward Fox McEnany. Mother: Virginia McEnany and Father: Alfred Fox.

I thought about young Nella's diary entry talking about Nanny Ninny getting fat and leaving the house. Of course, she left because she was pregnant. I wondered why Dr. Fox never publicly recognized his son.

A second file contained paperwork indicating a trust had been set up for Ed from the Fox estate. I skimmed through it, not entirely understanding the legalese. What I did understand was the signature. The trust had been set up by Clarence Engstrom.

"This was the confidential settlement," I whispered to myself.

Rob turned to me. "Did you say something?"

"Just mumbling."

By now, they had Ed on a gurney. It was time for me to leave. Bronte sat and waited by my side as they rolled him out. Ed noticed I had the file in my hand.

His voice was a mere whisper with a childlike cadence to it. "They called me Punky back then. But when I grew up, I became Ed. Never liked being Punky. Dumb name."

Bronte nudged me. Now that someone was taking care of Ed, she wanted to go home. I gathered the papers. "Come on, girl. Let's get the hell out of here."

Andrew's car was gone when I got back to mine. Driving away, the hospital was a black skeleton of a building that had held so many stories of life and death.

Chapter Forty-Six: Medical File

It was well after two in the morning when I finally pulled up to the darkened cabin. Bronte and I were both sooty and smelly and exhausted. Once inside, in the warm glow of the cabin, I checked her carefully to make sure she wasn't hurt. She sat calmly while I ran my hands through her fur and gently lifted each paw. I saw no evidence of injury. How she got out of that building without even being singed was a mystery I'd never solve. I suspected the hospital had a back entrance I hadn't noticed. Tucker must have known about it.

"Go rest," I pointed to her rug in the living room. "I'm taking a shower."

That night, I let her sleep next to me even though she reeked of stale smoke and gasoline fumes. Every once in a while, I reached over to pat her to make sure she was okay.

I fell into a deep, dreamless sleep. My phone woke me at seven. "Hullo?"

"Jamie, are you okay?"

"Jim?" I groaned as I sat up. My body ached from head to toe.

"I heard about what happened last night. I can be on the next plane if you need me."

I rubbed the sleep out of my eyes and yawned. "That would be nice." My sleepy smile turned into a grin. He was willing to fly home to me. I pictured him beside me instead of my smoky, smelly beast. Better sense prevailed, however. "Wait, Jim. I'm fine—really. Finish your classes—please."

Bronte lifted her head and licked my shoulder. Hairy dog didn't compare with sweet-smelling Jim. I recounted my evening to him. When I got to the part about Andrew, he interrupted. "Ah…was he helpful?"

I laughed. "Probably for the first and only time in his life. He saved me from running back into the burning building. He tackled me and nearly knocked me out."

We ended the call with Jim promising to phone again later today. "I love you," I murmured before I fell back to sleep.

My next call came an hour later from Clarence. I picked up the phone as I was eating my morning toast. "You are certainly up early."

"Well, you have caused another uproar in this town."

"Caused? I believe you can take credit for getting me involved in the first place." I filled him in on what had happened, including finding Ed's birth certificate. Clarence didn't sound surprised by this bit of news.

"It's probably breaking lawyer-client privilege to tell you this, but if they disbar me, fine. I have this new thing called The Internet. I can start a podcast for creaky, disbarred old lawyers." He chuckled. "Remember I told you that when I was a young pup lawyer fresh out of school, I helped Nella? Well, it was Virginia McEnany making claims against the estate after Dr. Fox died. Bless her heart. She only wanted to be assured that Ed would be taken care of when she died. Nella was in a tizzy because she had no idea Ed was her half-brother. We worked it out that he could stay as the caretaker as long as he wanted to, and we set up a trust for him."

"I should have picked up on it from the diaries."

"You weren't hired to be a sleuth. Just to write her story."

He told me they'd kept Nella in the hospital overnight, and they were going to place her in assisted living. "They had to involve me because she objected, of course. Said something like, 'When hell freezes over.' They were able to save the house, but it was severely damaged. The hospital was burned to the ground."

"Clarence, Ed told me he started the fire…Something about wanting all the snooping to stop. I suspect he might have pushed Tucker down those stairs."

Clarence made a humming sound before he spoke. "Let's let it sit for the time being. They air-lifted him down to the burn unit at Regions Hospital in St. Paul. Some pretty bad burns and smoke inhalation. If he survives, I'm not sure they could prove he was competent to know right from wrong."

"Clarence, that kid was hiding out in the building. He might have died if it wasn't for Bronte." I scratched behind her ears. "Something tells me there's more to the story about him."

"It would seem so."

"So you know, I'm on record to say, I'm not going to try to find it out."

"Wise move."

My next call was from Greg, the deputy. At least he didn't show up at my door. He wanted to hear the whole story. I told him about finding Tucker and getting him out of the building, and finding the boy.

"Do you think the kid started the fire? Maybe to cover that he'd been hiding in the hospital?"

I could have told him about Ed's confession, but I decided the less I said, the better. "I only talked with him for a few moments. He did tell me that Barrett Fox fell down those stairs."

"He witnessed it?"

"I think he spooked her, and she fell running away."

"Ah. Thought he was a ghost."

I pictured Tally on the grass, looking so scared. "How is he doing?"

"The doctor thinks he'll be okay. His parents are flying in today." He lowered his voice. "I'm not looking forward to dealing with them."

I sensed Greg wasn't really interested in digging into the start of the fire. I silently wished him good luck—especially with Tally's parents.

The gentle rhythm of the lake comforted me as the water washed against the shore. My head was still filled with memories of the fire. I took deep breaths to wish it away. Closing my eyes, I concentrated on the myriad of sounds around me—the water, the chorus of birds chirping, the chittering of the chipmunks teasing Bronte.

Just as I was feeling the muscles in my shoulders relax, my phone rang. Andrew. Of course, I'd have to talk with him.

"Hey," he sounded lively. "Just checking. How are you?"

"A bit sore. How about you?"

"Ready to try out as a tackle for the New York Jets."

"Oh, come on, you downed a 110-pound girl. I don't think that qualifies you."

He laughed. "Maybe not. I thought you should know. I stopped by the hospital. They're sending old Tucker to Duluth for surgery on his leg. I'm guessing we didn't help the fracture much. They've got him doped up, but he kept asking for 'the file.' Know anything about where it went? Could be valuable."

"No. He had it on the staircase and everything after that is kind of a blur." I honestly couldn't remember what had happened to the file.

"Maybe he dropped it before we got him out." He sounded disappointed. "Might have been worth something."

Scheming as usual. I remembered the fliers for the missing teenager on Tucker's bed. "Andrew, do you know if Tucker had anything to do with the missing kid who was hiding in the hospital?"

He hesitated a moment too long.

"Andrew?"

"Ah, well, I have a theory—kind of."

I waited. Sometimes silence could spur him on.

"Tucker said he had this 'thing' going and might be coming into some ready cash. I figured it had to do with the estate—like he'd uncovered something, and the old lady would pay...."

"Yes?"

"Well, after everything last night, I put it together. I think Tucker was helping the kid hide and that he would suddenly find him in the woods or something and get the reward money. Like maybe he'd split it with the kid?"

"They were in on it together?" I pictured the flier with the kid's birthdate. Next week he was turning eighteen. I could see Tucker telling him that when he turned eighteen, he would be considered an adult, and his parents couldn't send him back to Camp Six without his permission.

"They think Ed, the caretaker, probably started the fire. You know, when I asked the old lady to use the phone, she pointed to the hospital and muttered something about not minding if the place burned down."

"Really?"

"I wonder if she said something like that to the old guy, and he took her seriously."

"Hmmm. I guess it's a matter for the police."

Up to that point, I was thinking charitable thoughts about Andrew. He'd helped me get Tucker out of the building and saved me from foolishly running back in for my dog. Like the old Andrew, though, he managed to throw cold water on those thoughts when he spoke again. "I was thinking, we saved that kid. I mean, we were in the building, and I called the fire department. I wonder if we could claim the reward."

I stared at the phone. Was he really looking at this tragedy as a way to get money?

"Andrew, are you serious?"

He hesitated, and I abruptly ended the call and turned off my phone.

With the sun shining brightly, the temperature rose to seventy degrees. Warm enough for Bronte to chase some sticks into the lake. I didn't have the heart to give her a bath, but she still smelled like stale smoke.

"Hey, girl. Let's go after some sticks."

Bronte sauntered over to me and lifted her head. Her expression told me she was less than enthused. "I know you're still tired. It was quite a night, but I can't stand how you smell."

She responded by licking my hand. When I looked out on Lake Larissa, I saw a snowy egret land near the reedy part of the shoreline. I took it as a good omen.

I threw a stick into the water. Bronte watched it from where she sat but didn't dash into the water.

"Oh, come on. I don't want to give you a bath." Maybe she was injured, and I simply hadn't seen it. I reached over, grabbed another of her chewed-on sticks, and threw it up the incline. Wagging her tale, she sauntered after it.

"What kind of a lab are you—avoiding the water and not fetching with enthusiasm," I sighed. I would have to bathe her after all.

After a couple of tepid fetches, she settled at my feet to chew. I finished my coffee and was about to go back into the cabin when a truck rattled up my drive. Bronte lifted her head and began to wag her tail. Before she could get up the hill to greet the visitor, Rob came striding down. For a big man in his sixties, he walked like a teenager.

"Hey," he called. "I had some work at the lodge and wanted to see how you were doing."

I patted the rock beside me. "Have a seat. I'm enjoying the fresh air and lack of a burning building."

He sat down next to me. I held up my coffee. "If you want some, you'll have to fetch it yourself. I'm kind of sore."

"Coffeed out. Brad was so relieved when I got home safely last night that he made a wonderful breakfast this morning. Poor boy, he hates that I'm on the volunteer fire crew."

I smiled. "He worries about you."

"Yup."

Bronte was uncharacteristically quiet as she chewed on her stick. I reached down and patted her. "I'm worried about her. She doesn't have much energy."

Rob slid off the rock and squatted beside her. "Are you tired, young lady?"

She looked at him with adoring eyes as he slid his hands down her back and checked her paws. Although not formally trained, Rob was as close to a veterinarian as we had in Killdeer right now. I watched while he carefully massaged her back and her haunches.

"Some Native American spiritual technique you learned from your ancestors?" I asked.

"Nope. Got this technique off YouTube."

Rob worked on Bronte for a few minutes, whispering softly to her. When he was done, he sat back on the rock. "She'll be okay. A bit traumatized, but she told me if you promise not to give her a bath, she'll chase a stick into the water this afternoon."

"She told you that?"

He grinned. "I have great powers to communicate with the animals."

I tsked.

We talked a little about the fire and the aftermath. I told him Ed was sent to Regions in St. Paul to the burn unit, and he was probably responsible for the fire."

He raised his eyebrows. "You have the most interesting adventures."

"Really, all I want to do is get my favorite pot-bellied pig back to his author."

He didn't bother to ask me what I was talking about. He pointed to the truck. "I have something for you. Found it near the ambulance. You can probably get it to where it needs to go."

I followed him up the incline feeling every step in my aching hips. Rob reached into his truck and handed me a file. As soon as I saw it, I recognized it as the one Tucker had held on to. I took it, wondering what secrets it held.

Chapter Forty-Seven: Another Fox

After I waved good-bye to Rob, I brought the file in and put it on the table. Did I want to know what was inside? Bronte came in, ate a few nuggets of food, and settled with a loud sigh on her rug in the living room. I took a couple of ibuprofens and sat at the table staring at the file.

It was an old medical record in a heavy cover. The pages inside were held together by a metal clasp at the top so the pages could be flipped up. The record was for Nella Fox, and the front was marked with a red stamp "Confidential."

I had no right to read it, but curiosity overcame my qualms. The pages were written in black ink, and over the years, some of it had faded, and some of it had leached onto subsequent pages. The record started several weeks before Nella had gone into labor. It read like what I assumed was a normal pre-natal visit. Dr. Heller noted *I've assured the patient this record will be completely confidential. Only the matron and I will have access to it.*

I skipped through the notes until the delivery. It was hard to decipher some of the writing due to the cramped cursive. What I found, though, caused me to exclaim, "What?"

Bronte walked over to me from her rug and nudged my leg. "It's okay, girl. Just a surprise."

Dr. Heller's note described the baby girl as small, perhaps a bit premature, but healthy in appearance.

"Nella's baby wasn't born dead according to this."

He added only a brief note, *Patient's uncle will transport baby to St. Paul as previously arranged.*

The rest of the record chronicled Nella's rocky post-partum course. The details of her treatment and her medications meant little to me, except I understood she was very ill and came close to dying. No other mention was made of the baby.

In the very back of the record were papers signed by Nella in a shaky, almost unreadable hand giving up rights to the baby. I wondered if she really knew what she was signing or if Dr. Fox knew she'd given up the baby.

I stood up and stretched, suddenly very tired. Too many secrets.

"Nap time," I called to Bronte as I walked into the bedroom and sank into my unmade bed. The story of the Fox family clearly was not over yet.

In my dream, I was running from the burning hospital. In my arms was a baby. When I looked down at it swaddled in a pink blanket, it wasn't a baby but a doll with blonde curls and a perpetual smile.

I woke up to Bronte licking my cheek. I'd been asleep for over two hours. My body felt heavy and groggy. When I let her out, the sun was high, and the temperature had gone up to eighty. Bronte bounded to her place in the woods. It appeared Rob had cured her.

I turned back to the file on the table. I needed to talk with Clarence.

Clarence's kitchen held the sweet aroma of cinnamon rolls as he studied the file. I watched him trying to piece it all together. Nella's baby didn't die but was put up for adoption. I was sure she wasn't aware of it. She seemed so distraught when she talked about not being able to hold the baby. Who was responsible for the adoption? Dr. Heller? Dr. Fox? Virginia McEnany?

"Well, this is a kettle of day-old fish," Clarence slipped his glasses off and rubbed his eyes.

"Somewhere out there is another Fox."

I remembered the letter from Josie Heller about Nella's situation. "Clarence, I think the Heller family might be the key. I asked Jim to see if he could locate them. He sent me an email I haven't read yet."

By the time I drove back to the cabin, the sun was settling behind Bear

Island. I took in the air and the smell of the lake water, and the sound of the frogs and crickets. Time to put all the pieces together.

Jim's email with the Heller family information contained an address and phone number for a Dr. Cady Stanton, Josie Heller's daughter.

I called Jim. When he answered, he sounded harried. "Jamie, for god's sake, I've been trying to reach you for hours."

"Oh, geez, sorry. I turned my phone off after I talked with Clarence."

"Well, don't do that again."

Jim was rarely testy with me. I liked his irritation. "No, sir."

We talked for a bit about how he'd tracked down the Heller family. I assumed with marriages and name changes, it would be difficult.

"Obituaries are very helpful. I found one for Josephine Heller Wilson and worked from there."

"Are you sure it's the right family?"

I could almost see his shrug over the phone. "I guess you won't know unless you call."

We talked a little longer about when he would arrive back here, and I signed off with, "I love you, Jim. Can't wait."

His reply left me with a smile.

I hesitated before calling the number Jim had found, wondering what I would say. As a fact-checker for several New York magazines, I often made cold calls. I put myself back in that mode.

The phone rang nearly six times before a raspy female voice answered. "Dr. Stanton, how can I help you?"

"Cady Stanton?"

"Yes, who is this?"

"This is Jamie Forest. I live in Jackpine County, and I've been working with a woman named Nella Fox on her memoirs. I'm hoping you can help me."

Dr. Stanton hesitated. "That name is familiar. My mother used to talk about a Fox family. I think her brother worked for them."

I had the right family. Taking a deep breath, I thought about how to word my next question. Cady might not have been adopted, and I might be heading down a rabbit hole. "Uh, this is a bit of a long shot, but we're trying to locate someone who might know the whereabouts of Nella Fox's daughter. Did your mother ever mention an adoption?"

The line was quiet for a few moments. When Cady came back on, her tone had a tenseness to it. "Why do you want to know?"

"I apologize. It sounds like I'm prying—and I am. As I was working on Miss Nella's memoir, I came across information that she had a baby girl that was placed for adoption."

Cady was silent long enough that I wondered if we'd lost the connection. When she spoke, her voice softened. "Tell me more."

I told her about discovering the medical file for Nella Fox and the note about a small, but healthy baby girl who was going to be taken to St. Paul. "Nella, the mother, was only sixteen and, near as I can determine, didn't know the baby lived."

"Oh, my word." I heard a sharp intake of breath. "I was adopted, but my mother said very little about my birth parents. She called me her 'gift.' In those days, no one talked about birth parents of adopted children. When I grew up, I never approached it with her because they adopted me at such a difficult time."

"What do you mean?"

"You see, my mother's brother, a doctor, disappeared about the time they got me. Having me helped them through some very hard times."

We talked for nearly two hours while I took down notes about her life and her upbringing. She was a doctor herself, now close to retirement. Her mother, Josephine, died twenty years ago. It was always a big mystery in the family about what happened to Frank Heller.

"I used to call him my mystery uncle."

I murmured something, not sure how to respond. I suspected her mystery uncle had been murdered.

She continued in a gentle voice. "I'd like to meet Nella if possible."

I hesitated, searching for the right words. "Since she was told her baby died, this will probably be quite a shock to her. She's elderly and quite frail. I don't know how she might take this news, but I'll speak with her lawyer.

He can let her decide if she wants to meet you."

I left her with my phone number. When I crawled into bed that night, Bronte was already nestled in. She lifted her head, yawned, and went back to sleep. I stared at the ceiling, wondering if my call to Dr. Stanton would result in the opening of a painful wound for both of them. If Miss Nella didn't want to meet her, how would Cady feel? And what would Miss Nella think about meeting a daughter she thought had been dead for all these years?

Chapter Forty-Eight: The Reunion

I spent the next day going over the medical record. I had to look up some of the drugs and many of the medical terms in an effort to put together what happened to Miss Nella after the baby was born. I consulted my friend, Norma, the hospital nurse manager, asking her questions in general terms without revealing this was information from Miss Nella's confidential medical record.

"This doesn't sound like a modern delivery. It's an unusual post-partum course," she commented.

A week later, I sat with Clarence in the small living room of Miss Nella's assisted living apartment. She was dressed in a red pantsuit, and her snowy white hair was styled in a way that emphasized the blueness of her eyes. She sat regally like a queen. Clarence had told her about Cady Stanton, and Nella was still undecided about whether to meet her.

"She's been dead to me since the moment I gave birth. I'm not sure I want to know her. It was such a terrible time."

"Perhaps what Jamie has to tell you will help you make a decision."

She peered at me but said nothing.

I pulled out the old medical file. "I hope you will forgive me, but I went over the medical record Dr. Heller kept on you. Clarence knows you told me you pushed Dr. Heller down the stairs and were responsible for his death."

Miss Nella's cheeks reddened. "You promised not to tell."

"I'm only telling you and Clarence. He's your lawyer, and it's confidential."

She sighed, "It was a long time ago. I'll carry it with me to the grave."

Clarence patted her on the hand. "Actually, you need to hear what Jamie has to say."

"Miss Nella, according to the notes Dr. Heller made on the day we think he died, you couldn't have pushed him down the stairs. You were so sedated you were unable to even sit up. It's in the record. I think you heard the commotion, and after he disappeared, you put it together and made it your fault. Near as I can tell, you weren't physically capable of pushing him down the stairs."

Miss Nella's eyes widened. "Young woman, is it true?"

"I don't think there's any other explanation. You were far too sick to have done it."

If I was expecting tears of joy or happiness, I didn't get them from Miss Nella. She gaped at me for a moment, cleared her throat, and said, "Well. That's good. But if I didn't do it, what did happen?"

Clarence spoke in a gentle tone. "I was able to talk with Ed in the hospital in St. Paul. He was only seven at the time, and his memory isn't exactly reliable, but he thinks he heard what happened. He often played near the nurse's station when his mother was on duty. He said his mother, Dr. Heller, and Dr. Fox were, and I quote, 'playing a game of who could shout the loudest.' He said one would yell, 'Tell her,' and the other would yell 'No!' His mother made them go to the back staircase because they were making too much noise for the patients. He heard a smacking sound and some thumping. His mother rushed out and grabbed him and said he needed to go back to their cottage for tea."

Nella wrinkled her eyebrows. "I wasn't there?"

Clarence squeezed her hand. "No, Nella, you weren't."

"My father knew, and he kept it from me?" Nella's eyes filled with tears. "Imagine that."

Two weeks later, we sat once again with Miss Nella in her apartment. She had on her red pantsuit. It looked like she'd gained a little weight and had a rosiness to her cheeks. When the knock finally came at the door, she was composed. "Please come in."

Two women walked in. One was in her seventies but carried herself straight and tall. I had not met her before, only talked with her on the phone. My jaw dropped a bit at the resemblance. The other, the woman's daughter, was in her forties and appeared overwhelmed.

Clarence, who had met both the women, made the introductions.

"Nella, I'd like you to meet Cady Stanton and her daughter Louise."

Cady stepped forward and took Miss Nella's hand. "So nice to finally meet you."

Miss Nella's eyes sparkled. "Why, you look so much like my father. It's amazing. You have his face shape."

Louise exclaimed, "And she has yours."

I realized I was holding my breath at this reunion. More Foxes in the room.

After everyone sat down, Clarence took charge of the meeting. "As you know, my friend here," he pointed to me, "uncovered a medical record that documented your birth."

Cady nodded.

"And another friend, who isn't here, did the research to find you."

I smiled to myself at how Jim had worked the magic of the internet to discover Cady.

Nella hadn't taken her eyes off Cady during the introduction. She repeated, "You look so much like my father. This is hard to believe."

Clarence glanced at me before turning to Cady and her daughter. "The secret is out. I know it will take some time to get used to this."

Louise spoke. "I only wish Grandma was still alive to see this. She would have been pleased."

With her words, Miss Nella started to cry. "Oh, I'm so sorry for Josie and for Frank. It shouldn't have happened that way, but Papa could be a tyrant." She turned to Clarence. "I suspect Nanny Ninny did all she could to cover up what happened. She wanted to protect Papa—and Punky."

Cady talked about growing up in St. Paul. "My mother wanted to be a doctor, but she said when I was brought to her, she fell in love with me. She and my grandmother raised me as their own. I never knew the story behind how I came to be with them."

Louis interrupted. "Grandma didn't get to be a doctor, but Mother did. I know Grandma was so proud."

Nella smiled. "I'm proud, too, even though I had nothing to do with it."

"I guess we have doctor genes in the family," Cady said.

Clarence and I sat on the sidelines while grandmother, daughter, and granddaughter got to know each other. After an hour, Nella closed her eyes. "Maybe we can talk again. I'm tired."

Clarence and I escorted the women out. He told them as they walked to their car. "Thank you for driving all the way up here from The Cities. I hope you will come back. I think Nella would like that."

He shook hands with them. In the car back to his house, he took a deep breath. "I'm glad it was a happy reunion. I've been involved in worse."

"What bothers me is why Dr. Fox never told Nella that her child was alive and being cared for."

"Unfortunately, we can only speculate. I think Alfred Fox was more worried about the reputation of his hospital than the well-being of his child. That's probably why he kept Ed's heritage secret. Especially after it was known that Ed was slow."

I pulled up to the curb. "I'm guessing it's more complex than that and maybe more criminal. He shoved Dr. Heller down the steps in a fit of rage and then covered it up by burying him as if he were one of the patients. It was deliberate and ugly. Josephine and her mother lost him." I couldn't tamp down the anger I felt at the doctor who was supposed to heal, not murder.

By the time I returned to the cabin, it was twilight, and all the windows glowed from inside. I pulled up next to Jim's truck. Inside, Bronte barked a welcome. When I stepped out of the car, Jim stood in the doorway, tall and not-quite handsome. He handed me a cold beer.

"Hard day at the office, dear?" He held the door for me.

"Well, at least I wasn't having to deal with comma placement, just family placement."

I told him about the reunion. "It wasn't exactly a lovefest, but I think they will see each other again."

Jim had supper waiting for me, his special venison stew. I hesitated only a second before eating it. "Tell me this wasn't the deer who ate my tomatoes."

Jim shrugged. "Not hunting season yet."

The stew turned out to be delicious. I'm sure Apple Pie would have approved. I even thought about sending the recipe to Opal for her next book.

After supper, we sat on the rock with red wine and listened to the sounds of the lake as an evening mist rose. The crickets chirped in force. With Jim's arms around me and Bronte at my feet, I couldn't ask for more perfection. It was broken only by the ping of my phone.

"Don't," Jim grabbed my hand. "It can wait."

"I have to know."

It was a text from Andrew. **Good news! Mr. Right Digestion is back in New York and back in the commercial business.**

I showed Jim the text. He squinted in the darkness. "I guess that means I don't have to challenge him to a duel."

"Not unless it's on a New York stage."

I didn't reveal to Jim that I used the money from *Apple Pie a'la Murder* to buy him a plane ticket back to New York. I'd convinced him to sell his only possession, the silver SUV, go home and pay off all his debts.

Tomorrow Jim would be leaving for St. Paul to work for a few weeks before his resignation went into effect. He'd already interviewed with Jackpine County to be the acting sheriff when Rick Fowler stepped down. When he came back to my cabin by the lake, we would figure out our future.

Jim grabbed my hand when I stood up, "Wait." He pulled me over to him. "I have a question for you."

I hoped it didn't involve ghosts and murders. "Yes?"

"Will you consider marrying me?"

My jaw dropped. I wasn't expecting a proposal. "Uh…" I thought about Andrew and my last marriage. Would I jump in again?

Bronte nudged the back of my knee as if to push me further toward Jim. It was all I needed to answer him. "Of course. What took you so long?" I laughed as the tears rolled down my cheeks.

As we walked up to the cabin, I thought about Nella and her discovery of a family. For now, I had mine, and it was a fine one. I reached down and gave Bronte a pat on the head. "Girl, you're sleeping in the living room tonight." I don't think she minded.

Acknowledgements

Thank you to Shawn Reilly Simmons, my Level Best editor, and Dawn Dowdle, my agent, who have both been great supports and advocates. To my writer's group, Jan Kerman, Carol Williams, and Randy Kasten who are honest and astute in their critiques. A huge thanks to Mark Roberts who has such an eye for detail and a willingness to let me know when I go astray. To Jerome, always my first reader. And most importantly, to Grace Stone, my neighbor, who survived both the London Blitz and tuberculosis. Grace's stories, shared over a cup of tea, inspired this book.

About the Author

Linda Norlander is the author of A Cabin by the Lake mystery series set in Northern Minnesota. Books in the series include *Death of an Editor* and *Death of a Starling* and *Death of a Snow Ghost*. Norlander has published award winning short stories, op-ed pieces and short humor featured in regional and national publications. Before taking up the pen to write murder mysteries, she worked in public health and end-of-life care. Norlander resides in Tacoma, Washington, with her spouse.

SOCIAL MEDIA HANDLES:
   Facebook.com/authorlindanorlander

AUTHOR WEBSITE:
   lindanorlander.com

Also by Linda Norlander

A Cabin by the Lake Mysteries:
- *Death of an Editor*
- *Death of a Starling*
- *Death of a Snow Ghost*

Printed in the USA
CPSIA information can be obtained
at www.ICGtesting.com
LVHW041302190224
772243LV00006B/71